Just Go With It

MADISON WRIGHT

This is a work of fiction. Names, characters, businesses, events, and incidents are products of the author's imagination. Any resemblance to actual person, living or dead, or actual events is purely coincidental.

Just Go With It © 2022 by Madison Wright

All rights reserved. No portion of this book may be reproduced in any form without written permission from the publisher or author, except as permitted by U.S. copyright law.

First Edition April 2022

Cover Design by Sam Palencia at Ink and Laurel

Editing by V.B. Edits

Proofreading by Amanda Chaperon at Written Word Nerd

Instagram: @authormadisonwright

To Josh, for giving me a better love story than anything I could ever read or write.

Prologue

LO

Eight Years Ago

"No," I say, shaking my head emphatically, sending my curtain of copper hair swishing around my shoulders.

"Please, please, please," Camilla, my roommate and lifelong best friend, begs.

"Absolutely not." I turn around and start walking to the parking lot.

Camilla grabs my arm and hauls me back. Theatrically, she presses her long fingers to the floor-to-ceiling window of the coffee shop. "He's beautiful, Lo."

I know immediately who Camilla's referring to. She came back to our dorm room earlier this week raving about the tall, dark, and handsome junior she met in the student union, Rodrigo. He's all she's talked about for two days.

But it's not Rodrigo who catches my attention—it's the guy with him. He stands a few inches taller than Rodrigo, with broad shoulders and skin that looks kissed by the sun. His blond hair curls around his head, falling over his forehead like it can't be tamed by gel. His eyes crinkle as he laughs at something Rod says. He is magnetic, and I feel drawn to him like a moth to flame.

"Yeah, he is." My voice comes out a breathy whisper.

"So you'll come inside?" Camilla squeals, breaking me out of my trance.

"No."

Camilla, ever the dramatic, bends to her knees. She pushes her dark braids over her shoulders and clasps her hands together in front of her. "Lo, my best friend for all eternity, please, please allow me to go in there and go on a date with this man."

I cross my arms over my chest and lean against the window, relishing in the cool of the glass against my skin in the summer heat. "Just go in alone."

"He brought a friend!" She points through the window at Rodrigo's companion, and my focus drifts once more, catching the way the light reflects on the golden bits of his hair, making it look like sunshine on silk.

"Please, Lo," Camilla begs once more, now starting to sound desperate.

I pin her with a stare. "Did you tell him to bring a friend?"

She stands and bites her lip, avoiding my gaze. I can tell from the hunch of her shoulders and the faint pink creeping into her dark cheeks that I hit the nail on the head.

My jaw falls open. "Camilla Jones!"

"I thought it would be fun! When I met them in the student union, I thought you would be perfect together."

"You planned this the whole time?" I ask, my voice rising in disbelief.

"I knew you'd never say yes if I asked." Camilla at least has the decency to look sheepish.

I glance at the two guys again and let out a breath. My stomach does a little flip at the sight of the blond one's smile, the way it hitches up on one side before stretching across to the other. "Do they think this is a double date?"

"No," she assures me. "I told them this was not a double date. Just four friends hanging out."

"We're not friends with them," I remind her and press my lips into a flat line.

Camilla grabs my arm, tugging me toward the door, and I don't resist. "How about we fix that?"

The bell above the door chimes as we walk in, drawing the attention of the guys. Rodrigo's friend's eyes connect with mine, and I look away rapidly, heart racing.

Why, oh why, did I let Camilla talk me into this?

Camilla pulls us to a stop in front of them and drops my arm. Rodrigo gives her a warm hug, and I can tell from Camilla's shining eyes that she's on top of the world.

"Guys, this is Lo Summers," Camilla says, gesturing to me.

Rodrigo hugs me too, although much quicker than he did with Camilla. "I'm Rod. So good to meet you. Camilla talked about you a lot the other day."

I flash Camilla a look, and she winks.

Finally, I look up, up, up at Rod's friend. His eyes, a striking pale green I couldn't see from outside, meet mine, sending a rush through me. Normally, I could think of a thousand ways to describe those eyes—the way the light refracts in them, the unusual color, the barely contained energy—but my mind has gone utterly blank, a sheet of canvas wrapped in plastic.

He extends his hand. "I'm Weston King," he says, his lips tilting on one side before revealing straight white teeth. His low and husky voice chafes across my nerves as surely as the calluses on his fingers scrape against my skin.

"Nice to meet you." I clear my throat. "You both. Nice to meet you both." I cringe inwardly at my inability to function.

"Ready for coffee?" Rod asks.

Camilla grins up at him, leaning into his side like she can't help but be sucked into his orbit. "I'd love some."

They step into line, leaving Weston and me alone behind them. A thick, awkward tension pulses between us, leaving my skin clammy.

"*Pride and Prejudice?*" Weston asks. I blink at him, confused, and he points at the book sticking out of the top of my purse.

"Oh, um," I stumble, shoving the book further into my bag. "It's one of my favorite books."

Wes arches his brows. "You've read it more than once?"

"Oh, dozens of times," I reply. "It's—"

"I can help the next person," the barista says, cutting off my words. She gives Weston a flirty grin, leaning over the counter. "What can I get for you?"

Weston doesn't seem to notice though, his gaze still fixed on me. "Do you know what you want?"

"Actually, no. You go ahead." I quickly scan the menu.

Weston's eyes sparkle mischievously at me as he leans a hip against the counter. "Let me order for you."

"Why?" I ask slowly, not bothering to hide my skepticism. I force myself to meet his gaze. He's so...vibrant, he's almost hard to look at.

"Do you trust me?" he asks.

I can't help but laugh. "No, I just met you."

He bends toward me, and I catch a whiff of something musky and woodsy. "Come on, just go with it."

I hesitate for a moment, scanning his face. Those pale green eyes are locked on mine, startling in their intensity, and a curly lock of golden hair has slipped over his forehead, making him look almost boyish. The warmth of his bronzed skin radiates off him, and suddenly I'm overwhelmed. I might have watched Camilla get sucked into Rodrigo's orbit a few minutes before, but this is like a wave crashing over me, pulling me under.

Stepping back, I answer, "No, it's fine. I know what I want."

Weston's smile dims ever so slightly, and I think I see disappointment flash across his expression. He gestures me forward. I order my go-to—a vanilla latte. When I try to pay, Weston waves me off. I move aside, staring up at him as he places an order with a complicated series of steps and ingredients.

If I had ordered that, the barista would have fixed me with a withering glare, but for Weston, all she does is beam at him and nod—and, I think, unbutton the top button of her white shirt.

We make our way over to where Rodrigo and Camilla are standing. Camilla's grin is wide, her gaze expectant as we reach them. "Did you order the Weston Special?"

I glance at Weston, who looks smug, before turning back to Camilla. "The Weston Special?"

"I'm not sure what all is in it," she says with a shrug. "Rodrigo said Weston came up with it."

The barista calls our names, and we head over to the counter to pick up our drinks. Weston holds his out to me, and I notice ten digits written across the cup—the barista's phone number.

If Weston notices, he doesn't acknowledge it. "Here, try it," he tells me.

"I'm good."

His mouth quirks up at one corner, and I try to ignore the way my heart stutters at the sight. "You know you want to."

I hold Weston's gaze for a moment longer before I take the drink from him. The warmth seeps through my fingers and into my body, already flushed with awareness. Wary of his steady attention, I lift the cup to my lips and take a small sip. It's hot, almost too hot, but it's hands down the best cup of coffee I've ever had.

Weston grins down at me with that crooked smile, knowing he got me. "Good, huh?"

I nod, handing him the drink back and watch as he tastes it. Weston lets out a contented sigh. "Next time," he says with a wink, "just go with it."

One

LO

Eight Years Later

"Do not make me regret this," I whisper-yell around the dressing room curtain. Peeking my head out, I stare down Camilla, who is lounging on the couch on the showroom floor.

"Bringing me to your bridesmaid dress fitting? For my own wedding," Camilla says.

"Exactly," I tell her. "You know what you did last time."

"That sales associate agreed with me that you have amazing ta-tas," she responds calmly and crosses her legs.

I wrinkle my nose. "Of course she agreed. She was trying to make a sale. Which is why she told me I looked *fabulous* in a dress that my boobs were literally falling out of," I grumble. "Who even uses the word *fabulous*, anyway?"

"Are you going to come out or not?"

"Are you going to behave yourself?" I cinch the curtain tighter, not allowing her a peek at the dress.

Camilla replies, "Absolutely not."

I want to be annoyed with her, but I can't hold back a smile. When I step out, Camilla presses a hand to her chest with dramatic flare.

"Lo," she whispers, and from the lines of silver rimming her dark eyes, I can tell she's about to cry. Camilla has no filter when it comes to her emotions.

I make my way to the platform and meet her gaze in the mirror. It may be my dress fitting, but she looks radiant with her deep brown hair swept back and a faint, pleased flush coloring her cheeks. "Do you like it?"

"It's perfect," she breathes.

"Thank you for not putting me in red."

Camilla lets out a wet laugh, swiping under her eyes, and her signature fierceness returns. "I would never. You are my maid of honor and my only bridesmaid. Besides me, you deserve to be the hottest person at my wedding."

I turn around and grin at her over my shoulder, my waist length hair swishing behind me. "I can't believe you're getting married in nine days."

"I know!" Camilla squeals, smiling back at me, eyes sparkling.

I look at myself in the mirror and appreciate the way the pale blue fabric hugs my body. The spaghetti straps have been tightened so the draped sweetheart neckline only shows a church-appropriate amount of cleavage. The satin tugs gracefully across my hips and lands with a whisper across the tops of my toes. I was worried this style of dress wouldn't look good on my tall, curvy frame, but I'm pleasantly surprised.

"Let me make sure you don't have any underwear lines," Camilla says from where she's perched on the couch behind me. "Bend over."

I follow her instructions, shaking my head at the scene we must be creating. I'm standing atop a platform in a fairly revealing dress, bending over in a twerk position. My mother would be so proud.

"Now look over your shoulder," Camilla tells me.

"What?" I ask, turning my head to look at her.

I hear the snap of a photo being taken on her phone, and I'm off the platform before she has a chance to stop cackling. Camilla shoves the phone down her bra as I try to grab it.

"Give me that phone!" I yell, causing the sales associate to give us a questioning look.

I give the woman a placating smile and try reaching down Camilla's shirt for the phone. *Nothing to see here, ma'am.*

Camilla's laugh is hysterical as she flails her arms and legs to keep me back, giving everyone in the bridal shop a clear view of her lacy undies under her skirt.

"Oh, my gosh, who wears lingerie under their clothes on a Thursday?" I smack her on the shoulder and take another swipe for the phone.

"Some of us stopped wearing boy shorts in middle school, Lo."

"How dare you?" I say in mock outrage. "I'll have you know my Hanes are sexy as—"

I'm interrupted by a tap on the shoulder, halting my blows to Camilla's legs. I swivel to face the sales associate, who wears a sour expression, eyebrows furrowed and thin lips pressed into a flat line.

"Maybe you should change back into your clothes and check out," she suggests pointedly, eyes narrowed into thin slits.

I give her a gracious smile before shooting Camilla one last glare. "Delete that photo."

She kisses my cheek. "Gotta go!"

Great. Camilla Jones, one. Lo Summers, zero.

"Do not leave without deleting that picture!" I slide the curtain closed and change as quickly as possible.

When I come back out, Camilla has already left, needing to get back to work before her lunch break ends. I pay the ridiculous price for the dress and head to my car, texting Camilla as I go.

> **Me**
> Did you delete it?

> **Camilla**
> New phone. Who dis?

I shut myself into my sweltering car. Nashville in late July is not for the faint of heart. Or people who need prescription strength deodorant. Luckily, I am neither of those.

With the AC blasting, I pull up the GPS app on my phone. Another text dings at the top of my screen. It's from my sister, Alexa.

> **Alexa**
> Good luck at your appointment today!

I type a quick response before digging in my purse for my travel bag of medicine. After swallowing a pain reliever to dull the throbbing in my head and the aching in my muscles that started during the fitting, I drum my fingers on the steering wheel. *Here we go.*

An hour later, I'm shifting on an uncomfortable exam table, my dangling feet tingling miserably. It's negative forty-three degrees in this office, yet Dr. Paulus looks cool as a cucumber. She perches on her teeny, tiny rolling stool and crosses one leg over the other. "How are you feeling?"

That's a loaded question to ask someone with a chronic pain disorder, and I bite my tongue to keep from sarcastically telling her so. For some reason, doctors never seem to appreciate my humor.

I nod even though she didn't ask a yes or no question. "I'm feeling okay. The medicine is still working and really helps to control the pain. I'm living somewhat normally when I'm not having a flare-up."

"Good," she responds calmly. "How's the fatigue and insomnia?"

I make a so-so gesture with my hand. "Manageable, I guess. Who needs sleep anyway?"

"Well, sleep is actually vital to your health," Dr. Paulus says and stares at me. I blink, at a loss for words.

"Yes, of course," I say finally.

"And how is the brain fog?"

"What disease do I have again?" I ask cheekily and flash her a smile.

She doesn't miss a beat. "Fibromyalgia." She places her folded hands atop her clipboard and cocks her head, looking concerned for my mental health.

I splutter. See what I mean about the doctors and humor thing? "Sorry, that was a bad joke about brain fog," I respond, shoving my shaking hands under my thighs. "Right, um, the brain fog is one of the more annoying symptoms of the disease, but it's fine."

"And you said the medicine is still working well." Dr. Paulus consults her clipboard. "How's the dosage? Do we need to adjust it again?"

"No, I think everything is working as it should."

It's been a real process of trial and error trying to find a good treatment plan since my symptoms started during my junior year of college. That just so happens to be the reason I don't have a diploma hanging on the wall in my high-rise office. Or an office in general. It took three years for me to get a fibromyalgia diagnosis, and during that time, I had no relief. I dropped out of college, moved back in with my parents for a while, and worked when I could stand it.

Now things are more stable, if not what I had always envisioned for myself. I found a job working as a nanny and moved into a small house with Camilla. Last year, I finally felt good enough to start pursuing my real dream—what I went to college for before I dropped out. I wrote and self-published my first novel—a romance. I've grown a decent following of readers who are impatiently requesting another book. Things are good.

Or they have been. Pretty soon my life will be one epically disastrous train wreck.

"Great," Dr. Paulus remarks. "So tell me why you're here."

I clear my scratchy throat, hesitating, but finally decide to just rip off the bandage. "Okay," I say, wincing at how squeaky my voice sounds. "I'll be losing my insurance coverage next month."

In a fantastic, horrific series of events, I turn twenty-six and will be kicked off my parents' insurance just a month after

Camilla gets married and moves out of our duplex. And I can't afford the high premiums associated with having a chronic illness. Or I can, but then I can't pay rent. And if I ever want to quit nannying and write full time, then I need to have my finances under control.

I study Dr. Paulus' face, looking for judgment or encouragement.

She gives no indication that she even understood what I said. I'm sure she cries at home watching *This Is Us* like any sane human being, but here her face betrays no emotion.

"I need to know what visits will cost without insurance." I cringe to myself, not sure I want to know the answer to the next question. "And my prescriptions."

Office visits happen infrequently now that I have my fibromyalgia somewhat under control. But prescriptions are a monthly expense I don't think I'm prepared to pay for. Not to mention the other things I do to keep my disease under control—vitamins and supplements, massages, even cryotherapy and acupuncture on occasion. All of those are things I've been able to pay for out-of-pocket since my essentials are covered under my insurance. Now life is looking bleak.

Dr. Paulus leans forward, looking pensive. "Before I research this for you, I want to start off by telling you that there are options for affordable healthcare. I want to encourage you to look into them before you attempt to pay for this all on your own. Without health insurance, this will be an incredible financial burden."

Well, that sounds hopeful.

After staring at a computer over Dr. Paulus' shoulder for the next half hour while she totals my monthly medical bills, my head is swimming. I barely make it through giving the woman at reception my beautiful, amazing, wonderful health insurance card and paying my copay before hurling myself out of the building.

I dial Camilla as I stumble across the parking lot to my car. It's so hot that heat ripples are waving above the asphalt, making me even more disoriented.

I hear Camilla's voice through my phone as I lift it to my ear. Without explaining what's going on, I yell, "What the heck am I going to do?"

It speaks to the closeness of our friendship that she knows exactly what's wrong. Camilla knew about the appointment today, and although she doesn't know all the details of the terrible news my doctor just gave me, she knows it must be bad.

"Take a deep breath," Camilla tells me. I try to do as I'm told, but it feels like a pregnant elephant is sitting on my chest. That elephant had its baby, that baby grew up, and now they're both hanging out on top of me. They've gotten comfortable. They bought homes. They will die on my chest, and I will never breathe again.

"There's not an elephant on your chest," Camilla states.

Did I say that out loud? I think to myself.

"Yes," Camilla answers the question I must have asked aloud again. I'm losing my mind.

"Oh my gosh," I heave.

"It will be okay." Camilla's voice is calm, and while it should soothe my nerves, it bristles harshly against them like wool on a rash.

"Camilla, you're moving out in a few days. Our lease is up next month, and I can't sign again. I can't afford rent because my medicine is in the triple digits each month."

"We'll figure it out."

I'm in my car, on the verge of hyperventilating, and my best friend is not helping at all. The AC hasn't cooled down the car yet, and all of a sudden, I can't handle the stifling heat inside my black SUV anymore. I tug open the door none-too-gently and heave myself out. I'm sure I look like I've had a little too much to drink as I stumble around the doctor's office parking lot, gasping for air like I'm walking on the moon without my space suit.

The phone isn't even up to my ear anymore—it's clasped in my hand as I slide down the side of my car and onto the pavement. The asphalt burns the underside of my thighs, but I don't care. I barely feel it over the crushing weight on my chest.

Camilla is yelling through the phone for me to answer her, and I realize I must be breathing loudly. Picking up my phone from where I dropped it next to me on the ground, I stare at it like it's 1990 and I've never seen one of these newfangled contraptions before.

Camilla's voice sounds warbled when I press the phone to my ear. I don't know if she's in a tunnel, which seems unlikely in downtown Nashville, or if my ears aren't working properly. Maybe it's because I went to too many free concerts in college. I stood too close to the speakers in the pit and now my ears are permanently damaged. It's weird that this is just manifesting six years later, but who am I to argue with science? I never even took anatomy—the textbook made me blush, so I took earth science instead. I learned a lot about rocks and—

"Louise Olivia Summers!" Camilla screams, and this time she is perfectly clear. So clear, in fact, that if my eardrum wasn't damaged by all of those concerts, it definitely is now.

"*What?*"

"Why haven't you been answering me?" She sounds frantic, and I don't understand why. She wasn't talking for that long without me responding.

I check the timer under Camilla's name and see that we've been on the phone for thirteen minutes. Maybe I didn't answer for a while. How long have I been sitting on the ground?

I look up toward the entrance to the doctor's office and see a group of nurses peering at me through the blinds.

Crap.

Pushing myself to a standing position, I grimace at the tight feeling in my lower back and get into my now ice-cold car.

"Are you okay?" I hear Camilla ask.

"Yes," I say, slumping against the steering wheel. "I don't know."

My head is swimming and my heart hammers in my chest. The air is too cold and the leather seats are too warm. Everything is *too much*.

I let out a shaky breath. "No. No, I'm not."

Two

WESTON

"Do it for the 'Gram!"

I'm really getting tired of that saying, especially since I rarely post my videos on Instagram, but I guess "do it for the 'Tube" or "do it for the 'Tok" doesn't really have the same ring to it. Truthfully, I'm getting pretty tired of doing these kinds of videos in general. I mean, I'm on the wrong side of my twenties, approaching my thirties at a breakneck speed, and yet I'm still pranking strangers on camera. It's gone too far, but I don't know how to stop it.

Which explains what I'm about to do. Taking a deep breath, I get down on one knee and propose to the stranger next to me in the tamale line on Santa Monica Pier.

"Will you marry me?"

The girl's blonde hair glints in the sunshine, and her eyes crinkle in confusion as she stares down at me. "What?" she asks, clutching her phone to her chest and looking to her friend for help.

The wooden planks of the pier dig uncomfortably into my knee below my board shorts, and the summer sun beats down heavily on my shoulders.

"Will you marry me?" I repeat louder, and I feel the stares of people all around us as they start to notice.

She laughs then, as if finally realizing this is a joke, but I'm not done. I stand up and force myself not to look back at my best friend and cameraman, Camden, filming this whole interaction from his hiding spot around the corner.

"How dare you?" I shout, willing myself not to back down at her conflicted face. "I loved you! I waited for you for three years while you dated your cousin and slept with my dad! And now, you're still saying 'no?' I wanted to build a life with you!"

The woman is speechless, mouth hanging open. I give her one last pained look before I turn around into the sea of onlookers. Ignoring them, I run straight toward the railing, not thinking twice as I catapult off the side and into the turquoise water below.

I hit the waves hard, and water surrounds me in a warm and vigorous embrace before shoving me back toward the surface. One of my flip-flops slides off and I know it's gone forever, so I kick the other one off too before breaking through the waves.

Knowing there are dozens of people watching, I flip my head back, and salty droplets kiss my slick skin. I grin up at the camera before looking around to find the girl I'd talked to. I find her gripping the railing, staring down in unabashed horror and shock.

Waves jostle me, making it hard to focus on her face, but I give her one more piercing look and shout, "I'll always love you!"

As I swim to shore, I know Camden will handle getting the girl to sign a waiver to give us permission to post the footage of her on all my social media platforms. Now I've got to handle the lifeguards, and potentially the cops.

I DON'T KNOW HOW I make it off the beach without at least being questioned by police or security, but the lifeguards just seem to want to get rid of me—after taking a few photos, of course.

"Don't tell anyone we let you go without calling the cops," one of the lifeguards warns me, swiping through the pictures we took together on his phone.

"Scout's honor," I say, holding up three fingers.

I pat them both on the back before heading across the sand to the parking lot. When I'm halfway back up the beach, the sand scorching my feet, someone calls out, "Just go with it!"

I turn around, looking for the fan yelling my catchphrase. I spot him, a big burly guy about ten feet away. "Just go with it!" I holler back with a wave.

"Hey!" He motions for me to come to him. I try to ignore the burning sensation on the balls of my feet as I make my way to where he's stretched out on his towel, covered in sand and hair.

As I approach, I say, "Hey, man. What's your name?"

He stands and holds out a hand to me. "Chris. I'm a big fan."

"Nice to meet you, Chris. Want a picture?" I smile and shake his proffered hand.

He waves me off. "Nah, I saw you lost shoes in the jump, though." He motions to a pair of flip-flops at the bottom of his towel. "Take mine."

"Ah, no, man. It's fine," I say as he bends to pick them up.

"Really, dude."

I try to object again, but he's already placing the worn out sandals in my hands. "Thanks," I say before dropping them back into the sand and slipping my feet into them. They're much too small, but I just smile and thank him again.

"Just go with it, man!" he yells as I start toward the car again. I turn to give him a wave and smack right into someone. Reaching out, I grab the petite woman by the shoulders to steady her.

"I'm so sorry," I say quickly.

"It's fine. I—" Her voice cuts off as she looks up at me, recognition dawning. I flash her my most winning smile, hoping to move this along quickly so I can finally get back to my car.

Instead of asking for a picture or talking about one of my viral videos, her tiny hand cracks against my cheek, leaving a stinging sensation in its wake. I'm at a complete loss for words.

"What you did to Talia Benson was terrible," she spits before stomping furiously away, her steps being swallowed up in the sand.

I rub my cheek and finally make my way off the beach. *God, I'm really sick of this.*

Rounding the corner to where my car is parked, I see Camden leaning against the open trunk of my black Range Rover. He's fiddling with his gear in the back when he hears me approaching.

He turns the camera to me, and I force myself to look more upbeat than I feel. "There he is!" Camden shouts.

I flash the camera my signature grin. "The lifeguards were fans so I got off scot-free."

Cam tosses my phone. "Liz, the girl you proposed to, put her number in your phone and told you to text her later."

I wink at the camera. "Thanks so much for watching my video. I hope you enjoyed watching me jump off the Santa Monica Pier. Don't try this at home, kids. If you liked this video, give it a thumbs up and subscribe to my channel. Just go with it!" I smile again before Cam clicks the camera off.

The minute we're done filming, my shoulders droop. "I'm too old for this," I tell him.

"Now just imagine you're almost thirty and following your best friend around while he does these stupid stunts all day."

I punch his shoulder. "You love it." Camden has been filming my videos for me since I moved to LA six years ago. Brandon, my manager, helped connect me with Cam, an up-and-coming photographer and videographer, and we've been friends ever since.

While Cam finishes stowing his gear, I line my seat with a towel and get in. After settling into the driver's seat, I finally get a chance to check my phone. It's been probably two hours since I've looked at it, with setting up the video and dealing with the lifeguards and fans—and the one not-so-fan.

As if I haven't had to deal with the Talia fiasco enough already today, I see Brandon has texted me a link to an article.

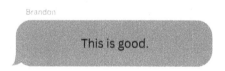

Which leads me to believe that the article is anything but good. Brandon and I have differing opinions about publicity.

I click on the article—*Talia Benson Tells All.* Talia's practiced smile fills the screen.

The article reads, "*I'm so grateful this album has been so impactful to so many people,*" Talia Benson shares. "*I had such a hard time when Weston broke up with me. We had been dating for so long when I asked him to commit to me and be exclusive. I never thought he would say no. This album was born out of* the heartache. I wrote it for myself, as a way to cope. It wasn't for anyone else—not for the fans and definitely not for Weston King."

Yeah, okay.

I exit the article's webpage, not wanting to read any more about "our *devastating* breakup." Scrolling past all my social media notifications, I notice a text from Camilla. Which is odd because she doesn't usually text me outside of the group chat between her, Lo, Rodrigo, and me. I tap the notification, and my jaw drops open. Below three fire emojis is a picture.

I click on it, and the screen fills with an image I couldn't unsee even if I wanted to. And I really, really don't want to.

It's Lo. She's standing on top of a platform in a dress the color of the California sky. The silky material was *made for* hands to be run all over it, and my own itch with desire. Her hands are propped on her knees, leaving her fiery red hair to tumble down her arched back in long luscious waves.

I *definitely* shouldn't be looking at this.

Maybe just one more peek.

The passenger door opens, and I chuck the phone at the dash so hard Cam looks at me like he just walked in on me snorting crushed up Froot Loops.

"What's on your phone?" he asks, suspiciously.

"Nothing," I say, putting the car in reverse and backing out of the parking spot. "Let's get out of here."

We're quiet for a few minutes as I maneuver out of traffic and Camden scrolls through his phone. "That was our last video together," he finally comments, breaking the silence.

I scrutinize him for a moment before turning back to the road. "I know—the last video before I move. It's kind of sad."

Camden doesn't say anything, but I know he's thinking this is the end of an era too. I moved to LA straight from college after I signed with my manager. My whole career and adult life have been here, but I'm over it.

"I expected Brandon to be more pissed about you moving," Cam muses, pushing a hand through his chestnut waves.

I let out a breath. "Me too. I mean, he's not happy, but there's not really anything he can do."

"Yeah, but with everything…" Cam trails off, and I know he's referring to all the bad press post-Talia. "I thought he would be giving you all kinds of stuff to do around here."

My jaw clenches. "Yeah, well, he gave me all kinds of things to do with Talia—parties to be seen at, things to post, everything—and you saw how that turned out. I'm ready to do things my own way."

"I don't know if that's all on Brandon," Camden hedges, his deep blue eyes widening slightly.

"No," I say, tightening my grip on the steering wheel. "It's not, but I told him I didn't think I should pretend to date Talia, but he talked me into it. He said the publicity would be good, and now look."

"I think he thinks this *is* good publicity."

"Exactly, which is why I need to get out of here. He can't talk me into going out with a model or collabing with someone for clickbait if I'm not here."

It's not the whole reason I'm leaving, but it's a big part of it. Mostly, I'm just disillusioned with this life. I had something worth sticking around for back in Nashville, and I left—for this.

Camden doesn't say anything else, and we ride in silence for a while, both lost in our own thoughts.

"I'll have to see if Brandon can find me a hot girl in Nashville to work with. I'm sick of seeing your ugly face behind the camera," I say as I turn onto his street.

Cam laughs then, loud and long. I really will miss him. I'm excited to move back, to be with my friends and closer to my family in Florida, but there are only a few things about my life in LA that I will miss, and Camden is one of them. He and his sister, Hazel, have been my closest friends here. I still haven't found a videographer in Nashville—I've been holding out hope they would move with me.

"Good luck with that," he responds. "No one is going to put up with you."

"I am a gem to work with."

"Whatever you've got to tell yourself, man."

"You could always move too," I say, trying one more time.

Camden laughs, straightening in his seat. "There's not enough money in the world."

Three

LO

I'D LIKE TO SAY that I spent the rest of the weekend thinking and praying about my situation and I'm okay with it now. Everything will work out. It always does. No need to worry.

Ha.

Not worrying is not a position I am familiar with.

"Morning!" I call out as I walk into work on Monday.

Elizabeth, my very pregnant employer, comes around the corner holding Maddox, the three-year-old I nanny. Both cars were parked outside, so I know John, her husband, hasn't left yet for the day. Elizabeth has already started her maternity leave, so she has been getting things ready for the baby that is due in two weeks.

"LoLo!" Maddox yells, squirming out of his mom's grasp. She lets him down, and I notice a pinched expression on her face as he barrels toward me.

I squat down and let him run into me. "Did you have a fun weekend, Maddy?" My fingers sift through the downy softness of his blond curls, smoothing them back from his delicate face.

"I did! We went to the park and got ice cream!" Maddox has yet to learn how to speak without screaming. I worry for his parents if he doesn't figure it out before puberty.

I press my lips to his cheek before turning back to Elizabeth, who still looks pained. She rubs a hand absently over her protruding bump and avoids my eyes.

"Are you feeling okay?" I ask her.

She keeps her eyes averted as she nods. "After you get settled, would you mind coming into the office?"

Dread pools in my stomach, and I feel all the blood rush from my head, leaving me unsteady. The three-year-old wrapped around my legs doesn't help.

I don't have any reason to worry, I tell myself. I've worked here for two years with no complaints. But who doesn't get an ominous feeling when their boss asks to see them in their office?

"Maddox, come with me, and we can turn on a show," Elizabeth says. Maddox lets go of my legs and follows Elizabeth to the living room, but I still feel off-kilter.

I swallow hard against the lump in my throat and press a shaking hand to my chest, hoping to steady the erratic beating of my heart.

I fuss around in the kitchen until I hear Elizabeth make her way to the office on the other side of the house. My breath is coming out in shallow gasps, and I have to tell myself to calm down before I follow her.

When I enter the office, I immediately know something is wrong. John is leaning back against his desk, his shoulders stiff and his law hard. Elizabeth sitting on the couch across from him, wringing her hands in her lap. My every nerve stands on end, making me feel like a bowstring pulled too tight.

I force a polite smile on my face and sit next to Elizabeth on the loveseat, pulse hammering in my throat.

It's so quiet that Elizabeth's gulp can be heard over the sound of the clock ticking on the wall.

I absolutely will not speak first. Under no circumstances...

"How was your weekend?" I ask. I hate myself.

"Lo, we have some bad news," John states, his voice flat and businesslike, although not entirely unfeeling.

Oh, okay. We're diving right into it. Whatever *it* is. This is fine. I'm fine.

"I know we just signed another year contract, but we're going to have to terminate it."

My heart stops, taking my breath with it. Tears sting behind my eyes, but I zero in on a spot on the wall and hold it, knowing if I lose my concentration, I'll melt down.

The details of my contract swirl in a fuzzy haze in my mind, like mist I can't quite grasp. There was a termination clause, but for the life of me, I can't recall the particulars. I never considered I would need to know it.

Elizabeth sniffles next to me, snapping me out of my trance. "We're so sorry. This entire pregnancy I've been trying to decide if I wanted to go back to work after the baby is born."

This is brand new information for me.

"It just took us so long to get pregnant this time, and I think this will be the last kid we have," she says on a shaky exhale. "I wasn't around enough with Maddox. I missed so much, and he's about to go to school. I just don't want that to happen again."

I nod, unable to speak. On one level, I completely understand. I know why she would want to stay home with her baby. Maddox is amazing. He's smart and kind and gentle, and his little sister is going to be wonderful too.

And Elizabeth did miss a lot. I was the one who caught Maddox's first steps on video and fed him his very last bottle. She should get to experience all of that with this baby if that's what she wants.

But I'm also about to be unemployed, homeless, and without medical insurance. I won't tell them that, though. I can tell from the pinched expressions of guilt on their faces that this decision has weighed heavily on them. They didn't make this decision lightly, and my financial struggles aren't their problem.

Tears fall unchecked down Elizabeth's face, and I reach out, instinctively rubbing her back. It's maybe a little backward that I should be comforting *her* right now, but my heart hurts for her anyway.

"We will still pay you for the next three months, as it states in the contract," John says, watching the interaction between me and his wife with sad eyes.

The band around my chest loosens a little at his words, but not much. It took me two and a half months of interviewing with families before I got this position. I don't want to interview for months for a job I don't really want. My plan had been to work for John and Elizabeth until I could go part time and write part time. And then eventually write full time. But there is no chance of that now.

"When is my last day?"

"We were thinking you could just head home now if you wanted. We realize it may be too hard to work today. You're welcome to stay if you want. If not, you're welcome to come take Maddox out for the day at any point to spend some time with him. And we obviously want you to come visit after Elizabeth delivers." John pauses, gentling his voice, "You're a part of the family. We're incredibly thankful for everything you've done for us."

Clearing my tight throat and blinking back tears, I say, "I think I'll head out if that's okay."

John regards me sympathetically. "Of course," he assures.

My legs quiver beneath me as I stand and make my way to the door. The metal handle is cool beneath my fingertips.

"Please come back and see us. We're going to miss having you around," John says, his tone soft.

I don't trust my voice, so I just give them a small smile and a nod before slipping out the door.

Wanting to avoid breaking down in their driveway like I did in the doctor's office parking lot, I barely stop to give Maddox a tight hug before letting myself out of the house. It's not until I'm parked beneath the shade of a large tree at the park down the street that I allow myself to cry.

Uncontrollable sobs wrack my body, and my vision is so blurred by tears that I can't even find my phone. I don't even know who I would call.

Camilla is probably on her way to work and would turn right around to take care of me, but she doesn't need to miss work the week before her honeymoon. Plus, she doesn't need more of my drama this week. She's getting married in six days and has plenty on her plate. My sister, Alexa, just had a baby a few weeks ago and I'm sure she doesn't need to hear any more crying.

This isn't the first time I've wished for someone to share the load with. It's impossible to have an incurable chronic illness without wishing for a partner. I have a great support system, but I'm realizing now how thin it is. I relied so heavily on my parents those first few years. And then I moved in with Camilla, and she's been helping lighten the load ever since.

Even if I wanted to move back in with my parents, I couldn't. After I moved out, they sold the house and started traveling around the country in an RV.

Camilla is getting married. She makes good money and could have been living on her own the past few years but stayed with me because she knew I needed her. I've been preparing for this scary independence for a year now, and I thought I could handle it.

Wiping my face, I stare blankly at my phone. For long moments, I rack my brain for someone—*anyone*—to talk to. My phone slips from my shaking hands, falling to the floorboard, but I don't bother to pick it up. There's no one to call anyway. My supportive foundation has cracks. I've opened the walls up to find termite damage. Everything is crumbling around me, and I don't know what to do.

Four

WESTON

"Hey, Brandon," I say, answering my manager's phone call on Wednesday morning.

"Hey." His authoritative voice rings through the speaker as I continue packing. "I spoke with the publisher again."

I halt, hand still inside my suitcase. "And?"

"They're not interested." His words are a hit to my solar plexus. I fall hard onto the corner of my bed and lean back. I've been wanting to write a book about my experience as a content creator—more specifically, spill the beans about my life as an influencer. I want to tell the world who I really am and why I got into this business.

"Why?" I ask, pinching the bridge of my nose to relieve the pressure building there.

"Same reasons."

I sigh and scrub my hand down my face. "I've been working so hard on my image. The book is supposed to help, but they won't publish the book because my image is so bad."

"It's fine, Weston. You're getting all kinds of press from this." *Bad press*, I think miserably. "You don't need the book." His voice is gruff, somewhat unfeeling, and I try not to let it hurt.

Brandon is more than a manager to me. After my videos started going viral on Vine in college, Brandon reached out to me. He told me this fun hobby I'd taken up could actually turn into a career for me. He had been working as a talent manager at a large agency for most of his career and wanted to make a change. Brandon quit his job and started his own business, taking me under his wing as his one and only client.

My team has grown since then—adding a publicist and an agent—to lighten Brandon's load a little, but it's Brandon I owe everything to. *He* was the one to believe in my vision. *He's* coached me in making every choice I've made as a content creator. It's as much his career as it is mine at this point. I've trusted every decision he's made and haven't wanted to change anything until recently.

"You haven't signed those documents that I sent over earlier this week," Brandon reminds me. "It's an easy ad, Wes. They just want you to make a few posts and videos and tag them."

"I'm just getting tired of doing this same stuff," I tell Brandon, like he hasn't already heard it all.

"I know," Brandon responds absentmindedly, and I can hear him tapping on his laptop in the background. "But these are the kinds of gigs you're getting offered. You can't just decide you don't want to do it anymore."

"I don't want to quit doing this," I say on an exhale, trying to sort through my thoughts. "I love it. I just want to do things differently."

"Yeah, well, there's a lot at stake here, and what you want to do isn't working." He sounds agitated, and it grates on my nerves.

My next words blurt out before I can consider them. "I know more than my job is at stake here, which is why I thought you'd be working harder to get me the kinds of jobs I actually want."

Brandon is silent, and I know I went too far. Standing, I pace across my room. "I'm sorry, Brandon. I was a jerk. I didn't mean it."

He's quiet for another moment. "I told you this direction wouldn't work, but you didn't listen. I'm the manager here, and I know this business. You need to stop trying to take things into your own hands and let me do my job."

I let out a breath. We're at the same point we always get to. Suddenly, I'm too exhausted to have this conversation. Again.

"Listen, I've got to go," I say finally. "I need to finish packing."

"Yeah, okay. Talk to you later."

Frustration gnaws at me as I flop back on my bed. Brandon and I have been having the exact same conversation for months—me saying I think we should try things a different way, him reminding me that he's the one who got us here in the first place. He's been right so far, something I don't like to admit. Any time I've tried going against his judgment, it's failed. Moving—something he's been decidedly against—is probably the wrong decision also, but I just can't stay here anymore.

After Talia released the album—the one telling everyone I couldn't commit to her after a months-long *relationship*—which, by the way, isn't true, every last thing I liked about living here dried up. Except for my friends, there's nothing I want here anymore.

Everything I want is back in Nashville. It's only taken me six years to figure that out.

Peering around my empty room, I feel like something is finally clicking in place, bringing a relief I haven't felt in a long, long time. I'm ready to go back. Start over—or try again.

Figure out how to keep doing the job I love, but in a way that actually makes me proud of myself.

I stand and pull open the dresser drawers, making sure I got everything. It needs to be cleared out before the moving company shows up here tomorrow to load up the furniture and ship it to Nashville. I tug the final drawer, the one I have always kept mementos in. It's empty—everything packed safely away.

As I'm shutting it, something catches my eye—a red sliver of paper. I yank it free and startle at the photo. It's me and Talia in a photo booth the night we met. Back then, I was enamored with her beauty and fame. I thought being seen with her was the best thing that could ever happen to my career.

If only I had known how wrong I was.

Without giving it another glance, I toss it in the trash.

"I HONESTLY BELIEVE THIS was the first time our pilot has ever flown a plane," I say to Rod on the phone and earn a glare from the passing flight attendant.

My flight landed at the Nashville airport ten minutes ago. My seatmate, who introduced himself as Bruce the moment I sat down, stands in the aisle as if, by doing so, the doors will magically open faster. This has rewarded me with some extra legroom that I unashamedly take advantage of. Even though I'm in first class, the window seat is not the friend of the six-foot-three man on a four-hour flight from Los Angeles.

"That bad, huh?" Rodrigo asks as he drives around the airport for the third time.

Oh yeah, I forgot to mention that the already super uncomfortable flight next to Bruce, a burly guy with body odor, was delayed on the runway at LAX for thirty minutes and stuck in line to the terminal at the Nashville airport, so I am now exactly one hour and twenty-three minutes late for my arrival time.

"I almost had to use my barf bag," I tell him.

My seat buddy looks down at me from his stance, half in and half out of the packed aisle, and grimaces. "Want a breath mint?"

I feel bad for being annoyed with Bruce earlier. He really is a nice guy. He offered to let me share his earbuds with him and listen to One Direction on his iPod. Yes, his iPod.

I politely declined, saying I had a rare kind of ear infection that can be spread by sharing earbuds.

"I'm good, thank you, though."

"What?" Rod asks.

"Nothing," I say back and wave off the Altoids Bruce is holding in front of my face. He pops no less than six of them in his mouth (doesn't he know they're dangerously strong?) before shoving them into his travel bag.

I tell Rod, "I'm sorry my plane was late."

He must have me on speaker because Camilla responds. "It's all good," she says. "It's not your fault Rod didn't check the live flight info you sent him." I can hear the teasing accusation in her voice.

Most men would have a defensive remark to lob back, but Rod is the most laid-back person I've ever met, and I can practically hear the shrug of his shoulders. It's the busiest week of his life, but he would have waited at the airport for hours for me if need be.

Which, I guess, he did. Oops.

The doors to the plane finally open. I say my goodbyes to Rod and Camilla and tell them I should be out in a few minutes. I make my way quickly through the airport, avoiding the eyes I feel on me as I get my bags and exit. I'm really not in the mood to deal with a Talia fan today.

Rod pulls his SUV to a stop in front of me. I'm pretty sure Camilla is the one who actually puts the car in park because Rod jumps out while it's still moving and wraps me in a big hug. Rodrigo Ramos is a hugger. I am not, but that's never stopped him.

As I reach around him to hug him back, I hear a loud whistle. I turn to see a security guard motioning for us to hurry up so we don't back up the line. "Keep it movin'!"

Rod opens the trunk, and we throw my suitcase and gym bag inside before I slide into the back seat. Camilla turns around and squeezes my knee.

I smile at her. "Hey, Camilla. How are you doing?"

"Very happy and slightly stressed," she replies with a smile.

"I guess that's better than being very stressed and slightly happy."

I couldn't be more excited for my friends. I was there the day Rod and Camilla met at the front doors of our campus Student Union, and immediately, I knew there was something special there. Then, when Camilla brought Lo out with us that first time, we all became inseparable. The four of us were together almost constantly until I moved to Los Angeles two years later.

We've all stayed in touch, texting most weeks in our group chat, but it hasn't been the same. Rod and Camilla have been out to visit, but except for when I came out here to house hunt a few months ago, I haven't been back at all.

My heart beats a little faster at the thought of seeing Lo again—after six years, and knowing how we left things. Now that Rod and Camilla are getting married and I'm moving back, I wonder if everything will go back to how it was, or if I messed things up too much back then.

Camilla claps her hands together as we pull out of the airport and into traffic. "I can't wait to see your house after all the renovations!"

A smile tugs at my lips, and I realize it's my first real one in a long time. I'm back in Nashville with two of my best friends, about to see my new house, and I'm here to stay. "Me neither."

I remember visiting Nashville a few months ago and touring houses with Rod, Camilla, and my realtor. Rodrigo's relentless positivity and Camilla's blunt honesty made it quite an undertaking. I hoped Lo would be there to balance them out, but she was on vacation with her family. I never realized how much I value her opinion until she wasn't there when I needed it.

When I'd found the house, though, I'd known it was the one immediately.

We pull into my new neighborhood in East Nashville, and my stomach clenches in anticipation of seeing my almost finished home. The 1950s Tudor had been in some dire need of updates that I've been overseeing from LA. They should be finished up in the next week, which works out perfectly since I'll be house-sitting for Rod and Camilla next week while they're on their honeymoon.

"So," Camilla starts. "Did you like that picture I sent you yesterday?"

"What picture?" Rod asks, turning onto my street.

Camilla answers quickly. "Nothing."

"Camilla," Rod whines. "Are you meddling again?"

She looks deeply offended, pressing a perfectly manicured hand to her chest. "I would never."

I lean forward. "Meddling?"

Rod says nothing, just flashes Camilla a look before he quickly turns back to focus on the road.

Camilla huffs out a breath and crosses her arms over her chest. "I just want them to fall in love," she whines.

My heart seizes before beating again at a faster rhythm. "Me and Lo?"

"Camilla..." Rod says, his voice deep with warning.

"It would be perfect."

"Do I need to be here for this?" I ask, growing uneasy at the direction of their conversation. They both know how things turned out last time, so I'm not sure why they're pushing it now.

"Nothing is going to happen there, Camilla. You need to let it go. Right, Wes?" Rod's deep brown eyes scrutinize me in the rearview mirror.

Camilla turns around to face me and pushes a lock of dark hair behind her ear. My pulse pounds, and I consider how to answer. They only know Lo's side of the story, and I'm happy to let them go on believing it.

I rub a hand along my jaw, stalling for time. Camilla frowns, taking my lack of response as agreement with Rod. Spinning back around, she glares out the window. The tension grows thick, the past a writhing undercurrent threatening to pull us all under.

Rod steers the car into the driveway and around the back, parking in front of the detached garage. I catch my first glimpse of the new paint and renovated back porch. We all stare through the car windows at the beautiful house.

"Lo will love this house," Camilla comments quietly.

"I know," I respond, my heart tightening in my chest.

Camilla spins around to face me, eyebrows pinched together. She searches my expression, and I'm not sure how much I want her to see.

I forgot that Camilla sees everything. Turning back around, a smug smile forming on her lips, she says, "I can work with this."

Five

LO

Ask any Nashville native, and they'll tell you there is no worse way to spend your Friday night than going down to Broadway. If you're from here, you have definitely been asked by many tourists what bars you like, what steakhouse you prefer, and which museum you like to spend your time at. What they don't understand is that we wouldn't accept a cash bribe to go to any of the places where they blow hundreds of dollars.

Needless to say, going downtown is never a way I would choose to spend my night—especially not after the week I've had. I didn't tell anyone that John and Elizabeth let me go, not with everything going on. I'll tell everyone after the wedding.

I just need to make it through the next two days. While I would love to spend my second to last night at home with my best friend, Camilla has other ideas. Since Rod and Camilla are only having a best man and maid of honor, they decided against traditional bachelor and bachelorette parties in favor of hitting the town with Wes and me.

Which means that I am now sitting in a honky-tonk bar off Broadway wearing a crop top that says "Would Rather Be Reading" across the front so everyone knows what to expect from me tonight. I paired it with a mid-thigh length denim skirt because I plan on dancing and not showing my biker shorts to everyone. And lastly, Vans because, while we may be doing terribly touristy things tonight, I refuse to wear cowboy boots and look like a complete idiot.

To my left, Camilla is whispering in Rod's ear in a way that makes me blush. I choose to avoid looking at her, and I especially ignore the way she looks at Rod as he whispers back to her.

On the dance floor, a drunk bachelorette party makes fools of themselves trying to take pictures in "Bride Tribe" T-shirts that they've tied up to show off their matching heart-shaped belly button rings.

I really hate coming downtown.

The ice in my drink clinks against the glass as I stir my straw with clammy hands. My gaze drifts over my shoulder to the doors once more, and I let out a relieved breath when I don't see *him*.

I was out of town when Weston visited a few months ago and I wasn't able to take time off work the few times Rod and Camilla went to visit him, meaning it's been six years since we've seen each other. But there's no avoiding him now. He's not only going to be here, but he's back for good. Which is fine. No big deal. I may have been secretly in love with him in college, but it's over. It's been six years.

It would have been easier to get over him if he wasn't all over the internet, playing the same pranks on other people that he used to play on me. Popping up on my Explore page on Instagram, asking a stranger to do something adventurous that I never would. Getting a notification on YouTube that he posted another video (how do I unsubscribe again?). Or seeing his photo on a gossip rag after he dated and broke up with a very famous musician that I used to love. Or listening to the breakup album she made about him. And then hearing the songs literally everywhere. If I have to see one more TikTok set to a song about their great love, I will lose my mind.

But all that to say, I'm definitely over him. Any feelings I had for Weston King are gone—capital G. My stomach isn't cramping. My foot isn't tapping on the floor. My fingers aren't twisting my necklace around and around until I feel it choking me. I'm fine. It's no big—

He's here. And wow. Time has been good to him.

I mean, I've seen him on social media. We all still talk fairly often in our group chat. But we haven't seen each other in person.

And pictures really, *really* don't do him justice.

He's always been tall, making me feel almost small next to him. But where he used to be a little lanky, he's filled out quite nicely. His shoulders are rounder, and the sleeves of his heather-blue T-shirt pull tight against his biceps. His dark jeans ride low on his tapered hips. He's strong but not built. Lean and muscled but not ripped. He looks effortless, and I kind of hate him for it.

His eyes connect with mine across the room, and my heart stops in my chest. Thousands of memories flash through my mind, but it's the last time I saw him that threatens to strangle me. I can imagine him perfectly, waving goodbye to Rod, Camilla, and me as he stepped through airport security—taking my heart with him.

I think I'm going to be sick.

I shove my elbow into Camilla's side. Her head swivels to me so quickly I'm scared she'll have whiplash on the big day. "What are you doing?" she yells into my ear, loud enough to be heard over the country music coming from literally every direction in this godforsaken place.

When I don't answer, she starts to look worried. "What's wrong?" Camilla asks.

"I can't do this. I need to get out of here," I yell back at her.

"Hey guys." I hear a deep voice over my shoulder, and I know there's no way the owner of that voice didn't hear me.

Slowly, I swivel to face him.

Rod jumps up to clap him on the back, but Wes continues to assess me. His pale green eyes are intense, and his signature half smile hitches up one side of his mouth, but I can't read the emotions beneath.

Standing on tiptoes, Camilla hugs Wes around his neck. His thick arms wrap around her frame in a tight, quick hug before he releases her, but his gaze never leaves mine.

"No hug for me, Lo?" Wes asks.

Under no circumstances will I be hugging that man. I'll die if I have to touch him. Racking my mind, I try to find an excuse.

"I took my shoes off under the table," I finally force out. "Don't want to get up and step on a shard of glass. People are always dropping drinks around here." All three of them look down at my covered feet, which are clearly visible under the table.

Wes looks like he's about to say something, but a woman stops next to our table. She gapes at Weston.

"Are you Weston King?"

Standing, I say, "He sure is," before moving past them, desperate for some fresh air.

"You guys ready to head to the next place?" Rod yells over the din of live music a few hours later.

I've been studiously avoiding Wes, choosing instead to talk to Camilla or excuse myself to get a refill or go to the bathroom. At this point, they probably all think I have a bladder infection.

I can't ignore him now, though. As we exit, Rod and Camilla find two rental scooters. "Oh, my gosh. That would be so fun!" Camilla squeals, her voice still at the decibel she used to be heard over the music inside.

"Let's see if we can find two more," Rod says.

Wes waves him off. "You two go ahead. Lo and I will meet you at the next place."

"You sure?" Rod asks, checking with both of us.

I cannot be left alone with Weston. I open my mouth to say that, no, it's not fine.

"Of course. Go ahead," Wes urges before I get a chance to respond.

Rod and Camilla take off on the scooters, leaving Wes and me incredibly alone—in a sea of tourists, of course. We follow after them in silence. This is good. I can do silence. It's much better than talking.

Wes bumps his shoulder into mine. "You've been quiet tonight," he points out.

I release a pent-up breath and allow myself to quickly observe him—the blue sleeves covering his biceps, the tan skin of his neck, the impossibly sharp squareness of his jaw. He peers down at me with eyes the exact color of fresh cut grass.

My stomach twists. I have a ridiculous urge to tell Wes everything. He's never been much of an emotional guy, not a shoulder I would seek out to cry on. But he undoubtedly could make me laugh and forget about my worries for a bit.

I bite my tongue, though. Laughing with Wes is just the first step down a slippery slope I spent months trying to crawl back up last time. Instead, I train my gaze on the busy sidewalk in front of us. "I'm fine. Just a headache."

It's not a lie, but it's not the whole truth, either. The stress of losing my job and the anxiety at seeing Wes again have been eating at me all week. Now that the moment of truth is here, my body has revolted, and I'm in pain all over.

"I'm sorry. Is there anything I can do to help?" he asks, his voice strained with concern.

I look up at him, a little surprised. I figured he'd make a joke or try to distract me—get my mind off the pain.

"What?" he asks.

Shaking my head, I turn back to face forward. "Nothing. I'm, um, fine. Thank you for asking."

He stays quiet, once again shocking me. Wes has never been one for comfortable silences, whereas that's my preferred state at all times. But now, despite the sounds of downtown—honking cars, music drifting from bars, and hundreds of voices—the quiet between us envelops me.

Just as I open my mouth to elaborate, a woman stops right in front of us. She gawks at Weston. I see that the soft expression he wore earlier has been replaced with a smile that would look natural to anyone else but appears stiff to me.

"Weston King?" The woman practically yells and launches herself into his arms. He holds her up but flashes me a somewhat pained expression.

When she drops back down to her feet, Wes sticks his hand out. "Hi. Yeah, I'm Weston," he confirms. "What's your name?"

"It really is you!" she screams, shaking his hand and using her other one to clutch her chest. "I'm Mary Lee. I love your videos. Can I get a picture?"

She spins around and seems to notice me for the first time. Thrusting her phone in my hand, she asks, "Would you mind?"

I shake my head and watch as she moves to stand next to Wes. His arm, the one that brushed mine as we walked down the crowded streets, settles over her shoulders. She flashes a winning smile at her phone in my hand, and my stomach clenches uncomfortably at the sight, dragging me back to a memory from seven years ago.

"Rod," Wes yells. "You've got to take a picture of me and Lo. No one is actually going to believe that I convinced Lo Summers to spend a night out on the town unless there is photographic evidence."

I look up at Wes, shaking my head. "I still think I should be back at my dorm. I have a paper due in my Creative Writing class in two weeks."

"Do you hear yourself?" Wes asks, nudging my shoulder with his own. "Two weeks, Louise. That paper will still be there when we get back. I promise."

I roll my eyes. He knows I hate it when he calls me Louise.

"Wait," Wes objects, holding up his free hand to stop Rod from taking the photo. A second later, his fingers slide gently across my skin, pushing a stray lock of hair off my forehead.

When he speaks, his voice is just a little lower, his green eyes boring into mine. "A hair."

I swallow thickly. "Thanks."

The moment lengthens and stretches, folding us in an intimate bubble, until Rodrigo yells, "You ready?"

Wes wraps an arm around my shoulders and pulls me into the warm solidness of his side. We fit together like puzzle pieces, and

I feel his heat everywhere our bodies touch, from my scalp all the way down to the tips of my toes.

"Smile!" Rod snaps the photo.

"Did you take it?" Mary Lee asks, pulling me back to the present.

"Oh, um." I look down at the couple of blurry photos I captured. "One more," I tell them.

A moment later, she takes the phone from me and inspects the photos. Spinning to face Wes, she ignores me altogether. "Thank you so much."

His full lips tilt in that winning grin that makes everyone feel like they're sharing a joke with just him. "Nice to meet you, Mary Lee."

"Sorry about that," he apologizes after she walks away. His hand rubs roughly at the back of his neck.

"Not a problem," I respond, trying to ignore the barrage of thoughts and feelings swimming around inside me. Wes opens his mouth, but I cut him off. "We better head to the next place. Rod and Camilla are going to worry."

I spin around and pick up my pace, weaving through the sea of people.

"There you are," Camilla yells a few minutes later when we arrive. She and Rod are waiting at the entrance, and I breathe a sigh of relief that I don't have to be alone with Wes and my memories anymore.

AN HOUR LATER, I am officially over this night. While we took a dancing break and ordered some appetizers, no less than ten women approached Wes, asking for photos.

Weston was doing pretty well for himself online before Talia Benson, but dating her tipped him over the edge into fame.

"Ready to go back out there?" Rod asks, throwing an arm over Camilla's shoulders as the band announces another dance. She smiles up at him, and he presses a quick kiss to her lips.

Needing a moment alone, I tell them, "I think I'm going to sit this one out."

"I will too," Wes says, and I resist the urge to smack my head against the table. I *really* just need one moment away from him and all the feelings he's resurrected inside me.

I fell hard for Wes in college, but I never deluded myself into thinking I had a chance with him. It wasn't because I thought he was too good for me or anything, but we were much too different. He was wild and adventurous and getting somewhat famous on the internet. And I was...not.

I thought I'd gotten over him, but as I lift my eyes to meet his, my stomach tightens painfully. I'm screwed.

Pulling my phone out, I hope to lose myself in a book on my Kindle app. Before I even unlock my phone, though, Wes leans his head back on the booth and rolls it until he faces me. His gaze is intense as he assesses me, a brand on my skin. "You're not going to read, are you?"

I must look like a deer in the headlights because he sits up, soft laughter rumbling from his chest. "You really were going to read, weren't you? I guess some things never change."

I motion to the bar where a few of the women who asked him for photos are staring daggers at me over their drinks. "I could say the same thing."

Weston drums his fingers on the table, looking away. "Things were never like this in college."

"You're right," I nod, agreeing with him. "In college, girls wouldn't leave you alone because you were hot. Now it's because you're rich and famous."

His grin returns. "Hot, huh?"

My face flushes, and I'm instantly annoyed because I know Wes never feels self-conscious. In two years of seeing him nearly every day, he never once got embarrassed, whereas I constantly looked like I had a bad sunburn. Worse, actually, because I don't get a cute rosy tint to my cheeks when I'm embarrassed. My chest and face break out in bright red splotches. I look like I have a rash. Which always humiliates me more and makes the whole thing worse.

Wes leans into my shoulder, his mouth quirked in a contented smile, his eyes soft and warm. "You've always been so easy to mess with."

I shoot him a glare, and he grins wider. We're quiet for a moment before he nods to where Rod and Camilla are dancing out on the floor. "I can't believe they're finally getting married," he comments, his tone no longer teasing, instead taking on a smooth, reflective quality.

When my gaze settles on Camilla, I find her laughing loudly at something Rod said. Her mouth is split open, her head thrown back, her eyes squeezed shut, her hair falling down her back like a thick dark fountain.

Heaviness settles over me like a weighted blanket, but I push it back. I really am happy for them. Ecstatic, even. Camilla looks like she's gotten everything she's ever wanted.

"Is it hard for you?" Wes asks, and I'm startled by how easily he can read my thoughts.

I search the strong lines of his face, not bothering to hide my surprise. He's not trying to make me feel better, not cracking a joke to distract me. His expression is steady, waiting for my response.

"Maybe a little," I say, turning to look at our friends, my heart straining in my chest. "Camilla's my person, you know?"

Wes hums deep in this throat, and I chew my lip, unsure how to describe what I'm feeling. "I just don't want things to change."

"You've never liked change," Wes replies quietly, his voice almost tender. I'm feeling reflected on his face—happiness and sadness, contentment and longing.

I want to look away, but I can't. I'm riveted, pulled in by the eyes that have haunted me for so long, unchanged and yet hiding years of differences. "No. No, I haven't."

Six

WESTON

"Camilla just remembered a few things that she needs for tomorrow. Can you and Lo duck out early to get them? We won't be able to leave for a little while," Rodrigo says, collapsing in the seat next to me. It's the day before their wedding, and we've been at the rehearsal dinner for the last couple of hours.

"Yeah, no problem," I say, monitoring the hallway Lo disappeared down. She's been gone for a while, and my unease grows stronger by the minute. I turn back to where Rod is stretched out in the seat next to me, eyes closed, exhaustion etched in the lines of his tan face.

"Did Lo seem weird to you tonight?" I ask, my voice sounding strained even to my own ears.

He opens one eye and regards me curiously. "No, I don't think so. Why?"

I try in vain to put into words what's troubling me about Lo, but I can't pinpoint it. "She was just really quiet."

He closes both eyes again, as if unbothered by my reasoning. "Lo is always quiet."

It's true, but I don't think that's the problem. She seemed off last night too—saying she just had a headache—but I didn't buy it. Tonight, she barely ate any of her food. She alternated between pushing it around on her plate and folding her napkin in her lap over and over.

Rod groans next to me, dragging my attention back to him. He digs his palms into his eyes. "I'm so tired. I can't wait for this honeymoon."

I muster a smirk I don't quite feel. "I'm sure you can't."

Shoving me in the shoulder, Rod says, "I've gotta get back out there. I'll text you what Camilla needs." He hops out of his chair as if the two minutes he sat down filled his energy meter right back up.

I watch as he grabs someone in his perfunctory tight bear hug before finding his way to Camilla. He slips an arm around her shoulders, and she smiles up at him before stealing a quick kiss. An uncomfortable pang resonates through my chest at the sight.

"Hey," Lo says as she slips back into her chair next to mine. "Did I miss anything?"

She still seems a little off, but I can tell she's trying to hide it. Her eyes are puffy and red-rimmed, making me think she's been crying, and my heart squeezes painfully.

Her phone beeps in her lap, drawing her attention before I can ask what's wrong. As she regards whatever is on the screen, her nose wrinkles in confusion.

"Rod just texted me a list of random stuff," Lo says.

"He asked if we could pick up a couple of last-minute things," I tell her.

"Oh." She nibbles on her bottom lip. I feel a strong urge to reach over and run my thumb across its smoothness, to tug her lip until it's free. I shake the thought away.

Lo looks apprehensive. "Okay, um, ready to go then?"

After saying our goodbyes, Lo and I close ourselves in my Range Rover. It was delivered yesterday, along with the rest of my stuff, which I will have to deal with getting out of storage later.

Lo stares out the window at the dock lights over the marina where the rehearsal dinner took place. Warm light spills through the windows, bathing her delicate features in shadow. She doesn't even notice me staring at her.

Unease stirs in my chest. "Okay, spill," I say.

"What?" Lo blinks, turning from the window to face me. Her face is wrinkled in confusion, and she looks so small and vulnerable that an ache blooms beneath my sternum.

I cross my arms against the hurt and try to focus on the matter at hand. "What's up with you? You've been acting weird for the past two days."

Lo's vulnerable expression forces me back to the last time she looked at me that way. Something was bothering her tonight, but I didn't consider it could have been me. A sick feeling spreads through my gut. I hoped things could go back to how they used to be *before*, but now I'm not so sure.

"Nothing's wrong," Lo finally says. I know she's not going to budge when she turns her focus back out the window, her jaw set in a firm line.

I stare at her profile, lit in a burnished gold from the streetlights, and decide to try another tactic. I've always been able to pull Lo out of her head by making her laugh—or blush. "Want some company after we run errands?"

Lo doesn't say anything. I lower my voice and lean closer, inhaling her sweet and spicy scent. She's so close, so soft and warm, I almost forget I'm supposed to be teasing her. "I bet we could find something fun to do."

She looks back, brow furrowed. "Sorry, did you say something? I think I zoned out for a bit."

I rub my jaw, leaning back into my own seat. My attempt at humoring her obviously went right over her head. "No, it was nothing."

Lo pulls up the list Rod sent her. "Looks like we should head to Target. They're closing soon."

Fine.

I don't bother Lo while we make our way through the store, only watch as she moves through the aisles with purpose. A half hour later, after finally getting everything Camilla needs and settling back in my car, I can't stand this awkward silence anymore.

"I know something's bothering you," I say, and Lo's eyes meet mine briefly before she turns away.

I clear my throat, the tension between us suffocating. "Is it...? Is this about the lake house?"

Her forehead wrinkles, as if the thought had never crossed her mind. It feels like a swift kick to the gut. "No."

Right. Yeah, I'm not thinking about it, either.

My mind scrambles for something—*anything*—to say to lighten the mood. I give her an easy grin I don't quite feel, the corners of my mouth tipping at the edges. "I never think about it either—definitely not at night." My smile widens genuinely at the flat, unimpressed look she gives me. "I'll keep going if you don't tell me what's going on."

Her face clouds over, and I curse myself for upsetting her again.

She looks down, fiddling restlessly with the zipper on her wallet. For a long time, she says nothing, and although I want to break the silence, I force myself to stay patient. Until I hear a sniffle. Haunted eyes meet mine, and the heart that normally races in my chest when she's near breaks right in half. Without thinking, I lean over the console and drag her into my arms.

Hot tears deep through the fabric of my shirt as she buries her face in my shoulder. My hands slide behind her neck, sifting through her silky russet locks without thought. Despite the circumstances, I can't help but recall the last time—the only time, really—I had her in my arms. Feelings and memories I thought I'd long since buried rise to the surface.

Lo leans into my touch, her back arching on instinct as I trail my fingers down her spine. My pulse jumps in my throat as her nose brushes the sensitive skin there. The moment stretches, and I still, holding my breath.

As quickly as she fell apart, Lo pulls herself together, sitting back as if she'd been burned. Cool emptiness washes over me. I've only held her in my arms one other time, and I remember feeling this exact way after that ended, too—like a piece of my body was missing.

Lo wipes her cheeks, roughly clearing the tears away. Mechanically, I open the console between us and pull out a fast-food napkin. With trembling hands, she accepts it, and dabs at her eyes. "I'm so sorry, Wes. I didn't mean to break down on you like that."

She looks so wrecked, with her bloodshot eyes and bright cheeks, that I want nothing more than to pull her back to me.

"I'm so sorry," Lo says again, her voice barely above a raspy whisper.

I clench my hands in my lap to keep from reaching for her. "Why are you sorry?"

She crinkles the napkin between her fingers. "I shouldn't have…" she trails off, letting out a breath. "I didn't mean to cry on you or burden—"

My body acts on instinct, reaching out to lay a comforting hand on her knee before I can stop myself. At my touch, the swipe of my thumb against her bare knee, she stops talking, her eyes trained on the point of contact.

"It's okay, really. You don't need to be sorry," I force out, my voice rough. I pull my hand back, shoving it beneath my thigh once more. "What's going on, Lo?"

She looks back at her lap, fiddling with the napkin once more. Her full bottom lip is held captive between her teeth as she seems to war with herself about what to say.

"Camilla doesn't know," Lo finally says on a resigned exhale. "Or at least, she doesn't know all of it. And I don't want her to know until after the honeymoon. I don't want her to worry."

My heart hammers at her words, knowing it must be *bad* if she won't even tell Camilla. Pressing my back against the cool glass of the car window, I say, "Okay."

"I lost my job Monday," she tells me, her voice passionless and resigned.

"I'm really sorry, Lo."

"That's not all," she says, and dread sinks like an anvil in my stomach. "My medical bills for my fibromyalgia are crazy expensive, and I'm losing my insurance next month."

"Wow, Lo. I—"

"Still not done," she interrupts. I gape at her, unsure how it could get any worse. "Because of all of that, I won't be able to renew the lease on my house. I was going to ask for a slight raise at work to make it all work in my budget and leave me with some wiggle room. I was going to be able to make it on my own." The hitch in her breath is heartbreaking. "But now…"

My hands itch with the need to comfort her, and I feel as if her body is a magnet, pulling me in against my will.

But I hold myself back, knowing it wouldn't be the right move, not when she's so vulnerable and I'm so confused by this onslaught of…wanting. Again. Instead, I slip my hands around the bottom of the steering wheel and grip hard.

"It's just a lot," Lo says hollowly. "Camilla has been there for me so much over the last six years." *And I wasn't,* I hear the echo of the words she doesn't say. "She's helped me with it all—talking me through the pain, staying home with me when I couldn't go out, helping me not feel guilty for having to tell someone 'no' again." She takes a shaky breath. "I knew her getting married and moving out was going to be hard, but with everything else…"

"I'm really sorry, Lo. If there's anything I can do to help…"

I swear I've never seen a soul look bruised until this moment. I want to fix it for her, but even if I tried, I can never replace Camilla, and Lo would never ask for my help.

Swallowing hard, Lo shakes her head before looking out the window. "Thanks for letting me spill my guts. Camilla has been in the crunch time period for this wedding, and my sister just had a baby, so I haven't had anyone to talk to." Her voice breaks on the last word and, screw it, I reach for her.

Lo hesitates for a moment, and I hold my breath, strung tight. Finally, her smooth arms slide around my neck and her head comes to rest at the hollow of my throat. I rest my chin on the top of her head, letting my hands move on instinct, smoothing and caressing, comforting and consoling.

"I'll be okay. I'll figure something out," she says, almost as if she's convincing herself.

Seven

LO

I FEEL RAW AND groggy, like I have an emotional hangover, as I let myself into the duplex. The emptiness of the house envelops me, and I'm glad for some alone time before Camilla returns. The gravel outside crunches as Weston's car reverses down the driveway. He wanted to see me inside, make sure I was okay, but I begged off. I need to be far away from Weston King. He has always been my kryptonite and six years apart didn't change a thing.

The promise of a warm bed and comfy clothes calls me to my bedroom. I strip the dress from my body, remembering how it felt for Wes's hands to ghost across the fabric at my back. Shivering at the memory, I open the door to my closet. A box shoved in the back catches my eye. I tug on a pair of leggings and my favorite "Readers Gonna Read" sweatshirt before I allow myself to examine it.

I drag it out of the closet, bending down to blow the dust off before I settle on the floor next to it. On the top, in my own faded handwriting, it says *College*. My heart tugs painfully. I thought things were hard then—with classes and working part time. Little did I know, things would get much more difficult.

A scratching noise echoes loudly in the silent room as I slip my finger beneath the folded cardboard and open it. On the very top is an old, worn stuffed bear. My heart constricts at the sight of it. I remember packing it in this box and shoving it far into my closet at my parents' house. I had just dropped out of college midway through my junior year, unable to keep up because of the constant pain I'd been in. I'd spent every night crying into this stupid bear, feeling its downy softness against my skin, and holding on to the memory of something—or rather, someone—thousands of miles away. When I couldn't take it anymore, I'd crammed it in this box, never to be seen again. When I'd moved here with Camilla, I'd brought the box, but I didn't open it, still wary of the contents.

That's not the memory my mind focuses on now, though. That one goes a little further back.

"Come on, Lo. Just go with it." Weston dimples at me.

"I'm not going to sit over a dunk tank," I tell him flatly.

He gestures at his phone. "It's what the people want to see."

I roll my eyes. He's talking about Vine. He made one video scaring me and now he thinks he's going to get famous playing pranks on his friends. To be fair, it did get a lot of views. But seriously, who actually gets famous doing this?

"Make Camilla do it," I say, doing my best to ignore his charm.

Camilla looks at me, deeply offended. "Do you not see my intricate face painting?" she asks, gesturing to the butterfly she paid fifteen dollars to have painted on her face.

"Rod, then."

"Oh, I would love to, LoLo. Wes asked me to film though," Rod says, smiling cheekily at me. Wes flashes me an identical grin.

"Ugh, fine."

Wes managed to dunk me on the first try. To console me, he won me a bear at another game. I named him Elvis, saying I much preferred *that* King to the one standing in front of me. It was a lie, though.

The sound of the front door opening echoes through the house. "Lo, I'm home! I'm ready to watch *Pride & Prejudice* and sob!"

I shove Elvis, along with all the rest of the memories I've managed to keep hidden over the last six years, back into the box. *Into the closet you go.*

I WAKE UP THE next morning in Camilla's bed, bittersweetness making my throat thick. Last night was our final night together as roommates. Today, everything will change.

I roll over to find Camilla awake. Her dark skin stands out against the milky white sheets, and her face is contorted in a frown that's way too mournful for the happiest day of her life. "What's wrong?" I whisper, reaching for her hand under the blankets. The feel of it it so utterly familiar.

"That was our last night together."

This is my best friend in the entire world. We met on the first day of kindergarten twenty years ago and have been inseparable since then. We roomed together in college and have lived in the same house for the last four years. Unless Rod seriously screws up, this is it. We will never live together again.

"I love you, *fried*," she says, and I really lose it. Back in the days of MySpace, Camilla posted a picture of us and mistyped "BeSt FrIeDs" instead of "best friends," and we've been calling each other that ever since.

Tightening my grip on her hand, I say, "I love you too, fried."

Guilt pricks at me over not telling her about everything going on in my life. When she gets back from her honeymoon and I tell her, Camilla will strangle me for keeping it to myself for so long.

I guess I haven't really kept it to myself. I told Wes last night, and his response shocked me speechless. I expected him to make me laugh and get my mind off of everything, but I got heart wrenching sympathy instead. It's a side of him I've never seen before. In college, he was the class clown. If someone embarrassed themselves, he deflected and made everyone forget about it. If someone was upset, he lightened the mood and made them laugh.

But last night he just allowed me to feel my feelings, and no one has held space for me to do that in a long time. Camilla would if I let her, but I've even shut her out of a lot of my hard feelings, not wanting to burden her any more than I already have.

I feel like she's always giving more in our relationship than she's getting in return, and so I've started holding back to balance the scales. I know that's not how friendship works, but I'm also incapable of stopping myself.

My expression must have changed because Camilla squeezes my hand. "Hey, are you okay?"

Nodding, I try to force all thoughts of my vulnerability vomit last night out of my head. Today isn't about me, regardless of what I have going on. "You're getting married today," I tell her, and my face stretches into a genuine smile.

Her eyes sparkle, and any sadness that lingers over the ending of this era is pushed aside by the excitement of starting a new one. "I'm getting married today!"

Later that night, thousands of twinkle lights sparkle against the inky backdrop of the night sky. A balmy breeze on the rooftop of the downtown hotel wedding venue catches my bridesmaid dress, the silky fabric skimming across my legs. Camilla and Rod sway offbeat in the center of the dance floor.

It's been ages since I stopped dancing and took up a spot against this post.

"Want to dance?" I startle at Weston's voice, low and husky, behind me. His warm breath brushes along my nape.

My heart hammers against the hand I pressed to my chest as I swivel to face him. "I didn't hear you walk up. You scared me. You should know at this point in the night there are only obnoxious frat boys and handsy uncles left at the wedding. It's a dangerous time to sneak up on a black belt."

Wes grins. His smile always lights up his entire face, making his eyes crinkle at the corners. I can't make myself look that happy, even when I'm trying, and he does it effortlessly about a hundred times a day.

"Black belt, huh?"

A hot blush creeps into my cheeks. "Not exactly…"

Twin dimples pop out on his cheeks, lighting up his face like the first stars in the night sky. I drum my fingers on my leg and huff out a breath, knowing he'll beat this horse until I give in and tell him.

"I went to one class," I mumble to Weston's toes.

"Hm?" he asks. "I didn't quite hear that."

"It was really hard," I say, barely any louder, still not looking at him. "So I dropped out and bought one on Amazon." I mutter the last words, hoping he doesn't hear me.

When Wes doesn't respond, I peek up at him, only to find his shoulders shaking with barely containing laughter. I shove one of them, feeling the hard muscles ripple beneath my palm.

"Don't laugh!"

"You *bought* a black belt?" he asks, wheezing.

I cross my arms, daring him to not find me intimidating. He doesn't. "Yes, I bought it. Best eight dollars I've ever spent."

Weston sucks his trembling lips between his teeth, and I watch as he struggles to contain his laughter. Shaking my head, I say, "Don't you do it."

Contagious laughter escapes him, and try as I might, there's no way I can resist. I've never been able to resist him when he laughs like this.

I can feel curious gazes drawn to us from all around, but I can't bring myself to care. It's been so long—too long—since I've felt like this. And with the way Weston's eyes are shining at me, I get the sense that the same may be true for him too.

When we eventually pull ourselves together, he leans one strong shoulder against the pillar beside us. He sobers and searches my face, trying to read my expression.

"Are you okay? You seemed a little out of it when I walked up," he tells me, and I know he's referring to everything I told him about last night.

I nod, avoiding his knowing gaze. "I'm fine. I'm sorry about last night."

Wes hesitates for a moment. "You don't need to be sorry," he says, finally. "I'm glad you felt like you could trust me."

The air between us changes, crackling like the dying embers of a fire, and when I meet his eyes, I see the same memories reflected there. Memories of the last time he asked me to trust him. I did then, but I swore to myself that I wouldn't again.

"What are you thinking about, Lo?" His voice is thick as honey and rough as the calluses lining his palms.

I glance away, hoping he can't see the raging pulse thrumming in my throat, and search desperately for a change of subject. My eyes lock on Camilla swaying in Rod's arms, a look of pure, contented joy on her face. Her bright smile is reflected against her dark skin, and she's glowing. Rodrigo looks down at her as if he's never seen anything better.

I nod in their direction, thankful for the distraction. "What they've got seems nice," I say.

"Yeah, it really does," Wes responds, and I think I hear the same longing in his tone that I feel deep beneath my chest. Surprise glances through me.

"I'm shocked. I didn't think you ever wanted to settle down. You've dated almost every girl in LA." Wes raises his eyebrows, and the heat creeps back up my neck and over my cheeks again. "At least that's what it looks like."

He stands back up to his full height and crosses his arms over his chest, his biceps pulling the fabric of his suit jacket tight over his arms. "You can't believe everything you see online, Lo."

The moment stretches between us, and my mind runs wild with all the possibilities that one sentence holds.

Clearing his throat, Wes turns his attention back to the dance floor. He nods toward Camilla and Rodrigo. "What do you think they're saying out there?"

"Most likely things that should never be repeated."

A low chuckle rumbles from his chest and I want to put my hand there, to feel it vibrate beneath my fingertips. "You're probably right." He nonchalantly points to a couple sitting alone at a table. The man is talking animatedly to his very disgusted date. "What about him?"

I intone a deep, excited voice. "'Did you know there are earthquakes on the moon, and they're called moonquakes?'"

Wes shakes his head seriously. "No, she looks too repulsed for him to be talking about something as mundane as moonquakes."

"'Ground up beaver testicles used to be taken orally as a form of contraception,'" I say again in the false voice.

Wes doesn't say anything for a moment, and when I turn back to him, he's staring at me with his mouth hanging open. "What?" I ask.

"Beaver testicles?"

"Yes. People used to grind up beaver testicles and soak them in alcohol and drink it as a form of birth control."

Wes is dumbfounded. "How do you know this?"

I shrug, turning back to the uncomfortable-looking couple. "Internet, I think."

That low, deep laugh returns, and I can't help but join in. "That's the most disgusting thing I've ever heard," he says, wheezing.

"I have more," I tell him between breaths.

"Oh, please, no."

It takes a few minutes to calm down because every time we're almost done, we end up looking back at each other and lose it all over again. The strange tension, the one that's been building for six years without release, finally begins to dissolve.

Pale green eyes sparkle down at me, and Wes extends his hand, palm up in my direction. "Want to dance?"

I hesitate a moment before slipping my hand in his, marveling at the contrast. Weston's hand is big and warm and golden. Mine is pale and freckled, with long, slender fingers that are always cold no matter the weather.

Wes turns, leading me through the crowd onto the dance floor. Spinning to face me, his free hand settles heavily on my hip. The heat of his skin through my thin satin dress sends a pleasurable warmth through my belly. He pulls me closer, leaving almost no space between us, and I can't help but lean into him.

But I can't make myself meet his eyes. I've been here before, just once. I can't bear to look up at him and see those exact same memories written on his face. Instead, I let my cheek hover right above the exposed hollow of his throat where he's unbuttoned his shirt. His head lowers, and his stubble scrapes against the sensitive skin of my neck. When I shudder, he closes the remaining distance between us, lining us up perfectly.

Despite the circumstances, despite all the reasons I shouldn't, I relax. I'll probably regret this tomorrow, but I can almost hear it, a faint echo in my mind, urging me to just go with it.

Eight

LO

I PLAN TO SLEEP in the morning after the wedding, but the buzzing of my phone on the hotel nightstand wakes me before the sun has a chance to. My whole body aches, and I know today will require extra medicine and a heating pad. Groaning, I fumble for my phone in the dark and silence it. Immediately, it vibrates again, the sound grating against the last vestiges of my nerves. Blearily, I peer at the screen.

Camilla. Camilla, who is supposed to be flying out for her honeymoon this morning.

Suddenly wide awake, I swipe open the phone. "What's wrong?"

"Have you been on social media this morning?"

I peel the phone from my face to check the time. It's 6:54 A.M. "It's barely morning," I tell her. "What are you doing up?"

"We never went to sleep!" Rod yells through the speaker.

"Ugh." I sigh, my lip curling. "What do you guys want? You better not be calling me just to rub that in."

Camilla's voice dims as she talks to Rod in the background. They better not be having this conversation naked.

"You haven't been on your phone?" Camilla asks me again.

"No, Camilla, I haven't been on my phone. It's been on Do Not Disturb. I only got your call because you're on my favorites list."

"Aw," she says, drawing the word out.

"What do you want, Camilla?" I ask, trying to keep my voice from sounding exasperated.

"Oh, yeah!" Camilla says, as if just remembering why she called. "Get on Snapchat and go look at the news thingies."

Pursing my lips, I do what she says. I notice a bunch of Instagram notifications but ignore them and click on Snapchat, waiting for it to load.

"Do you see it?" Camilla asks impatiently.

In the background, Rod says that they would know if I had seen it. My heart picks up speed a little at that comment, and I silently curse my Wi-Fi for sucking so bad.

Tsking, Rod says, "Such language early in the morning."

I guess I wasn't silent.

When it finally loads, I swipe over to the right and a picture of Weston and me fills the screen.

My fingers stop working for a minute, and I can't make myself click on the photo.

It's a picture of us from the wedding last night. My mouth is open mid-laugh, and Weston's eyes are doing that crinkle thing they do when he's happy. I remember the exact moment. We had been dancing to a slow song when Cotton Eyed Joe started blaring through the speakers. We looked at each other and lost it.

What I don't know is how it ended up on the internet. Or why. The words *Who Is Weston King's New Queen?* flash across the photo.

I open the article and scroll down. There are more photos of us, heads together at the rehearsal dinner when he was trying to talk to me, dancing last night with my head on his chest, high-fiving after he dazzled the crowd with his best man speech. It all looks ridiculously intimate. Which is ridiculously ridiculous.

"Oh, my gosh," I blurt, rapidly skimming the article.

Over the line, Rod yells, "There it is!"

"What *is* this?" My voice is shrill even to my own ears. The article lists my name. It mentions that I live in East Nashville. It talks about how Wes and I have been friends since college—how I was featured in many of his early videos.

Where did this information even come from? And what do they think they've uncovered? A sordid affair between me and an internet star? If I weren't freaking out so much, I would actually laugh out loud at the absurdity of it.

"Rod has been trying to call Wes, but he's not picking up. Want to meet us for breakfast? We don't have to head to the airport until ten." I don't answer her at first, greedily lapping up every word splashed on the screen.

Instagram notifications start to flash at the top of the display, indicating that it's now seven and my Do Not Disturb has turned off. I click the first one and cover my mouth. Yesterday I had a couple thousand followers, mostly friends and family and fans of my book. This morning I have over twenty thousand.

Dozens of accounts have posted the photos from the article and tagged me. I don't even bother looking at my DMs. How are this many people even awake right now?

"Lo?" Camilla asks. I shake my head as another notification pops up. "Breakfast?" Camilla repeats.

"Yeah, yeah," I say absentmindedly, continuing to scroll through the dumpster fire that is my inbox. Literally hundreds of DMs. Why did I click on this?

"See you at eight."

I nod, even though she can't see me. The call clicks off, and I just stare at the screen, mind uncomprehending. *What. Is. Happening?*

Suddenly, I just can't look at it anymore. I chuck the phone across the room like it burned me. It lands with a hard thump on the carpet.

I don't know what I thought would happen. Maybe I thought it would catch fire. Maybe I thought a genie would pop out and say this was all just a funny joke.

But, as I often have to remind myself, my life is not a Disney movie. The phone just lies there. It's then that I realize it's screen-down on the nasty hotel room floor.

Oh my gosh. How many toes have been on this floor?

Scrambling out of the bed, I pick up my phone and blow on the screen. Five second rule?

When I glance up, I catch my reflection in the floor-length mirror that doubles as a door to the closet. I look *wild*. My copper hair dried around my head in frizzy waves after my shower last night. When I try running a hand through it, it gets stuck. Leftover mascara smudges under my eye. I lick my finger and try to scrub it away, but have no luck.

Letting out a growl of frustration, I grab my sweatshirt off the desk and shrug it on before stomping toward the door. The door squeaks as I yank it open and my steps pound against the carpeted hallway floor. Without hesitating, I pound my fist against Weston's door.

The click of my door shutting behind me makes my hand freeze. I have made a grave mistake. If Wes doesn't open his door, I'm locked out. At this moment, I honestly don't know what would be worse—*Wes* or *everyone in the hotel lobby* seeing me looking like I'm driftwood washed up on a dirty beach.

Spinning around, I hop from one bare foot to the other, cursing my rare display of impulsivity while also debating what to do. Before I can decide, Weston's door opens. Slowly, I spin on my heel to face him.

Wes stands in the doorway, rubbing his jaw and looking like temptation itself in boxer briefs and nothing else. My throat works in a hard swallow.

Remember when I said Wes wasn't built? I've never been so wrong in my life. Taut golden skin stretches over muscles I didn't even know existed. He looks like he's been wrapped in expensive silk, the kind you luxuriate in touching. My hands itch with the desire to trace the ridges of his abdomen or the dips in his collarbones. I want to get a tape measure to find out how broad his shoulders really are. I wish I had a camera to capture this tribute to the male form.

Weston King *did not* look like this in college.

My brain is a computer with a virus, unable to perform even the simplest tasks anymore. I came here for a reason. I know that. But for the life of me, I cannot remember what it is.

"Lo?"

My eyes leave where they were trained on his chest and climb slowly back up to his face. *Move faster, eyes.* Belatedly, I realize my jaw is hanging open.

I may even be drooling.

"Can I do something for you?" Wes asks, and why did that sound so *dirty*?

My stomach clenches, and my hand settles over it instinctively. Looking down, I register that I am undoubtedly closer to him than I was a few seconds ago. It was not Wes who moved closer. His feet are firmly planted inside his room.

And, oh my gosh, so are mine. My feet shuffle back before I look back up at him. A smug smile tilts the corner of his lips.

Why am I here?

Oh, yes!

Now fueled with the same purpose that sent me here, I shove into his room. Wes has the audacity to look pleased.

Snatching up a shirt draped over the back of the desk chair, I chuck it at him. "Put some clothes on." The shirt smacks him in the chest, before falling to the ground. I stare longingly at it.

Wes cocks a brow. "That seems like a colossal waste of time if you're just going to be taking them right back—"

I put a hand up, trying to look menacing but knowing I look like a sunburned lobster with the way my face is flaming.

His smooth chuckle fills the space between us, but he grabs the pair of running shorts that were also hanging over the chair and pulls them on. The shirt stays in a heap on the floor, and I can't decide if that makes me happy or mad.

Perching on the edge of the bed, his lean, muscular legs stretched out in front of him, Wes asks, "What's up?"

After unlocking my phone, I toss it at his bare chest. He catches it with capable hands, which is just so unfair. I just woke him up and chucked a phone at him, and yet I'm still the one caught completely off guard.

I know the exact second Wes registers what's on my screen. Twin creases form between his brows and his full lips dip in a frown. Concerned eyes meet my own. "I am so sorry, Lo. Are your social media accounts private?"

"My personal accounts are. Not my author profile, though. I keep that public so I can engage with my readers."

Wes nods, as if that makes sense, but I can tell he's still lost in his thoughts. Belatedly, I realize he's problem solving, and it makes me feel a little better. At least I won't have to handle this alone.

"Okay," he says finally. "Maybe that's not too bad. It's just giving you some more exposure on that front."

That's true, I guess, but the entire situation still feels like an invasion of privacy.

I cross my arms over my chest, as if that can protect me from the scrutiny that is sure to come with this unforeseen moment of limelight. "What do we do?"

Weston's broad shoulders wilt, making him seem almost small and vulnerable. I have the overwhelming urge to comfort him as he drags a hand down his face and says, "I'll need to call my manager and see what he thinks."

I give into the impulse to sit down next to him, and bump his shoulder with my own. He gives me a small, weary smile before handing my phone back.

Staring at the screen, I read aloud, *"Who Is Weston King's New Queen?"*

"Clever," he murmurs.

"How did they even do this?"

"They have a way of manipulating a situation," he answers, his voice low and quiet.

Dragging my eyes up the bare expanse of his chest, I meet his eyes. They're filled with a rare intensity that makes my breath hitch. It takes me a moment to remember what I wanted to say. "Has this happened to you before?"

His muscled shoulder stiffens against mine, and although I can feel tension coiled beneath his skin, he holds my gaze. "Yes."

I swallow hard, mind racing, and his eyes track the movement of my throat. I feel like I've been set on fire, my every nerve flaming to life. Scrambling for a change of subject, I blurt, "Breakfast."

Wes blinks as if coming out of a trance and meets my eyes once more. "Breakfast?"

"Breakfast," I repeat. I am an author. My art is words. Yet I am unable to think of a single other one.

A knowing smirk tilts up one corner of his mouth. "Breakfast," he says again, his voice a slow, rumbling murmur. Heavens, why does everything this man says sound so suggestive?

I jump up from the bed, leaning against the dresser to put space between us. Breathing deeply to try and settle my racing heartbeat, I say, "Camilla and Rod want us to get breakfast with them before they fly out."

Wes leans back on his hands, and it takes everything inside of me not to let my eyes wander down his perfectly sculpted chest. *Maybe just a quick peek.* "Okay," he says, finally.

"Okay," I repeat, and he grins again.

Weston crosses his arms, and I track the movement of the rippling muscles. "Is there anything else I can do for you, Lo?"

Now he's just doing it on purpose.

I push off the tall dresser so forcefully that an old to-go cup of coffee sitting atop it starts to wobble. As I reach around to steady it, it tips over the edge, spilling cold liquid across my cream sweatshirt.

Wes is up in an instant, handing me some napkins from the desk as I stare down at the stain on my stomach. Uselessly, I try to mop it up. I let out a breath and sag against the dresser again.

"What?" Wes asks, hands slightly extended as if he's ready to slay whatever to-go cup sized dragon tries to harm me again.

"For the first—and definitely the last time in my life, I did not overpack. This is the only thing I had to wear today." Irrationally, tears prick at the back of my eyes. It's ridiculous, but nothing is going as planned today, and I suddenly feel overwhelmed.

Wes leans down so he's eye-level with me and meets my gaze. His green eyes are soft, his brows bunched in concern. Warm hands settle on my shoulders, giving them a gentle squeeze. "Hey, no big deal."

Taking a step back, rummages through his duffel before putting a faded gray T-shirt in my hands. It's soft as butter and thin from many wears. "You can borrow one of mine."

Sucking my bottom lip between my teeth, I chew on the delicate skin to keep from crying. "Th-thanks." Avoiding his knowing gaze, I step quickly away and head toward the door.

"Lo?" Wes asks, and I risk a glance back at him. "You okay?"

I nod a little too eagerly and hope he doesn't notice. "Yeah, of course." Letting myself out, I lean against his door and release a deep breath. I need to get myself together. Wes is back for good, and these kinds of situations are going to keep happening. I can't keep falling apart every time I'm in his presence.

After allowing myself one more moment to gather my wits, I push off the door and walk across the hall. It's not until my hand grasps the cool metal of the handle that I remember I forgot my room key.

Spinning around, I try to work up the courage to knock on Weston's door again. I move in front of it, fist poised to knock. The sound of his shower kicking on stops me.

Nope. Nope. Nope. Hell will freeze over, pigs will fly, and whatever other crazy, impossible things will happen before I knock on the door of a naked Weston King. Even I'm not *that* stupid.

After awkwardly running into every single person from the wedding and dealing with a receptionist who definitely recognized me from one of the countless articles circulating about me and Wes, I let myself into my room and slump against the door.

I glance at Weston's shirt, still balled in my fist, and shrug out of my soiled sweatshirt before pulling it over my head. The cool fabric skims over my torso, hanging to mid-thigh. It's soft and supple and smells like Wes, like spices and wood. It feels like being wrapped in his arms, and I don't know what to think about that.

On the front, in block letters surrounding a coffee cup, are the words "Just Go With It."

I shake my head as I peer at my reflection in the mirror. Full circle. I never really noticed the coffee mug in his logo, but I'm guessing it dates back to the first time we met—the first time he urged me to just go with it. He never stopped after that, either, always trying to get me to go along with his shenanigans. Then he started making videos using the tagline and got famous for it.

And now, here I am, sporting the phrase that started it all. Something about it makes my heart squeeze painfully. I tug at the hem and allow myself one more minute of standing in front of the mirror before I move to finish getting ready.

A knock sounds on the door a little while later. When I swing it open, his dark blonde hair curls in wet, wild waves all over his head. An olive green shirt stretches over his broad chest and his legs are clad in dark-wash jeans. It's completely unfair that he looks this good right now, when I look like a truck stop diner waitress after working third shift.

He leans against the doorframe. "You ready to head to breakfast?"

Spinning on my heel, I retreat into the room. "Let me get my shoes." Wes props a foot against the door to hold it open as I tug my Vans on. His eyes, glazed over with a look I can't quite decipher, track my every movement.

I straighten and smooth my hands down the planes of my stomach. Stepping past Wes into the hallway, I try to think of something to say. "Thanks for the shirt."

"No problem," he responds, a rough quality lacing his voice.

When we climb into the elevator, I can feel Weston's gaze on me, and it takes all my strength not to look up at him. The elevator dings at each floor we pass, the only sound echoing through the small space. When the doors slide open, I move to step out, but Wes cuts in front of me. I finally look up at his face, close enough to notice the pale stubble covering his cheeks.

The usual teasing is missing from his voice when he speaks. "I like the shirt on you."

My throat works in a hard swallow, and I search his green eyes, not sure what I want to find there. "Oh, um, thank you."

"Just like old times, huh?" His mouth quirks in the barest of smiles.

Hundreds of memories flood my mind, and I can hear the echo of Weston's voice urging me to let go and just go with it. "Yeah, just like old times."

And it's true. It seems whatever feelings I buried long ago are scratching back up out of their graves now that he's standing in front of me again.

A throat clears behind Wes, and we both turn to see a man standing at the entrance to the elevator. "Are you getting off?"

"Sorry, man," Wes says.

The gentle pressure of his hand at the base of my spine urges me forward. As soon as the doors shut behind us, I shrug off his touch. At his questioning glance, I say, "People are going to think we're together."

"That ship has sailed, Lo." The words, spoken so cavalierly, do nothing to calm the thumping of my heart.

Camilla and Rodrigo are already in the dining room when we arrive a moment later. I slide into the seat next to Camilla and wrap an arm around her thin shoulders. "Hey, married lady."

She's practically glowing as she smiles at me. "Hey, Queen."

Across the table, Rod chokes on his orange juice.

"This isn't funny," I say, fixing them both with equally withering glares.

Camilla waves me off, reaching for her glass. "I think you're missing how good of a thing this could be."

I glance around the table, checking to see if the guys have any idea what she could possibly be referring to, but they both seem as lost as I do. "How, exactly, is that?"

Camilla looks at me like I told her the live action *Beauty and the Beast* is better than the original. "Lo, you are a romance novelist! You just 'scored' one of the most famous men on the internet. Your book sales are going to skyrocket. You could spoon-feed them drivel for your next novel, say it's based on your love story with Wes, and everyone would eat it up."

I sigh loudly, feeling a headache start creeping up the back of my neck.

"And you," Camilla points at Weston. He has the decency to look like a cornered animal. "You could use some good publicity." She waves her hand dismissively. "Especially after what's-her-name."

Camilla knows exactly who Talia Benson is. And it's true that the breakup album she wrote about Weston didn't exactly paint him in the best light.

"You know what you guys should do?" When neither of us respond, her eyes maniacally widen. I know whatever she's about to say is going to be even worse than when she convinced me to get a perm in the eighth grade. "You should just get married!"

My heart screeches to a stop, tires squealing and burning on the pavement of my chest cavity. Of all the bad ideas I imagined, this *never* would have crossed my mind. Under no circumstances will I be marrying Weston King. "You're insane."

I turn to Wes, expecting to see a similar horror-struck expression on his face, but he's focused only on Camilla. His gaze is hard as flint, but she ignores it, regarding us both in turn. When her dark eyes meet mine, she says, "It would solve all your problems."

Nine

WESTON

My heart gallops like a team of wild horses in my chest as I stand outside Lo's door later that evening. This could work. I've been trying to figure out how to change Lo's mind—how to make her see that we weren't a *mistake*—and this opportunity just fell in my lap.

I've been dealt a stellar hand of cards, but I know I have to play it right or she will shut me down entirely. Taking a fortifying breath, I rap my knuckles against the door. It swings open like it's being carried on a phantom wind.

"No," Lo says before I get a word out.

Right. Off to a good start. I step past her into her living room.

Her head shakes so violently that I'm surprised she's not dizzy. "Nope. Nah. No, thanks. No," she says emphatically as she maneuvers through the maze of boxes in her tiny duplex. I don't know where she's moving, and I don't think she does either, but it's exactly like her to prepare anyway.

I lean against the front door, arms crossed over my chest, as she sorts through boxes, mumbling under her breath and completely ignoring my presence. I track her movements, distracted by the way her curls slip from her messy bun, hanging loose over the silky nape of her neck. My eyes skim over the delicate flush to her cheeks, and a thousand ideas come to mind of other ways to keep it there.

"Do I need to be here for this conversation?" I ask a minute later when Lo still hasn't stopped murmuring to herself.

Not stopping her task of packing up books from her bookshelf, she says, "Not at all. You can let yourself out."

This isn't working. As she tries to fit more books into an already full box, I decide to try another tactic. My feet carry me across the room before I can consider my next actions too closely.

I stop in front of the waist-high stack of boxes, place my hands on either side of the open one on top, and lean into her space. Pinned between the bookshelf and me, her chest rises and falls with rapid breaths. Silently, she studies me, and I wonder how many of my thoughts are reflected on my face.

I had a plan, a barely formed one, but a plan nonetheless. With her blue-green eyes locked on mine, close enough to see the faded gold ring around her pupils and the white flecks in her irises, only two words come to mind. "Marry me."

For a moment Lo says nothing. That spicy, floral essential oil she's always worn tickles my senses, and I want to lean into the curve of her throat where it smells the strongest. Against my will, I inch closer.

Something soft smacks on the side of my head.

Looking down, I see a throw pillow from the couch in Lo's hand. Her eyes are wide and unblinking, like maybe I won't notice she just accosted me with home decor.

My eyebrows inch up my forehead. "That's not how I pictured it going when I proposed to someone."

"See," Lo says on a breathy exhale. "That's exactly what I would have expected to happen to you."

The tension between us snaps like a rubber band. I'm sure my amusement is written all over my face as I lean back, allowing her some breathing room. Sliding from her position between the boxes and bookshelf, Lo retreats to the kitchen, leaving me still dazed in the living room.

My shirt hangs on her frame, catching on the swell of her hips as she reaches into one of the cupboards. An almost painful longing courses through me at the sight. The phrase on the front started not only my career, but also our friendship, and it feels so unbearably right for her to be wearing it.

I avert my gaze as she returns from the kitchen, not wanting her to see the stark desire I'm sure is written all over my features. She extends a cup of water to me and the cool glass feels like heaven against my clammy hands. I follow her lead as she walks around the coffee table to sit on the couch.

Lo doesn't say anything as I sip my water. The strain slowly leaves my muscles as I watch her mentally sort through what to say. *This* feels like familiar ground, nothing like that anxiety that's been swirling in my gut since the gravel of her driveway crunched beneath my shoes.

The longer she takes, and the more often she looks as if she's about to say something and stops herself, the more at ease I become. By the time she looks like she's finally figured out exactly how to convince me this is a terrible idea, I'm holding back a smile.

"We're *not* getting married," she says, confidence oozing from her voice.

I can't help myself. I laugh. "It took you that long to come up with 'We're not getting married?'"

Her glare is icy. "I don't even understand why this is a conversation we need to have."

I raise my hands up in mock exasperation, our banter making me feel lighter than I have in months. "I know! You should have just accepted my proposal immediately."

"I am not marrying you!"

I try my best to look compelling, but know I'm failing miserably by not being able to keep the grin off my face. "Louise." Her eyes narrow at me—she really hates it when I call her Louise, which only makes me want to call her that more often.

"Lo," I say, and she looks slightly more placated. For just a moment, as I sort through ways to convince her, I let her think she's convinced *me*. As her shoulders relax, I begin listing my reasons, ticking them off on my fingers. "You need health insurance. You need a place to live. You need to write more books without having to worry about paying silly things like bills." My mouth quirks in a smile, and I point to myself. "I, despite my best efforts to squander my fortune on LA rent, am incredibly rich."

If looks could kill...

My attempts at humor are obviously not working on her today. Backpedaling, I decide to change my approach, and try to appeal to her practical side instead.

"I can pay for health insurance. You can stay with me in my beautiful, newly renovated home and turn one of my many rooms into a delightful office to write in. I can allow you to objectify me and use my devastatingly good looks as inspiration for your hero in your next novel."

The pillow smacks against my cheek again.

I exhale and gentle my voice. All vestiges of pretense are gone and I hope she can't see the raw longing reflected on my face. "Seriously, Lo. You need a place to go and health insurance. Would it really be so bad?"

Lo's jaw works, and she avoids my gaze.

Scrambling for something else to persuade her, I say, "I could use some good press. I've been wanting to take my career in a new direction for a while, and it hasn't been working out.

Everyone still sees me as that jerk on YouTube. Talia basically told everyone I'm incapable of committing to a two-year phone plan, let alone a woman."

"I wonder why," she mumbles, staring at a point over my shoulder. The words are a punch to the soft, vulnerable spot beneath my ribcage.

Rallying one last time, I move into her line of vision, and her eyes finally connect with mine. "We really could do this, Lo. You won't have to worry about health insurance or money. And you can help me too. You can help me change my image, help me show people I'm capable of more than..." I trail off, not sure how I want to end that sentence. "You can write your book and the publicity will drive up sales. It could all work."

Searching my face for sincerity, she finally seems to waver. Unwise hope surges in me. "We couldn't stay married forever," she says finally, and the hope withers and dies.

I sit back and rub my neck. "Right, of course. We could divorce whenever you're back on your feet." The words taste sour in my mouth, but I mean them. If she doesn't want to stay married to me, I'll let her go no matter how much it destroys me in the process.

For a long moment, Lo is silent. "It's not a good idea, Wes. We can't do this."

The air releases from me like a deflating balloon, and I let my head fall back on the couch before I stand up. "Okay." My hand settles on the door handle, but I can't leave without saying one more thing. "Let me know if there's another way I can help, Lo."

Alone in my car, I slump against the steering wheel. I messed this up. Lo has never been one to take a leap, and I just pushed her to the ledge and told her to jump. I should have known it wouldn't work, for the same reasons it didn't the last time.

At the end of the driveway, I decide to turn left, heading to my new house, instead of right toward Camill and Rod's. My house isn't done, and I was just there a few days ago, but I want to see it.

It's long before my headlights beam across the door of the garage. The moonlight spills across the white-painted brick, making the place feel almost magical. Staring at the house that I thought Lo would love, I feel like an idiot. What does it matter what she thinks of my house?

I climb out and let myself in through the back door, checking out the progress they made in the last few days. A few spots still need touch-ups, and the furniture will be moved in later this week, but all looks good.

My fingers trail along the kitchen counter as I admire the changes from the construction. Unbidden, an image of Lo cooking breakfast at the stove pops into my mind. The vision is so clear, I'm almost convinced it's real. She's standing at the kitchen counter, wisps of copper hair escaping from her bun to curl around her neck. Her long creamy legs peek out from under one of my T-shirts. The steam from the stove brings a flush to her cheeks, and a smile plays on her lips.

Blinking the image away, I climb the stairs. The owner's suite and the guest room are both on the first floor, but there's another room upstairs. It's smaller than the other rooms, but I smiled the first time I saw it. I remember Lo telling me once that she always wanted to live in an attic room full of books.

Standing in the doorway, I imagine how it would look as a library. Lo would come over and carefully pull a book from the shelves. She would study the back cover, promising to return it but end up loving it and keeping it for herself. I would let her, too, until every bookcase was bare.

I shake my head, trying to clear the image from my mind.

I didn't think moving back to Nashville would be this hard. I hid my feelings for Lo for two years before I acted on them, never quite knowing what she wanted. Sometimes she would look at me like she wanted everything I'd been dreaming of, and other times it was like she'd pulled a shutter tight over her emotions, blocking them out even from herself.

But I've been gone for so long. I thought the feelings would have gotten lost after all this time and all those miles.

Maybe they did, but as soon as I saw her again, they came right back. And stronger than ever, too, because I'm not a kid anymore, unsure of what I want. Now, I know what I want. It's just that, once again, Lo doesn't want the same thing.

Ten

LO

"WHAT ON EARTH HAPPENED?" My sister, Alexa, asks as she stands amidst the sea of boxes in my living room, looking horrified. Her caramel hair is twisted in a knot on the top of her head and baggy sweatpants hang from her hips.

"I'm moving! Hopping off on the next stop on this great train adventure we call life. Going wherever the wind takes me. Getting out of Dodge." I hope my plastic smile appears perky, but from my sister's dubious expression, I can tell I'm not convincing her.

This visit is as unexpected as Weston's was two days ago. More, actually. I could have guessed that Weston would jump on a hair-brained idea like us getting married more than I would have expected my sleep-deprived sister to trek from our hometown an hour north of here to visit me.

My newborn niece, Kara, is sleeping peacefully in her car seat.

Alexa looks thunderstruck as she takes in the state of my living room. "I know I've been a little MIA the last six weeks, but I feel like I would have known if you were moving," she finally says.

"I'm pretty sure I told you."

Alexa's eyes narrow, she perfected that mom-glare real fast. Kara doesn't stand a chance. "No."

I cave like a poorly constructed igloo after the light dusting of snow we call a winter storm here in Tennessee. It takes exactly eighteen minutes to catch my sister up on the mess that my life has become since she gave birth last month. Or mostly, since last week.

Alexa's jaw unhinges from her mouth like a snake devouring its next meal as I reveal each bit of information. "Why am I just now hearing about all this?"

Guilt pricks me. Yes, my sister just had a baby—a sick baby—but she would have been there for me anyway. I think about how I would feel if her life was falling down around her and she kept it all to herself. I would be upset that she didn't let me help bear her burden—that she carried around so much weight on her own, letting it crush her. And I realize that's what I've done.

Alexa must see the mixed bag of emotions crossing my face because instead of questioning me further, she takes a step forward and wraps me in her arms. I sink against her, barely able to hold myself up now that I feel the full weight of everything.

I'm tall, but my sister is taller. Her cheek rests gently against the side of my head. She feels different from how she used to, soft in places that used to be hard. She still smells the same, though, like lemon and vanilla and something distinctly clean. Alexa is pure sunshine, and I soak it in.

Finally, I pull back. I hadn't realized I'd been crying, but she wipes the tears from my cheeks. "I'm sorry, Penny," she says, calling me by her longtime nickname. Alexa is five years older than me, and when I was born, she had just been learning the different coins in her kindergarten class. She took one look at my hair, the exact color of a penny, and has rarely called me anything else since.

Sinking onto the couch, I wipe away the remaining wetness on my face. Alexa perches next to me, waiting while I clean myself up.

"Now," she starts, "tell me why you aren't marrying Weston."

I couldn't be more dumfounded if she told me she'd seen Santa Claus come through her chimney last Christmas Eve. "You can't be serious."

Sighing loudly, she crosses her legs at the ankles and pins me with an exasperated stare. "Of course I'm serious."

I bolt upright, uncomprehending. When I open my mouth, no words come out. After trying to regain my thoughts, I open it again. Nothing. My whirring mind is still utterly blank.

Reaching over, Alexa shuts my mouth with a hand under my chin.

"You look like a dead fish hanging on a wall," she says, unsympathetically.

Once again, I'm too stunned for words. It seems motherhood has burned away any pretense my sister used to have. The only thing I can think to say is, "Marry Weston?"

Alexa leans forward and plucks a piece of popcorn from a bowl I left on the coffee table earlier. She chomps down on it before saying, "Why not? It honestly seems like a perfect solution for both of you. Convenient, even."

I cannot form coherent thoughts. "Alexa," I splutter. "This is *marriage*, not carpooling."

Alexa ignores me, reaching for more popcorn. I grab the bowl from the coffee table and hold it out of her reach.

She is aghast. "I am breastfeeding, Louise Summers." She points at herself. "I need to keep my strength up."

It's unfortunate for Alexa that she points directly to a ketchup stain on her shirt.

"I think the McDonald's you ate on the way here will keep you plenty sustained for the time being."

Alexa looks down at her soiled shirt and frowns.

"No popcorn until you explain yourself," I tell her.

Finally, the amusement drains from her expression, replaced with a gentle sincerity. "Lo, you were just let go from your job. You're about to lose your health insurance. You can't sign another lease on this place. And—"

"You're really good at this pep talk thing," I interrupt.

Alexa rolls her eyes heavenward. "Let me finish," she says. "Your options right now are slim. You can come live with me. We just turned the spare room into a nursery, but we can put a bed in there and keep Kara in our room."

I start shaking my head before she's even finished the offer. "I'm not intruding on you weeks after you have your first child, Alexa."

"Okay, then your only other option is moving in with Mom and Dad—in the RV." Her flat voice clearly expresses her thoughts on that idea.

"You don't have to say it like that..."

"You're not moving in with Mom and Dad," she says dismissively. I pick at my nails, unable to respond with the lump rising in my throat.

Alexa places a hand over mine, stalling me. I turn to her, and her expression has softened. "Penny, being married to that man would not be a bad gig."

"Fake married," I correct her.

"Fake married," she repeats. "I remember Wes. He was a nice guy." At my raised eyebrows, she clarifies, "Okay, not a *nice guy* in the usual sense of the word. He was wild and impulsive and everything you've never been. But he was also kind and funny and thoughtful, at least from what I remember."

Wes has changed. A vision of him the other night, looking more earnest than I've ever seen him, flashes through my mind. I'd wanted to say *yes* when he looked like that, with all his wildness and impulsivity simmering below instead of blazing like hellfire on the surface.

"Plus," Alexa says, dragging me from my thoughts. "We all heard that album. And everything she's had to say about it."

I clutch onto her words like a lifeline. "Exactly," I say. "Talia Benson wrote an entire album about how Weston couldn't commit to her. How he broke her heart and didn't even care."

Alexa looks at me. "If you really think it's true, then I don't want you anywhere near him," she says, her eyes much too discerning. "But I don't think you believe it's true."

I don't, and she knows that. No matter my past with Wes, I know he couldn't have done all the things Talia accused him of. He would never lead someone on, and I know that from first hand experience.

"Marriage is a big deal," I say, grasping at any straw I can get my hands on.

"Both of your situations are a big deal. I think a fake marriage is probably less of a big deal than the decline of Weston's career and your homelessness."

Her words pierce through the thick walls I built around myself after Weston left and my world fell to pieces. For a long moment, I don't say anything, my mind swirling in a thousand different directions. Finally, I say, "I'll think about it."

Alexa pats my knee, her pale, slim fingers an exact replica of my own. "Of course you will. You're Louise Summers."

At my blatant confusion, she says, "You think through every possibility of every single situation. Camilla came up with the idea, and immediately Wes was knocking on your door. Like I said, he's impulsive. But you're not. You need time to think." She searches my face, as if expecting me to understand whatever meaning she's hidden behind her words.

When no lightbulb flares to life over my head, she leans forward and scoops out a handful of popcorn from the bowl resting in my lap. "You know what? I think if Wes had waited even twenty-four hours to think on the idea before storming over here, you would have had a different response to him. You would have thought about it all day and come to the conclusion that it was the best solution." She pops a few kernels into her mouth and talks around them. "But he didn't."

My heart beats faster at her words.

"He came over here without thinking." she continues, pointing at me with her popcorn hand. "And that scared you. Not the proposal. The impulsivity. The thought of tying yourself to someone who is reckless and dangerous and could wreck you if he wanted to." Alexa raises her eyebrows. "And maybe it scared you that it was so easy for him to say yes to this idea in the first place."

She doesn't know the whole story, what happened between us before Weston left for LA, but that just makes the fact that she's right all the more worrisome.

Alexa looks at me as if sensing my mind is elsewhere. She's right—it's back on a deserted beach six years ago. She stands, leaning forward to give me a hug. "I better go before Kara wakes up. I love you, LoLo."

"Love you too," I murmur, still lost in my memories.

When I hear the gravel crunching beneath her tires a few minutes later, I make my way back to my room. Opening my closet door, I grab hold of the dusty box in the corner and pull.

The word *College* taunts me once again. This time, I disregard Elvis the bear and instead pick up the frame beneath it, the one that's never sat out on a shelf or hung on a wall. This photo was just for me.

Swallowing hard, I examine the picture of a younger Wes and me. My hair is shorter, and his shoulders aren't quite as broad, but what strikes me is our smiles. Rod captured a moment of Wes looking down at me while my eyes were trained on the camera. He hasn't looked that happy in any of the photos I've seen of him online in the last six years. And since getting fibromyalgia, since becoming familiar with a much darker side of this world, I can't make myself look as carefree as I did back then.

In the photo, we're standing on a shore at a lake house Camilla and I rented to celebrate the guys' graduation. It was going to cost us basically everything we'd saved up during the spring semester, but we wanted to soak in all the time we could before Wes and Rod moved away from campus and to Nashville. It wouldn't be a long commute to see them, but it would be much different from all of us hanging at their apartment like we had almost every night over the previous two years.

Memories flash before my eyes. That was the night everything changed.

"That's a good picture," Wes says, looking at the image on the phone screen. He stands next to me, holding the phone out for me to see.

My breath hitches in my throat. If not for the happy smile on Weston's face, I would think he'd been teasing me at the moment Rod clicked the button. But his expression isn't joking. It looks like utter bliss.

His gaze is heavy on me when I look back at him. My pulse pounds beneath my skin as the moment stretches, pulling us into a vortex where nothing else exists.

"Hey, ready to swim?" Rod asks, snapping the moment like a rubber band pulled too tight.

Wes clears his throat, and I try to calm my racing thoughts. Surely he's not feeling what I've been feeling for the last two years. Not a chance.

It's not until later that night, after the sun has gone down and Rod and Camilla have both excused themselves to go to bed, that the feeling—like Wes and I are trapped together in the eye of a hurricane—comes back. I think maybe Wes and I could be on the verge of something, but I don't know what.

Across the firepit, Wes watches me, as if sensing my inner turmoil. The flames dance across his features, sending flickering shadows across his skin and making the golden hue of his hair look like the first rays of sunshine in the morning.

"Want to get back in the water?" he asks, snatching me from my thoughts.

My eyes drift back to the inky water, listening to the gentle lapping of the waves against the rocky shore. The sounds of the night envelop us, and there's no one else around to make noise. We're completely alone out here, and the thought thrills me as much as it scares me.

The fear—of trusting Wes, of letting go, of being wrong about this—wins out, though. I shake my head and stand. "I think I'll just head to bed."

Wes doesn't move from his spot on the wooden stump, but when he speaks, I can feel it as clearly as if he touched me. "Come on, Lo. Just go with it."

He's said it to me hundreds of times. There have been plenty of times—like that first night at the coffee shop—when I turned him down. Then there have been others—like the dunk tank—when I've said yes to whatever crazy scheme he's come up with. But now I waver in indecision. I could play it safe, go back to my room, and *crawl between my sheets. Or I could be brave for once and freefall into whatever Wes has planned.*

I swallow, making my mind up. "Okay."

Wes doesn't hesitate as he stands, stripping back down to his swimsuit with the ease and confidence of someone completely sure of themselves. I don't. I can't. *It feels different—too vulnerable—now that we're alone.*

I follow him to the edge of the water, still clad in my shorts and tank. The lake rises to greet me, lapping greedily at my ankles. Cool, loamy-scented water covers my skin, rising inch by inch, all the way to my chest as Wes moves deeper and deeper into the lake. For a moment, I think about all the critters that could be beneath the surface, but just as quickly, I decide not to think at all. I always think entirely too much.

Wes stops and spins to face me. I don't move any further, leaving feet of space between us. The water sluices over his powerful shoulders, and they shimmer in the moonlight. My hands itch with the desire to trace them, feel the silken texture beneath my fingers, but I hold myself back.

"Are you going to come any closer?" Wes asks, his voice a low rumble across the surface of the lake.

I hesitate, considering, but then shake my head.

"Okay," he says, before growing quiet for a moment. His eyes never leave mine. "Can I come closer?"

My heart beats so forcefully in my chest that I'm sure he can see it pounding through my skin. I contemplate for a moment before nodding ever so gently.

He moves toward me slowly, as if giving me time to change my mind. The water ripples between us until he's only a breath away. I've never been face to face with him, considering our height difference. But as he sinks down in the water, we are matched up perfectly.

"Hi," he says, his trademark grin finally tugging at his lips.

I release a pent-up breath, finally feeling like things are back to normal.

But then he moves a little closer, and my pulse pounds everywhere. "Do you trust me, Lo?" he asks. I think back on all our time together, from the first time he asked me that the day we met to now. Wes may be wild and impulsive, sometimes even reckless and dangerous, but he never is with me.

"I trust you," I tell him quietly.

The distance between us evaporates like smoke on the wind. One hand slides along my waist, beneath the loose fabric floating around my torso. The other gently cups my neck, and his thumb swipes along my jawline, leaving a trail of fire in its wake. His forehead comes to rest on mine, and for a moment, I almost think he's trembling.

"Just go with it, okay?"

My nose brushes Weston's as I nod, and I think it might be the most intimate thing I've ever experienced. That is until his lips find mine. I gasp at the contact, and he takes advantage of the opening, swiping his tongue in a lazy rhythm against mine. He nips and tugs at my mouth, before beginning a slow, lazy exploration, like he has all the time in the world. Like this might be our first kiss, but it surely won't be our last.

The kiss goes on and on, overwhelming me in the best way. I always thought drowning would be terrifying, being swept up in a wave, unable to control the outcome. But as I drown in this kiss, swept up and unable to control my racing heart, I can't imagine anything better.

A dog barking outside drags me out of my head.

I look down at the picture—stuck between the past and present, memory and reality—unsure of what to do next.

Eleven

WESTON

"Did you watch the Dodgers game last night?" Brandon asks, his voice coming through my car's Bluetooth as I drive down the highway.

"I don't watch baseball, remember?" I say, switching on my turn signal to change lanes.

"What?" he asks. "You always used to watch it with me when you slept on my couch when you first moved to LA."

"You said it right there, man. I was sleeping on your couch. I watched what you wanted to watch," I respond with a laugh.

It's nice to not be arguing with Brandon right now. We've hardly had a conversation the last few months that hasn't ended with us annoyed with each other.

"How are things in Nashville?"

"Things are fine here."

"Did you sign that contract—the one we talked about before you left?"

So much for not arguing. He's not going to be happy after what I say next. Dragging a hand down the side of my face, I decide it's better to just rip off the bandage. "No. I'm, uh, I'm going to turn it down."

Brandon's quiet for a long moment, and when he finally speaks, his voice is terse. "I don't think that's a good idea."

I'm not in the mood for this conversation, but I force myself to reply calmly. "I'd rather focus on other things right now. I'd rather create some good content than support a brand I'm not even using."

"Fine. Send me what you've got."

I swallow, knowing I'm in for a dressing down and not wanting to deal with one right now. "I haven't had much time to do anything yet with everything going on."

"You've been there for over a week now. You'd think you'd have found time to, I don't know, do your job—especially if you're not going to do what I'm asking you to do."

"I've been moving into my new house, and it's been crazy busy. I'm not going to become irrelevant by not posting anything for a week."

"Okay," Brandon says. I wait for the lecture to come on, sensing he's not done.

After a long moment, I ask, "That's it?"

"Yeah, that's it."

My breath comes out in one relieved huff. "Okay, good."

"Because I don't need to tell you that not just your career, but also mine, rides on whether you put out useful content. You know how high the stakes are."

Okay, here we go.

"I don't need to remind you that you're backed up on brand posts or that you were supposed to finish that sponsored video last week. You've got it under control," he continues.

What he fails to mention is that these are ads I didn't want to do for a dating app I've never even used. "Right," I say, not bothering to hide my irritation. "Thanks so much for the call, man. I'll talk to you later."

"Get your work done," Brandon retorts and hangs up before I can say anything else.

What Brandon doesn't know is that I've been working on my own stuff. Or trying, at least. I didn't tell him about proposing to Lo. He'd be livid that I made such a big decision without running it by him. He doesn't need to worry, though.

Four days have passed since I proposed to Lo in her boxed up living room, and I can't stop kicking myself for my stupidity. I've been racking my brain for months trying to figure out how I could get another chance with Lo. Then this one dropped in my lap, and I still screwed it up.

It was perfect—a way for me to spend lots of time with Lo without spooking her. And I would get to help her, the way I wasn't here to do before. Marrying her would help me professionally too, although that's not my only reason for wanting to. While making videos with Lo would help my image, I thought it might also help bring us back together. More than anything, I want a second chance.

But I forgot that Lo doesn't work the way I do. She has to be presented with all the facts—the good, the bad, and the ugly. And then she needs to deliberate and agonize over it for a ridiculously long time.

She doesn't do *sudden*. She doesn't make split-second decisions.

I moved too fast and ruined everything, just like last time.

My phone buzzes on the nightstand in my bedroom at the lake house, waking me. When I check the screen, I notice how late I slept. Memories of Lo, of the honeyed taste of her kisses and the soft slickness of her skin, threaten to pull me back into my dreams. I guess my moonlit swim—and staying up for hours thinking about it after—really took it out of me.

My phone buzzes in my hand, but I ignore the call from the unfamiliar number. I try to return to my dreams, but they pale in comparison to reality. I don't know what made me finally do it—kiss Lo. I've wanted to for so long, but Lo is a creature of habit, and I didn't know how she would handle a change like this.

But as the firelight danced across her skin, lighting her up in burnished golds and rich coppers, my fate was sealed. I wasn't sure what I wanted to do when we got out to the water, but when I saw the same desire reflected in her eyes, I broke. I knew I'd never be whole again if she didn't let me kiss her.

And it was the best kiss of my entire life.

I ended up staring up at my ceiling grinning like an idiot until the early hours of the morning.

My phone vibrates again, alerting me to a voicemail. I expect a telemarketer, but instead, I hear something much more shocking.

"Hey, Weston. My name is Brandon Phillips, and I currently work for a talent agency in LA. I saw some of your videos on Vine and wanted to talk to you about representation. I had some ideas on ways we could take your career to the next level."

My phone ringing through my Bluetooth speaker pulls me out of my memories. I answer without looking at the Caller ID as I maneuver into a tight parking spot. "Hello?"

"I'll marry you."

I hit the brakes hard. "Lo?"

"Have you proposed to someone else in the last three days, Weston?" she deadpans, her voice light, although I detect the veil of anxiety beneath it.

AFter finishing pulling into the spot, I lean my head on my steering wheel, my heart beating violently in my chest. "No," I tell her. "I'm just shocked. I'm pretty sure you said 'no' in ten different ways."

Lo's exasperated huff is loud enough to come through my car speaker, and I can't help but smile into my steering wheel. When she finally speaks, her voice is small, unsure. "Can we meet and talk?"

Sitting up, I lean back against my seat. "I have an appointment to look at some furniture in five minutes, but I'm free after that."

"Where are you?" Lo asks.

"In your neck of the woods, actually. I'm at the furniture store in Madison, so I can swing by—"

"I'm coming to the furniture store. I'll be there in fifteen," she says and hangs up before I get a chance to respond.

I guess I'll be furniture shopping with Lo, *my fiancée.*

Fifteen minutes later, after talking about my style and budget with the salesman and being shown some pieces I may like, I'm left alone to wander the store. I keep sitting on different couches, but I don't notice any of them. My eyes keep flitting to the door, and my palms are sweating.

While I still think this is a great idea, I can't say I thought she would actually agree to it. And now that she has, I feel unexpectedly edgy.

The door opens, and I see Lo step inside. She's wearing cutoffs and another graphic tee, this one saying *Synonym Rolls, Just Like Grammar Used to Make.* Some of the tension in my shoulders melt, and a genuine smile curves my mouth.

Lo's eyes connect with mine across the maze of furniture, and she makes her way to me as if pulled by an invisible tether. She traps her bottom lip between her teeth as she approaches, a sure sign she's nervous. I want to run my thumb along the surface and tug it free.

"Oh, no," Lo says, snapping me from my thoughts as she eyes the sectional I'm perched on. "This couch is terrible."

While I stare at the *perfectly fine* couch I'd already decided to purchase before she arrived, Lo turns and walks to one not far away. She collapses against it, letting out a wholly indecent moan.

Shaking myself from my thoughts, I look around until I spot her red hair peeking out over the back of a cream sectional. We're separated by two couches and a dining table, so I have to yell for her to hear me. "You seriously came here to accept my proposal and insult my taste?"

Lo's jaw drops at how loudly I spoke, and she spins around, making sure no one heard me. When she determines the coast is clear, she says at a much lower volume, "After seeing how bad your taste is, your chance of me accepting your proposal is looking more and more dismal."

An easy grin tilts my lips, and she smiles back, looking much less anxious than she did when she arrived. Standing, I weave my way through the furniture to her. As I get closer, Lo seems to sink deeper and deeper into the sofa, as if trying to back away from me.

Before I can think better of it, I walk straight toward her. But I don't sit next to her. Instead, my hands sink into the plush cushions on either side of her head. The heady scent of her envelops me, drawing me ever closer. The blue of her eyes is intoxicating, more potent than any drug, and the bow of her peach-colored lips has me wanting to lean down and see if they're as sweet as I remember.

I search her face, wishing I could know exactly what's going on in that head of hers. *What changed her mind?*

My voice is a rough, ravaged whisper. "So you changed your mind then?"

Lo doesn't respond with words, just nods.

I will my face not to betray the rush of relief I feel. "So you'll marry me?"

She nods again, unblinking.

"That's not an answer," I tell her. "I could get confused."

Her throat works as she swallows. "Yes," she answers. "I'll marry you, Weston."

Twelve

LO

WHAT HAVE I GOTTEN myself into? I think as Weston finally leans away from me, allowing me to take my first full breath in what feels like hours. He collapses on the couch next to me, rolling his head against the back so he's looking at me, his neck stretched in a long, lean line. Digging myself out of the cushions, I sit up, turning to face him.

"Under certain conditions," I say and Wes arches his eyebrows. I clarify, "I'll marry you under conditions."

"Hm," he says and pushes himself up, turning so we're sitting the same way. His knees brush against mine, and I try to ignore the prickle of awareness that bolts through me at the contact.

"And what, pray tell, are your conditions?"

I look down at my hands, unable to keep eye contact. Not with Wes so near and with us having such a delicate conversation. Instead, I pick at my nails, thinking through what I want to say.

I didn't tell Alexa, but what she said on Sunday shocked me. She was right, and I didn't like it. Six years ago Wes was impulsive and reckless with my heart, and I don't want to give him the opportunity to do it again.

But I realized that's up to me. Despite this sounding like the plot of an epic romance novel, it's not one. I can choose to not fall in love with him again. It's that simple. I will *not* fall for Weston King again.

Because despite everything, Wes is my only option. It just sucks that my only option is the sexiest man I've ever seen and someone I've also had the pleasure of making out with. I can still remember the precise texture of his lips, the feeling of his hands scraping over my bare skin, the heat of his body pressed against mine. And absolutely *none* of that is going to be helpful moving forward.

Reaching into the bag I stopped at my feet, I retrieved my notebook. Weston watches me with barely contained amusement that makes me want to slap that annoying smile off his face.

"I see you've really thought this through," he says.

I pause and glare at him before returning to flip through my notebook. "Someone had to." Taking a deep breath, I say, "Condition number one: We tell only our closest and most trusted friends and family that this is fake."

"That one seems obvious," Wes says, his green eyes lighting on mine.

"Nothing is ever too obvious that it doesn't need to be said," I tell him. "Condition number two: We both need to benefit from this marriage. We will help each other out with whatever is needed for our respective careers. I'll do videos with you if you need me to. You can help me with book things."

"Book things?"

"Since I'm self-published, I do everything for myself. Branding, marketing, interacting with readers. It leaves very little time for actual writing. You're really good at all that, obviously, so I could use your expertise."

"Done," he says, without hesitation. "Whatever you need."

Now, here's the hard part. Gnawing on my bottom lip, I avoid Weston's gaze. Tendrils of heat crawl up my neck and light my cheeks on fire. I just need to rip off the bandage. Forcing my eyes up to his, I say, "I have one last condition."

One of his dark blonde brows arches.

I clear my throat, not allowing myself to look away from him. "Wes…"

"Lo…" he responds, his tone teasing.

His ability to be calm in every situation grates on my nerves. Why, oh why, is this man not able to feel anxious?

Burying my face in my hands, I make an exasperated noise in the back of my throat.

Warm fingers wrap around my wrists, tugging gently, and concerned green eyes meet mine. "What's up?"

"We kissed," I blurt. He blinks at me, his face a portrait of stunned confusion. For the first time in his life, Weston King is *speechless*. If I wasn't about to be sick with nerves, I might actually laugh.

When he doesn't respond, a horrifying thought crosses my mind. What if he *forgot*? "We kissed six years ago," I tell him, feeling both desperate for him to remember and annoyed that he could have possibly forgotten.

His lips twitch in a smile that makes his dimples pop. "I remember. I was there."

I stare at him, unsure what that smile means. I grasp onto the one thing I know for sure. "We both agreed it was a mistake."

Wes drops my hands and leans back, rubbing his neck. His biceps flex with the movement, and I can't help but appreciate all the ways the years since we last saw each other have been good to him. "You did tell me that. Very kindly."

I fold my hands together in my lap to keep from smoothing back the hair he mussed up when he was rubbing his neck.

"Wes, the very next day you got a call from Brandon asking to represent you. To help you move to LA. It was your big break. Nothing could have happened between us."

"Right," Wes says, and it almost sounds as if his voice is a little harder. "We shouldn't have done it. We were better off friends anyway."

It may have happened six years ago, and we may have already had this exact conversation once, but it doesn't stop it from stinging a little. I had been in love with Weston for two years when he finally kissed me. It was absolute perfection. The way he held me—his hands on my face, his warm breath on my skin, his smile against my lips—it was everything I could have ever hoped for.

But then Brandon wanted to represent him and move him out to California. I was the one who said it was a mistake. I didn't want Wes to think he was crushing me or breaking my heart. He agreed with me, and it honestly hurt more than it should have. He chose LA and left. And yes, while I'm over it, it hasn't stopped feeling a little like salt in a wound any time I think about it, even now.

"What's your condition, Lo?" Wes prompts softly.

I clear my suddenly tight throat. "Right." Despite planning these conditions for days, I still haven't figured out how to phrase this. "We, um, well…"

Weston's gaze is steady on me as I trip over my words, and I feel like he can see straight down to my soul.

Letting out a shaky breath, I say, "It's just that we got confused before. We screwed up six years ago. If we hadn't been such good friends, it probably would have ruined our friendship." Things between us have been different since then, but I hope he attributed it to the distance between us and not my broken heart.

I wait for Wes to fill in the blanks of what I'm trying to say, but of course, he doesn't. "I think we should keep clear boundaries," I tell him.

The faintest of grins plays on his lips. "What do you mean by that?" he asks, his voice deep and rumbling. He leans forward, bracing his hand on the cushion next to my shoulder. His movements are slow, like honey pouring over biscuits, but my breathing is the opposite. His gaze dips to the rapid rise and fall of my chest before locking back on my eyes.

"You haven't answered my question, Lo," he breathes.

I swallow and try to ignore the quivering deep in my stomach. "No, um," I gesture between us. "No physical contact except in public," I finally blurt.

He leans a little closer, as if pulled by a gravitational force neither of us can control. "None?"

"None," I respond, willing my voice to remain even.

Weston's eyes drop, fixing on my lips, and darken almost imperceptibly when my tongue pokes out to wet them. "We're in public now," he says, meeting my gaze once more.

My breath hitches in my lungs, and I feel as if I'm standing on the edge of a precipice, unable to stop myself from falling over.

The spell breaks as Wes moves back, putting much needed space between us. "I'm just kidding. I agree. Better to keep things uncomplicated."

I hate the disappointment that courses through my veins at his words, but even more than that, I hate myself for being sucked back into his orbit so easily. I need to be on guard if this is ever going to work.

Taking a fortifying breath, I tell him, "That's it. For now, at least. I'm sure I'll think of more. What are yours?" I reach for my bag, stuffing the notebook back inside.

"I don't have any."

My hands stop moving as I focus on him. "None?"

"No," Wes says, broad shoulders lifting in a shrug. "You're the planner, not me. I trust whatever you come up with."

A pleased smile lifts my mouth. "Well, thank you for trusting me."

Wes watches me as I lean back into the couch cushions, an identical smile on his face. "Do you like this couch?"

I nod, relishing the way I sink into the cushions as they surround me like a warm hug. "I love this couch."

"Let's get it."

"What?" I ask, sure I didn't hear him correctly. I don't know why buying furniture together seems like a big step when we just agreed to get *married*, but it does.

Weston's smirking now, and I know he can see my thoughts written all over my face. "I mean, I can't tell the difference between this couch and the other one I was on."

"Well, that one was atrocious, for starters."

"It will be yours too. Might as well get one you like." He shrugs like this isn't the big deal that it is.

The weight of what we're doing finally starts to sink in.

"So we're getting married then?" Wes asks, his thoughts mirroring my own.

This may be the biggest mistake of my life, but I don't have another option. And although I'm not sure if it's a good or bad thing, there's no one else I would rather do this with. Grabbing one of the throw pillows, I hug it to my chest, and say, "I guess so."

One corner of his mouth quirks in a smile. "Now we just have to tell everyone."

"You're what?" Camilla screams and, I kid you not, does an actual spit take.

So maybe springing "We're getting married!" on Rod and Camilla the day they get back from their honeymoon wasn't the best idea. But we also don't have a lot of time. Less than a week, actually.

Wes hands me a wad of napkins that I use to wipe up the sticky soda Camilla just sprayed in my direction. "I said we're getting married." My voice raises at the end like I'm asking a question.

Wes smirks at me. My nervousness is highly amusing to him.

Rod's large brown eyes just flick back and forth between the three of us, trying to figure out if this is all a joke.

Camilla snatches the wad of damp napkins from my hand and fixes me with a fierce gaze. "Explain."

It's as if my voice box has ceased to function properly. How does one form words? How do mouths speak them? Have I lost the ability to talk? Will I live forever like this?

I turn to Weston. He's sitting next to me in the booth, one toned arm draped over the back of the seat behind me. We just picked up Camilla and Rodrigo from the airport and took them to lunch at mine and Camilla's favorite deli in East Nashville. I've been here so many times and made so many good memories that walking into the familiar place is usually like wrapping myself in a warm blanket.

Not today, though. Wes must see that in my eyes because he doesn't laugh at my panicked expression. His hand dips to squeeze my shoulder before he turns back to our best friends and explains the series of events that have transpired since they left.

The story is interrupted every few moments with questions and comments from a very excited Camilla and a shell-shocked Rod.

"So, then," Wes says. "Lo proposed to me in the furniture store."

He hisses softly and lets out a laugh as my elbow connects with his ribs. "That's not true. *I* agreed to marry *him*." I tell Camilla who is looking between Wes and I suspiciously. Bracing myself, I say, "I haven't been completely honest with you the past few weeks."

At the tone of my voice, Camilla reaches across the table and grabs my hand, knowing instinctively that it's not good news that I have to share.

"I was let go from work." I expect the pain of admitting that to be overwhelming, like it was when I first found out, but it's like a weight being lifted from my shoulders. My people all know now, and we have a plan.

"Oh, Lo," she says, her smooth, dark hand tightening on mine. "When? Why didn't you tell me?"

"It was the Monday before the wedding. Elizabeth decided to not go back to work and stay home with Maddox and the new baby. I left work that day, and I haven't been back."

"They can't just do that. You haven't done anything wrong," she says, her voice rising in indignation, but I cut her off, telling her about the three-month salary they offered. Her brown eyes still flame with indignance, but she looks a little less ready to pounce. "Are you okay?"

"Is there anything we can do?" Rod asks. I look between them, thankful for the help they've both been to me over the last six years. Camilla has always been there to cater to my emotional needs. Rod would be the one to leave work early to pick up medicine for me from the pharmacy so Camilla wouldn't have to leave me alone in pain.

I wouldn't have made it the last six years without them. I fight back the thankful tears that well in my eyes, knowing that even though things are different now, I'll still always have them to lean on.

"I'm okay," I tell them, my spirits lightening considerably. Leaning forward conspiratorially, I whisper, "If there were literally any other option…"

"Really?" Wes deadpans. "Not even trying to hide it, I guess…"

I flash him a genuine smile and try not to shiver as his fingers slip under my hair and squeeze the back of my neck.

Camilla looks between the two of us before fixing her eyes on me. "So, what's the plan, then?"

I slap my left hand down on the table. A gold band with a small solitaire diamond glitters under the pendant light above our booth. Wes took me to the jewelry store yesterday and told me I could pick whatever I wanted. When I'd chosen it, a faint smile tilted his lips, and he said it looked like me. I made a joke about it being plain, and he tested my resolve to keep my hands to myself by saying it was the prettiest diamond he's ever seen.

Camilla screams at the sight of the ring. People turn to gawk at us, and I wave awkwardly, praying that I'll melt into my seat.

Once everyone has turned back to their food, Camilla has the decency to look sheepish. "Sorry," she whispers, and I roll my eyes.

Rod wraps an arm around her. "You've got the ring, then? When's the wedding going to be?"

I brace myself, screwing my face up. "Saturday."

Rod's hand swiftly covers Camilla's mouth before she has a chance to yell again. Her cocoa eyes bug out at us.

"We want to do it somewhere private so we're not harassed by people, but we also need it to be somewhere nice looking so it looks convincing," Wes says.

"Right," thinking about how everything has fallen into place so easily. "There was an opening at one of the state parks not far from here. We found a photographer who was available on short notice." I shrug. "It just kind of worked out."

Rod looks at Camilla, silently asking if he can remove his hand. She nods spastically. "You're getting married *Saturday?*"

"Yes," I respond, shoving down the swarm of nervous butterflies that take flight in my belly at the idea.

Camilla scrutinizes us with narrow eyes before focusing on Wes. "And you're both okay with this arrangement?"

I chew my bottom lip, unsure what she means. *Does she think I'm taking advantage of Wes? Or worse, does Wes know about my feelings for him in college?*

"We're both good with it," Wes says, his voice low and steady, his gaze never wavering.

My heart pounds at the unspoken conversation they seem to be having, and I wish more than anything that I knew what the looks passing between the two of them meant.

"Okay," Camilla says, her easy smile cutting the tension. "Let's do this." The knot in my stomach loosens at her words.

"So, who all knows?" Rod asks.

"Just you guys so far," I say.

"You haven't told your manager?" Rod looks at Wes with wide eyes.

"No," Wes responds. I wait for him to elaborate, but he doesn't.

Rod leans forward, resting his elbows on the table. "Are you going to?"

Wes doesn't move, but his muscles strain. "I will after the wedding." His voice is calm when he responds, betraying nothing, and I almost wonder if I imagined it.

Rod holds Weston's gaze for another long moment, and I *know* there's something else going on here. I make a mental note to ask Wes about it later.

"So, what now?" Camilla asks, pulling me out of my thoughts.

"We need to tell our families this week and finalize some details for the wedding." I look at both of them in turn. "We're going to need your help."

Thirteen

WESTON

Today is my wedding day, and while most grooms would feel nervous knowing they're about to commit their life to someone, I'm nervous for entirely different reasons, most of them I'd rather not focus on.

I'm hoping we did enough to solidify this fake relationship. Camilla and Rod took pictures of Lo and me in different places wearing different outfits so we could hopefully make it look like the relationship has been going on since around the time I announced my move.

Our parents know the truth, but they won't be here today. Lo's parents are across the country in the RV, and my parents couldn't make the trip on such short notice. Plus, as we were quick to point out, it's all fake anyway.

The only people who will actually be in attendance are Lo's sister and her husband and daughter, and Rod and Camilla.

One person I intentionally didn't tell was Brandon. He won't like that I made this decision without consulting him, but I know this is what's best. So before we announce our marriage to the world, I'm going to have a very difficult phone call to make.

Brandon knows something is up. He's called me more since my move to Nashville than he ever did when he lived fifteen minutes away in LA. But I've either ignored his calls or kept them short. He's suspicious, but he doesn't know what's going on.

My phone vibrates somewhere, pulling me out of my head. I look across the cabin I rented to get ready in, searching for the noise, and find it on the desk in the bedroom.

"Hey, Cam. What's up?"

"How's married life?" he asks, slightly out of breath. He and Hazel also know the truth, and I wanted him to fly here for the ceremony and take our pictures, but he already had another wedding to photograph today. I'm honestly a little shocked he would call me while he's working. He's usually so wrapped up in his craft that he forgets the rest of the world.

"Not married yet."

"Oh, right," Cam says, his voice trailing off for a moment. "It's only four there, right? I always get the time difference mixed up. So an hour till the wedding, then?"

Despite it all being fake, I still feel a twinge of nervousness knowing I'm getting married in an hour. That's normal, right? *None of this is normal, idiot.*

I check my watch—4:06. The photographer should be here any moment to take pictures. "Yeah, a little less than."

"Nervous?"

"Not at all," I lie straight through my teeth.

Cam chuckles over the line. "Yeah, okay."

"Have you ever known me to be nervous before?" I ask, tugging on a thread on the quilt covering the bed.

I hear shuffling in the background before he answers. "No, but you've never done anything risky before."

I laugh a little. "My entire career is doing risky things on camera."

"Not like this." He says it so simply, most likely not giving it a second thought, but it wedges beneath my skin and lodges there. I'm about to take the biggest risk of my life. I'm about to marry Lo Summers, the girl who turned me down six years ago after the greatest kiss of my life.

I can't help but let my mind flash back to that day, after I got that first call from Brandon. I'd felt on top of the world—pursued by a Los Angeles talent manager and kissed by the girl who'd unknowingly held my heart in her hands for two years.

I round the corner into the lake house kitchen. It's bright, the early summer sunshine pouring through the windows. Lo sits at the counter, scrolling through her phone. She looks up at me as I walk in, and a pretty pink blush stains her cheeks. She's breathtaking.

"Where are Rod and Camilla?" I ask, not taking another step into the kitchen. I want to kiss her, and I want to kiss her now, but I know Lo needs to ease into things.

"They went out to pick up breakfast."

Instead of rushing to snatch her up in my arms, I lower myself into the seat next to Lo, feeling her shoulder brush against mine.

"Hey," I say, beaming down at her.

"Hey," Lo replies, but I notice she doesn't reciprocate the smile. Her eyes seem to explore mine, no doubt noticing the excitement contained there.

Slowly, the corners of her mouth tip up. "You're in a good mood."

"I got a call from a talent manager," I burst, unable to hold it in any longer. "In LA!"

Lo's smile falters slightly before it returns with full force. "That's really exciting, Wes. What did they say?"

"He's working for a big agency now, but he's wanting to branch out on his own. He saw my videos and thought I would be a perfect fit. I'm flying out there next week to meet him."

"Wow, Wes, congrats," she responds, but her voice sounds a little stiff.

My enthusiasm dwindles a smidge at her response. "What's wrong?"

Lo's gaze searches my face once more as she seems to debate something internally—expression troubled. Finally, she looks away. "About last night?"

Something leaden drops in my stomach at her tone of voice.

Her lips tighten. "It was a mistake," *she says quickly, and I feel it like a punch in the gut.* "We shouldn't have done it, right? We just got caught up in things. We're just friends."

All I can think is, No. No, you're not right.

But as I watch her struggling with herself, I know it would just be easier for her if I went along with it. She obviously doesn't want to hurt my feelings—ruin our friendship.

"Right," *I tell her, swallowing thickly.* "A mistake."

My thoughts are interrupted by a quiet knock at the door. I cut Cam off mid-sentence, although I haven't been listening to a word he's said. "Hey, Cam. I gotta go. Talk to you later."

I click the phone off before he has a chance to respond and make my way to the door.

It's probably Rod coming back with the snacks he went off in search of a little while ago. Or the photographer who should be here soon.

But when I open the door, I'm surprised to see Lo standing on the porch in her wedding dress, worrying at her lip.

I think I might be dying by the way my heart comes to a screeching halt in my chest. Lo has always been beautiful, always captured my whole attention anytime she entered a room, but today, she is a sucker punch to my resolve.

All her hair is swept to one side, exposing a creamy expanse of neck speckled with freckles that I want to taste. Her plump bottom lip is trapped between her teeth and my fingers twitch with the ridiculous desire to tug it free. All those soft, luscious curves are covered by a light, thin white fabric that looks impossibly smooth. I want to know what it would feel like beneath my palms. I want to see if she'd moan against my lips and sink into my kiss like she did the last time.

Looking at her, I know I've made a grave error, a lethal mistake. I've been here before, and it didn't go as planned. I don't know why I thought I could marry this woman when two thousand miles and six years couldn't erase the feeling of her lips on mine.

I'm screwed.

Lo's voice snaps me back out of the past. "Can I come in?" she asks, twisting her hands.

I move back reflexively. "Yeah, of course. Sorry about that."

Her steps are timid and unsure, arms wrapped around her body like a protective blanket. Although she's tall and broad shouldered, she looks small and...scared.

Dread, thick and cold, coils in my stomach, and I just *know* she about to back out.

"What's wrong?" I ask, not sure if I really want to know the answer.

Lo's quiet for a moment, staring at her feet. If I weren't so anxious, I would grin at the sight of her typical white Vans popping out from beneath her wedding gown.

Finally, Lo lifts her face to meet my gaze. "Are we making a mistake?"

This could be my out, my way of saving myself before I fall in too deep again. But even as I think it, I know I'll never do it. I'd jump headfirst off a cliff if it meant Lo was waiting at the bottom with open arms.

That image, my friends, is beside the definition of *pathetic* in the dictionary.

Letting out a breath, I lean back against the door and cross my arms over my chest. Lo tracks my movements with a furrowed brow. "No," I say finally, pounding the nail in my own coffin. "This will be good for both of us."

Lo nods, more to herself than to me, but I can tell she's not fully convinced.

"Lo?" When she looks at me, I speak slowly and deliberately, not wanting to leave any reason for her to doubt my sincerity. "I wouldn't do this with anyone else."

"Me neither." My knees nearly buckle under the look of complete trust she gives me. She's trusting me with *everything*, and I can't screw this up. Not again.

She looks away again, her eyes tracing the walls, the floor, anything and everything but my face. A blush stains her neck, contrasting against the creamy white of the dress.

Something inside me clicks at the sight of that blush, an instinctual part of me that has always seen it as an invitation to push. I can't help the smile that lifts my mouth as the tension starts to leave me. "What's wrong, Lo?" I drawl.

She rolls her eyes and scuffs her shoe against the wood floor, mumbling something under her breath.

I move closer, tilting my head down to hear her better. "I didn't quite catch that."

Quick as a whip, Lo stands straight up, fastening her gaze on mine. Firm resolution sets her shoulders. "I said we're going to have to kiss out there."

A laugh escapes me before I can think better of it. "You don't have to look like you're going into battle, Lo. It's just one kiss."

Despite her earlier bravado, her hands twist nervously together in front of her.

My eyes take a slow path from there, up the slope of her arm and the curve of her collarbone, pausing in all my favorite spots, before finally settling on her face. I could spend all day mapping out the constellation of freckles on her cheeks.

"Are you nervous, Lo?" I ask, dropping my voice a few octaves.

She squares her shoulders. "No."

I lean forward, pulled by an invisible string. "We could always practice," I say, one corner of my mouth curved in a half smile. "We wouldn't want to look like this is our first time. For the cameras, you know."

Lo inhales sharply through her nose, not letting her gaze leave mine. "It's not."

A fire ignites beneath my skin at the intention in her eyes. It's an expression I've never seen on her, and one I would give my left hand to see many, many times again. My muscles twitch when her palms slide in a slow path from my forearms to my shoulders.

My throat bobs in a hard swallow, and her eyes fix there and hold. The moment stretches, broken only by the firm pressure of Lo's hands on my shoulders, moving me out of the path to the door.

"See you out there," she says as she swings the door open, her white dress trailing behind her.

"Hey, Lo?"

She turns around, and her engagement ring glints in the sunshine, sending light refracting all over the cabin like stars in the night sky. "Yeah?"

"Do you still think this is a mistake?"

Her eyes search mine for a moment, as if looking for her answer there. "No, Wes, I think it's all going to be okay."

Fourteen

LO

WHAT THEY DON'T TELL you about a fake marriage that will be publicized all over the internet is that you still have to take all the intimate wedding photos with the person you're marrying. I have been dipped, caressed, and snuggled more in the last hour than I have in the last year. And kissed. Definitely more of that than in the last, well, it's embarrassing to say how long.

"Okay, Wes, could we get another dip and kiss?" Heather, the photographer, yells her question at us from her stance across the field.

"Another one. Lovely," I grumble.

Wes grins. "I've never had any complaints before."

I certainly didn't complain back in college.

Before I know it, my world tips upside down, and Weston's face hovers above my own, his eyes tracing the lines of my face, before he presses his lips firmly to mine. *This* is the exact reason for my whining earlier. The kisses he's given me all day are completely lacking any fire. I know what it's like to be really kissed by Weston King, and this is not it.

I should be grateful. I should be sending praises heavenward that Wes isn't kissing me like he did that first time. He's doing what we agreed—keeping this uncomplicated. I *love* uncomplicated.

This is exactly what I want.

I certainly don't nip at his bottom lip. I definitely don't notice the noise he makes in the back of his throat or the way his hands tighten on my waist.

Because. This. Is. Uncomplicated.

"That's it, guys!" Heather yells, and Wes pulls back, his eyes heavy-lidded. I avoid looking in his direction, unsure what to make of that moment. "I'm obsessed with you guys. You can just tell how much you two love each other."

I can't help but flick my eyes to him at that comment, and my erratic heartbeat slows at the glimmer I see there. He's been a trooper this whole time, making the awkward poses less uncomfortable. He whispered jokes and sarcastic remarks about the photographer's directives between kisses and staring deeply into each other's eyes.

And then I went and mauled his face. I broke my own rule on the first day.

I am doomed.

Heather sidles up next to us. "This was great, you guys. Thank you for letting me be a part of your day."

Wes wraps an arm around my waist, and the gesture of easy affection does nothing to help untangle my jumbled emotions. "You were amazing," Wes tells her. "Thanks so much for everything."

"Of course!" She looks sheepishly between us. "I know this is super unprofessional, but Weston, could I get a picture with you? I'm a big fan."

Something twists in my gut, but I push it down, reaching to take the phone she's grabbing from her back pocket.

Wes stops my retreat with a squeeze around my middle, holding me to his side. "Sure, let's take one all together."

I don't think it's what the photographer had in mind, but my heart pinches in my chest at his gesture.

We squish together, Weston's arm still draped tightly around me, and smile at the phone the photographer holds out in front of the three of us.

I can't help but notice the way Weston's head dips toward mine, his jaw coming to rest on my temple, as Heather snaps the photo.

"Thank you so much," Heather says, moving back, and I use it as an excuse to step out of Weston's embrace. I need a moment. "I'll get you a couple of preview photos in a few hours or first thing in the morning. It was so nice to meet you both."

With a wave goodbye, she disappears through the thicket of trees. I turn to Wes, rubbing my hands over my upper arms. "What now?"

He nods in the direction of the cabins. "I think Rod and Camilla and your sister and her husband are waiting back in my cabin."

Even though Alexa and her husband, Matt, know the truth about this marriage, they still wanted to show up as moral support. I could use some right about now.

"I can't wait to get out of this dress," I say, and when Wes cocks a single eyebrow, I shove my elbow in his ribs. His laugh echoes through the woods like leaves dancing in the breeze.

We walk in silence for a few minutes, our feet kicking up dust along the dirt path that stains the hem of my dress.

"Wait," Wes says and stops. He picks up the train of my dress and holds it in his fist, exposing my ankles. "So it doesn't get dirty."

The white fabric contrasts with his tan, calloused fingers, and I know that one day I'm going to write a moment like this in a book. "Thanks," I say before continuing down the path. "How do you think everything went?"

I can hear the smile in his voice as he answers, "I think we were very convincing. Especially since you kept trying to stick your tongue down my throat."

A hot flush colors my cheeks, and I'm very glad he's behind me. "I did not. And besides, you kept grabbing my butt."

"Only because the photographer told me to."

"Mm-hmm," I say, glancing at him over my shoulder. "I distinctly remember a few times you took it upon yourself without her direction. In fact, I don't remember her telling you to do so until she saw you doing it already."

His lips tilt in a smirk and his green eyes crinkle at the sides. "What can I say? I'm a butt guy."

When we make it to the cabin and unlock the door, I hear a great yell of "Surprise!"

"Even a fake wedding deserves cake!" Camilla yells from across the room and pulls the trigger on a confetti cannon, sending multi-colored strips of paper spraying in every direction.

"I'm going to embroider that on a pillow," Wes says under his breath, and I hold back a giggle.

Before I've even had a chance to snag a slice of cake, Alexa appears at my side and begins dragging me away from Wes. "Hi, Wes. So nice to see you again. Looking very fit." She winks, and I want to melt into a puddle. "Just going to take Lo to the bathroom with me. Girl stuff, you know?"

Wes winks right back. "Wouldn't want to intrude. Have fun, Lo." He waves his finger at me.

Alexa yanks me into the bathroom and shuts the door behind us. She arrived right before the wedding started, so I haven't had a moment alone with her all day.

"First, Penny, you look beautiful," she says, fingering the intricate braid hanging over my shoulder. "I love this look on you."

"Thanks, Ale—"

"Second, that man is sexy."

I roll my eyes and try to move around her to reach the door. Alexa smacks at my hand. I sigh and lean up against the sink.

"That kiss looked hot." She legitimately waggles her brows.

I sag against the counter, suddenly feeling very weary. For the first time today, I notice a twinge in my back and a heaviness in my bones—I forgot my medicine in the craziness.

There's a knock at the door, and Alexa moves to open it. Camilla's face appears in the doorway.

"Hey, hey!" Camilla lets herself into the bathroom, and I realize she's holding my purse. She sets it on the counter next to me and digs through its contents, producing a prescription bottle. "Figured you probably forgot to take your medicine today."

I take the pills from her gratefully and use one of the paper cups next to the sink to down them. When I turn back around, Camilla is smiling at me. "Probably forgot because you were dreaming about kissing Wes again, huh?"

"*Again?*" Alexa yells.

Oh no.

I drag a hand down my face, only to have it shoved away by Alexa. "You'll ruin your makeup." She looks between Camilla and me. "Now tell me what she meant about 'again.'"

I fix Camilla with a glare, but she doesn't even have the decency to look remorseful. I stare down at my white Vans that are peeking out beneath the hem of my dress. "Wes and I kissed in college," I mumble underneath my breath.

"*You what?*"

"Please stop speaking in exclamation points," I whine. I point at Camilla. "You know what? You did this. You tell her the story."

"Gladly," Camilla responds with a grin.

As I let myself out of the bathroom, she says, "It was a balmy May night. The moonlight glistened on the lake, casting shadows across Weston's chiseled face…"

Two hours later, Wes and I pull out of the state park, heading home. His home—mine now too, I guess. A trickle of unease and anticipation spreads through me at that realization.

Wes moved into his new house amidst all the chaos last week, and although we moved most of my things with his, I stayed at the duplex anyway. I wanted to spend my last week of "singleness" sleeping in my familiar creaky home, snuggling on my couch and steering clear of Camilla's empty bedroom.

There is no avoiding Weston's house now, though. During the wedding, movers packed up the last of my furniture and unloaded it at Weston's. We officially live together.

Excitement starts to bud as we pull into Wes's driveway. This part of East Nashville is about ten minutes from my old house and in a much nicer area. The houses around here are all big craftsmans or charming Tudors like this one.

Wes parks in front of the detached garage and comes around to let me out, remaining unusually silent, and I wonder if he's feeling as strange about all of this as I am. "Thanks," I say as he shuts the car door behind me and grabs my duffel bag from the back seat.

I follow him through the back gate and past the pool, the still water dappled with pale moonlight. The deadbolt on the back door clicks as Wes unlocks it, and the sound feels more like the beginning of this new *adventure* than signing the marriage license did earlier today.

"Welcome home," Wes says, his voice a soft, rumbling murmur.

The back door enters into the kitchen, and although I'm not a cook, you'd have to be blind to not appreciate this kitchen. Dark wood beams cross the ceiling. I run my fingers across the white marble countertops and marvel at how beautifully they contrast with the black cabinets. Wes told me he hired an interior designer who picked out the soft leather barstools and the brass pendant lights hanging from the ceiling. Something—although I can't quite name what it is—stirs in my chest knowing this place is mine now too.

My eyes snag on Wes, leaning against the island, one leg crossed over the other in his fitted black suit pants. His attention is wrapped up in something on his phone, so I take the opportunity to look my fill. His wild curls have long since lost the fight against his hair gel, and his tie hangs limply around his shoulders. A patch of pale blonde hair is exposed at the open collar of his shirt, which is still tucked in, and I can't help but wonder if I'll get to catch a glimpse of his toned stomach when he untucks it.

I yank myself back to attention. This is bad. It doesn't help that I can still feel his hands on my butt from earlier. They were big and strong and—

Wes looks up then, as if he can feel me staring, and I press a hand to my stomach. *Calm down, ovaries.* He holds his phone up. "The photographer sent a few pictures."

He closes this distance between us, although I really think he shouldn't, given the way my thoughts are *completely out of control*. His warmth envelops me as he sets the phone down on the counter between us, swiping through the photos. It's strangely intimate, standing in my new house with my *husband*, hours after our wedding, staring at pictures of us wrapped in each other's arms.

"We look convincing, huh?" Wes says, but his tone is heavier than I would have expected. I lift my eyes to meet his, and I'm startled by the intensity there.

I make an affirmative noise in the back of my throat, not trusting my voice.

For a long moment, he holds my gaze, looking like he's debating something in his mind. I hold my breath, although I don't know what I'm waiting for. Finally, he says, "I'm going to change. Meet me back down here in a bit so we can make a game plan for posting these in the morning."

Wes disappears into his bedroom, and I stare at the place he vacated, not sure if I'm relieved or disappointed with that way that turned out.

Fifteen

WESTON

I don't know what's gotten into me. This day has been a thousand shades of weird. First, the wedding. How many people can say they woke up this morning and got fake married? Except, in the eyes of the law, I guess it was real.

We took the vows in front of friends and family. Witnesses watched as we signed the license. We are legally married in every way. It was surreal—after everything we've been through—to stare into Lo's eyes and promise to love and cherish her for the rest of our lives. It made for a strange first kiss as husband and wife. Not bad, but certainly not my best either.

But that's nothing compared to what it was like taking pictures after. The photographer, having no idea this was anything but the happy wedding of two people madly in love, contorted us into every position imaginable for these photos. I am only a man. I can only have soft lips pressed against mine and a butt *in my hand* for so long before my mind begins to wander.

I'm not going to lie and say it wasn't pleasant, but it also won't be good for anyone for me to be thinking that way about my real *fake* wife that I royally screwed things up with in the past. We already almost messed up our friendship by blurring the lines once before, and not nearly as much was at stake then. I really need to get it together.

My phone buzzes. It's a text from Camden.

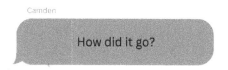

It's a good thing Camden couldn't be there today because he would have seen how much I was struggling and enjoyed himself way too much. If I thought this photographer was forcing us to look intimate, I can only imagine the torture Cam would have subjected me to.

I start to tell him it was fine, before erasing it. Today was good. It went better than I could have hoped, actually. It's only me who is feeling weird right now—and not because everything went wrong today, but because of how right it all felt.

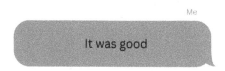

I attach the photos Heather sent, then toss my phone on the bed. Slumping down beside it, I run my hands over my face. The gold wedding band catches my attention, and I groan. It looks so foreign, but it also feels so right. I'm so screwed.

My phone buzzes again.

> Camden
>
> Those look really good, man

I scroll through the five photos again, able to look more closely now that Lo isn't hovering beside me. One was taken from far away, with us holding hands and looking directly at the photographer. We look like we're ready to take on the world together. It would probably be a good one to post with the announcement tomorrow.

Another is a closeup of us from under a veil. It was the first kiss after the ceremony, and I was determined to make this one a little better. It was gentle at first, but I surprised her by taking a soft nip at her lower lip. Instead of kissing me back, though, Lo smiled, and Heather caught that moment. It looked even more intimate than I suppose the kiss had—our eyes closed, noses pressed together like we were searching for each other in the dark, Lo grinning against my mouth.

The next three are much the same. After Lo laughed at my attempt at a better kiss, I realized there was no point in trying to prove my kissing expertise with someone I shouldn't get good at kissing anyway. Instead, I told jokes, and she did too, and we laughed through the whole thing.

That is, until that last kiss, when Lo had taken *my* lip between her teeth. I don't know if she was hoping for a laugh, but if so, she was sorely mistaken. My control had been on the verge of snapping like a worn-out hair tie.

I couldn't tell if Lo recognized that moment in the last photo Heather sent, but I did. As I stare at it now, something tugs painfully in my chest. It all looks so right, which is just so wrong.

Without thinking it through, I send it to Brandon with a text telling him I got married today, and promptly shut my phone off. I'll probably live to regret that in the morning, but I'm feeling a little reckless right now, and this seems like the safest alternative considering the temptation in my living room.

When I leave my room a few minutes later, Lo has changed into lounge clothes. Good. Something about her in that wedding dress was really starting to get to me. She looks up from her spot on the couch as I approach.

"I told Brandon."

Her brows inch up her forehead. "And?"

I grin, plopping down next to her. "I don't know. I turned my phone off."

Lo laughs, and the sound loosens the knot that's been forming in my stomach all day. This is good. This is normal. Just Wes and Lo—old friends. Who got married.

"What's the game plan for tomorrow, then?" she asks.

I lean my head back into the cushions and stare at the ceiling. "I turn on my phone. Brandon rips me a new one. We talk to my publicist and agent. We tell the world. We get ice cream."

She smiles at me. "Ice cream, huh?"

I nod gravely. "Yeah, I'm definitely going to need ice cream tomorrow. I'm going to need comfort after dealing with Brandon." A wolfish grin tips my lips. "Unless you can think of a more fun way to make me feel better."

A pillow hits me in the chest, and I chuckle, finally feeling the stress of the day melt away.

"You really can be the worst sometimes," Lo says, although her grin tells me she doesn't mind too much.

"You know what sounds really good right now?" I ask.

She pins me with a look. "If you say something dirty, I'm going to bed."

I laugh up at the ceiling before turning back to face Lo. Her cheeks are flushed. From happiness or embarrassment, I can't tell. Either way, with her hair tied in a bun atop her head and her face glowing, Lo looks absolutely beautiful. It's the first night, and I'm already screwed.

"A Weston Special."

She checks the time on her phone. "It's nine o'clock."

"Come on, Lo, just—"

"Yeah, yeah. 'Just go with it.'" She rolls her eyes. "Fine, make me a Weston Special."

She sinks down into the sofa and stretches out as I stand, but I tug her up with me. We're chest to chest, Lo pinned between me and the couch, and I know I should step back. After a moment's hesitation, I do. If Lo notices, she doesn't say anything.

Lo pads softly behind me into the kitchen before she takes a seat at the island. I pull two mugs down from the cupboard and start preparing the ingredients—cinnamon, vanilla bean paste, brown sugar, and milk. While the espresso maker brews four shots of espresso, I whip up the rest of the latte. I've done this so many times I could do it in my sleep, but I feel anything but relaxed as Lo tracks my every movement.

It's not like she hasn't seen me do this a hundred times, even back in college when I used a stovetop espresso maker and imitation vanilla flavor. But her gaze feels different tonight, just like it has all day. My skin prickles in awareness beneath her stare.

"Are you flexing?" Lo asks, a smile in her voice.

My knee-jerk reaction is to stop, but then she would know. Now I'll just have to stay tense forever. Shouldn't be that hard, seeing as how I have been all day.

"No, *Louise*, I'm not flexing," I reply as I pour the frothy milk mixture over the espresso. I carry our mugs to where Lo is sitting at the edge of the bar, placing hers in front of her. Her breath hitches as I lean in. At least I'm not the only one.

"Cheers?" I ask, extending my mug in her direction.

She holds my gaze for a moment before clinking our mugs together. "Cheers."

"To a short, uneventful marriage," I lie before sipping the hot liquid.

A grin splits her mouth, and she repeats, "To a short, uneventful marriage."

Sixteen

LO

When I wake up, the pale morning sunshine is casting unfamiliar shadows into my new room. I look around, appreciating how the sun slants through the curtains here more than it did at the duplex.

The light catches on my wedding ring and sends glittering rays across the walls. I'm not sure how to feel when I see it. There were so many times in college I dreamed of a future with Wes, but I never imagined waking up alone in bed with his ring on my finger.

My phone buzzes, shaking me out of my thoughts. I pick it up, ignoring the long line of Instagram notifications, and click on the text from Wes at the top.

> Weston
> Come downstairs when you wake up. I made breakfast :)

Groaning, I roll over in bed. My life is starting to uncomfortably resemble a romance novel, and I really can't decide how I feel about it.

Dressing swiftly, I exit my room, letting my fingers trail along the wrought-iron bannister as I head downstairs. When I enter the kitchen, Wes is sitting at the counter, eating cereal from a bowl roughly the size of a punch bowl. I stop in my tracks, trying to hold back a laugh at the scene in front of me.

He looks up and smiles before noticing my expression. "What's up?" he asks around a bite of cereal.

I suck in my lips, trying not to release the giggle bubbling in my throat. After yesterday, I wasn't entirely sure where we stood. Things at the wedding had been…different than expected. Despite the circumstances, it was intimate, albeit a little awkward.

But last night was good. The coffee woke us up, and we stayed up talking for hours about everything under the sun—college, Wes' life in California, my disease. What we didn't talk about was us, or rather, the us that could have been six years ago. I was glad for it, because I don't think I could have handled sitting on the couch in the low light talking with Wes about that night.

Everything last night felt really, really right. Weston's soft, green eyes focused on me. His rich laughter filling the room. His strong body stretched out across from mine.

I'd started to wonder if the mistake we made six years ago wasn't the kiss, but calling it off before we give ourselves a chance.

But I shouldn't have worried about it. I've read a lot of romance novels. Like *a lot*. When a man likes you, he stands shirtless in the kitchen and makes you scrambled eggs. It's a proven fact.

He does not, however, stare at you like you've grown two heads overnight while he has milk dripping from his chin into his punch bowl of cereal.

The whole situation is so comical that I don't even feel the twinge of loss at what could have been. Shaking my head, I sit next to him at the counter, still holding back a smile. "It's nothing." Wes may not be naked making me breakfast, but he did set out a normal sized bowl and three different kinds of cereal for me to choose from. "Which did you choose?" I ask, looking at his bowl.

"All three," he says with a grin.

I laugh and pour myself some Apple Jacks. "So," I say, pointing at his phone. "You texted me this morning, so I'm assuming that means you turned your phone on."

He nods, looking grim as he swallows a bite.

"And?" I ask before taking a bite of my cereal, savoring the cinnamony-sweet taste.

He sets his spoon down on the counter and turns to face me, his eyes serious. "Wanna go to LA tonight?"

I choke on my cereal.

Wes smacks my back none too gently. I hold up a hand, and he stops, but he gives me his glass of what looks like orange juice. I take a sip, and the tart liquid does nothing to soothe my sore throat.

My voice is scratchy when I finally speak. "You want to go to California tonight?" I ask.

"Not at all," he responds.

"Then why—"

"I don't want to go, but Brandon is, to put it very delicately, not happy. He says that, for many reasons, he should have known about this ahead of time. Mostly, he's annoyed that my management team wasn't able to set up some press stuff for us."

Weston's green eyes look troubled, and I can tell that his manager's unhappiness is weighing heavily on him. We didn't talk much about Brandon while we were planning this whole scheme. I asked if there was anyone on his team he needed to tell, and he said he would talk to them after the wedding.

When I pressed him, Wes said that they would be upset about it, but he didn't seem to want to expand, so I didn't push it. Now I'm wishing I had.

"Won't everyone assume we're on our honeymoon this week?"

He nods. "Brandon wants us to fly to Orange County. He's already rented us a house in Newport Beach. He wants us to stay there and take pictures and post as if we're on our honeymoon."

"Oh, okay," I say. A free vacation to Southern California doesn't sound too bad.

"Really, though, he and some other people on my team are going to be there with us, at least during the day, helping us form a plan of how to proceed."

"Don't we already have a plan?"

Wes runs a hand through his hair, making his blond curls stick out every which way. "We do, but I don't think they're going to like it."

I chew on my bottom lip, unsure what to say. Finally, I ask, "Are you having second thoughts? We haven't posted anything yet. No one knows but us."

His eyes snap to mine. We're sitting very close, I notice suddenly. I can see the dark green flecks in his bright eyes, and I notice how long and thick his lashes are. They're blond at the tips, so you can't tell unless you're a breath away. It makes me wonder what he's observing about me from this distance.

"No," he says quietly. "I don't regret it. I still think it's a good idea." He smooths his finger over the lip of his bowl before meeting my gaze again. "We just need to stick to our plan and not let anyone change it."

It hits me that he's nervous. He's so confident in every situation, but every time we talk about his manager or other people on his team, he tenses up. I don't understand why these people who are supposed to be running his career, these people he considers good friends, can make him so anxious.

Is it because he's lying to them, or is it something more? My mind flashes back to the conversation we had with Rod and Camilla when they got back from their honeymoon. I remember the look Rod gave Wes when he said he wasn't going to tell his management team about us until after the wedding.

Without thinking, I place my hand on his forearm. The muscles bunch and tense beneath my touch. "We came up with this plan without them, and it's a good one. We aren't changing it for anything we don't think is better."

He holds my gaze for a long moment, unblinking, as if he's taking my words and storing them somewhere important. A smile touches his lips, and his shoulders relax. Something inside me soothes at the shift in his body language, and it makes me irrationally happy to know that I'm the one who was able to do that.

Seventeen

WESTON

I SHOULDN'T BE NERVOUS about seeing my team. Rationally, I know they work for me and not the other way around. It's their job to support my decisions and help me figure out how to build my business around them. But that doesn't stop an oily anxiety from settling deep in my stomach.

It's been a whirlwind of a day. I knew when I woke up that I would have a thousand missed calls and texts from Brandon and the rest of my team. I was not wrong.

No one on my team was very happy with me, but Brandon seemed to be the only one actually upset about the marriage. The agent and publicist were annoyed that I didn't tell them first so they could start preparing for how to handle it.

Brandon booked Lo and me first-class tickets on a direct flight from Nashville to Orange County for the early evening, so we had a few hours to get things ready. We spent the day doing laundry, packing, and ignoring our phones.

I mostly forgot about what would be waiting for us when we landed, but now that the plane is descending, I can't help myself.

Lo reaches over and puts her hand on my knee, and I realize I was bouncing it incessantly. I still beneath her touch and she pulls her hand back. "Nervous?" she asks.

"Not at all," I lie, and notice the way she's fidgeting, bottom lip trapped beneath her teeth. "You're nervous," I say, not a question.

She clasps her hands together in her lap. "I mean, a little."

"Why?"

Her eyes dart away from mine, and she clutches her hands tighter together, knuckles turning white with the pressure. Without thinking, I reach for them, prying them apart before I pull one into my lap. Slowly, I knead her palm with my fingers.

"Doesn't squeezing your hands like that hurt?" I ask.

Lo hasn't answered me, and when I look back up at her, her eyes are saucers. I lift a single brow, and she clears her throat before speaking. "Um, yeah. It does actually. This is helping, though."

"Good," I say, still ministering to her hands. "Did you take your medicine? It's been kind of a crazy day."

Lo nods, but doesn't speak, still watching our hands. Hers is pale and white, dotted with freckles, and mine is tan and rough with calluses.

"Why are you nervous?" I ask again.

It could be my imagination, but when she answers, her voice seems a little shaky. "I mean, this is your team. They're unhappy about this marriage, and it most likely isn't you they're going to take it out on. Plus, I'm just bad in social situations in general."

I look up at Lo, releasing one hand before reaching for the other. As I massage that one, I say, "They won't take it out on you. And I honestly don't think anyone except Brandon is upset. If the rest of them are, it's not because we got married, but because I didn't tell them."

Lo nods but doesn't respond.

My finger bumps her engagement ring, and I trail it over the ridged surface. "What can I do to help?" I ask.

"Just don't leave me, okay? I know they're all going to want to talk to you, but I'm scared." It looks like it physically pains her to say it, and I wonder if it actually does. She told me stress makes the pain worse, and if she's feeling even a small amount of the tension coursing through me right now, she's probably hurting.

"Yeah, of course."

"I just need some time to get used to everyone before you leave me alone with them," Lo says quietly.

I realize I've stopped massaging, and that I'm simply holding her hand in mine. Giving it one last gentle squeeze, I return it to her lap. "Of course. Whatever you need."

It's not long before the plane lands and we disembark. As we exit the plane and step into the terminal, I notice someone's gaze pass by me before they do a double take.

"Lo," I whisper. "I need you to hold my hand."

The look she gives me is one of abject horror. Like we didn't make out in front of a photographer with my hand on her butt for over an hour two days ago.

"Why?" she asks.

"Don't freak out, but we have an audience."

Lo whips her head around, but I stop her by grabbing on to her hand. "Don't look." When she meets my eyes, hers are full of anxiety. I tug her a little closer, partly to comfort her and partly because I've been looking for an excuse to do this for days now. "It's fine. Just look at me like I'm the greatest thing to ever happen to you."

Lo rolls her eyes, and I can feel her calming down, even if only slightly.

"You know," I continue, "they say when you're nervous that you should picture someone naked. And if this were a real relationship, you'd have lots to imag—"

She shoves my shoulder with her free hand, and I can't help but laugh.

The first set of eyes are not the only ones I feel trailing us as we get our bags, but I don't mention it to Lo.

Brandon texted earlier that he ordered us a car. As we step out into the balmy Southern California night, a young woman—probably a few years younger than us—holds up a sign with my name on it. Before we know it, we're in the back seat, our bags stored in the trunk.

I've been making small talk with our driver, and when I finally look over at Lo in the dark, her face is practically glued to the window, the streetlights casting shadows over her skin. She is a kid on Christmas night trying to catch a glimpse of Santa.

A smile tugs at my lips. "What are you doing, Lo?"

When Lo turns to me, her eyes are bright, her face shining. "I didn't mention this since everything was so busy, but I've always wanted to visit Newport Beach."

I hold back a laugh, not because she's funny, but because she's cute when she's excited like this. "Why Newport Beach?" I ask.

She tucks a lock of copper hair behind her ear. "You're going to laugh..."

"I won't laugh," I promise, and Lo's eyes narrow as she seems to consider the grin on my face for a moment, as if checking for sincerity.

"I read a book series that takes place here." My smile grows, but I hold back any laughter that may want to slip out. "I always enjoyed reading in elementary school. We always had all these reading competitions in class. But it wasn't until middle school that I loved reading."

From the time I met Lo, reading was more than a hobby or passion for her. It was a personality trait. It was something everyone associated with her. She's always got a book stashed away somewhere like a squirrel hiding nuts for the winter.

"I read this series of books that were set in Newport Beach. They changed everything," Lo says, a wistful tone to her voice. "They made me love reading and made me want to become a writer."

"Did you ever write anything?" the driver asks, and Lo looks embarrassed. She forgot we had an audience.

When Lo answers, her voice is smaller and a little squeaky, but probably not enough for the driver to notice. "I did. I've published one novel."

"Oh, my gosh," the woman says. "That's so cool. Would I know it? I love to read too."

"Oh, probably not," Lo answers hurriedly. "I'm self-published, and this is my debut, so it's not super popular."

"It's really good, though," I say, and Lo's head swivels to face me. "Lo sells herself short. I'd never even read a romance before and I loved it. She writes the love interest so well..." I trail off. "You can really just picture those green eyes the main character loves so much."

Lo pins me with a glare, but I see the heat creeping up her neck. "Lots of people have green eyes, Weston," she whispers forcefully back at me.

"Less than two percent, actually, *Louise*."

"What's the name of it? I'll have to check it out," the girl interrupts Lo's retort.

"*The Lake House*," I respond, flashing Lo a satisfied smirk.

The driver gasps, and I flick my eyes to the windshield to see if we're about to wreck, but it's clear. "I love that book!" she practically screams. We come to a red light, and she spins around to face us.

"You're Lo Summers?"

Lo looks shell-shocked, but more than a little happy. "Yes, that's me."

"Oh my gosh, this is so cool. Hi! I'm Hailee," the driver yells again. "I read your book in one sitting! I stayed up till four in the morning even though I had class the next day. I could not put it down. And, wow, can I just say, Axel is the perfect book boyfriend."

"The perfect boyfriend," I say smugly.

"Book boyfriend, as in, not real," Lo responds before turning away from me and back to Hailee.

"Thank you," Lo says gracefully.

A few minutes later, Hailee slows down in front of a beach house on Balboa Peninsula. It's white and two stories, with Bermuda shutters painted in a seafoam green. The lights are on, although the shutters are closed so I can't see inside. What catches my eye, though, are the cars parked in the driveway. My stomach clenches when I notice Brandon's BMW.

Lo continues to talk to Hailee through the driver's window as I unload our bags. A grin curves my lips as I see them posing for a selfie. Hailee's phone is extended in front of her, and it flashes brightly as she snaps a picture.

"I wish I had my copy with me so you could sign it," Hailee says.

Lo swipes her phone open and clicks on something before handing it to Hailee. "Here," she says. "Type your address in here and I'll send you a signed copy and a little goodie when I get back home."

"Wow," the driver squeals. "That's so nice of you." She proceeds to type on Lo's phone before handing it back to her with an impromptu hug. "Thank you so much!"

As the car backs out of the driveway, I wrap an arm around Lo, giving her shoulder a squeeze. "That was really cool," I say, unable to keep the smile off my face.

Her cheeks are flushed, her eyes shining, and despite the long day of packing and traveling, she looks beautiful. "It really was."

"I hate to burst your bubble," I say.

She lets out a breath. "But we have to go in now."

I turn us around so we're facing the beach house. We stare at it for a moment, neither of us really wanting to go inside. Beside me, Lo stiffens slightly, and I hate that it's my people who are causing her anxiety.

"You ready?"

"No," she answers.

"Me neither."

I pull her a little closer, hoping the gesture is as comforting for her as it is for me, and lead us up the porch stairs. Taking a deep breath, I knock on the door, unsure of what waits on the other side.

Eighteen

LO

I'M NOT SURE WHAT I expected to find on the other side of the beach house's front door, but this definitely wasn't it. If I had to take a guess, I would have thought there would be a brooding Brandon. Or maybe that Weston's publicist would be glaring at my leggings and oversized T-shirt and thinking that if Wes was going to get married, it could have at least been to someone who dressed better.

What I definitely didn't expect was a petite woman to throw the door open, squeal loud enough to wake the neighborhood, and throw herself at me before I even have a chance to look at her face.

"Hi!" she yells in my ear. Backing up, she grips my forearms. "It's so good to meet you. And you're beautiful. Wes, you didn't tell us how pretty she is." Fixing her attention on Wes, she launches herself at him for a hug.

A laugh rumbles from his chest as he wraps his arms around her. "Good to see you too, Hazel."

I take a step back and bump into someone behind me. Spinning around, I say, "Oh, sorry."

Wes looks up at the sound of my voice, and a smile lights his features when he sees the man behind me. "Cam, you're here too."

The man—Cam—smiles, shrugging one shoulder. "I'd much rather be at home."

Some of the anxiety and tension from the last few days eases as Wes laughs. It's the laugh I remember from college, the one that's so genuine and carefree that it's impossible not to be dazzled by it.

Weston's eyes meet mine, glittering under the porch lights. "Lo, this is Camden and Hazel Lane."

I look between the two of them. They both have warm, tan skin and eyes that are an intriguing shade of dark blue. Their hair is brown, although Cam's is quite a bit darker than Hazel's caramel shade. Although Cam is tall, almost as tall as Wes, and Hazel is on the petite side, their resemblance is uncanny.

"Brother and sister," Cam says, as if reading my mind.

A grin touches my lips. "I can tell. Nice to meet you both."

"What are you guys doing here?" Wes asks.

Cam nods over his shoulder at the open front door behind him. "Figured Brandon might be a little less hostile if we were here."

The smile slips from Weston's face for a moment, almost too quick to notice before he plasters it back on. "Thanks, man." He lets out a breath. "Well, we might as well get it over with."

I want to grab Weston's hand and squeeze it for reassurance—his and mine—as we walk into the house behind Camden and Hazel, but our hands are full of luggage.

The house is bright and modern, everything you could want in a beach home. My eyes take in the shiplap walls and the giant rattan light hanging from the tall, arched ceiling. The calming shades of white, beige, gray, and blue-green settle my nerves slightly.

Hazel leads us through the hallway, past a powder room and an open bedroom, and into the main living space. The kitchen and living room are open, and the other three people in the room immediately draw my attention.

A woman leans against the marble countertops in fitted jeans that accentuate her long, long legs and a fitted blazer that probably costs my entire weekly paycheck. I immediately feel frumpy in my travel clothes and wish I had dressed a little better.

The other people, a man and a woman, look up from their seats at the kitchen bar as we walk through. The woman with dark skin with coal black straight hair, grins at us, her eyes shining as she takes me in. I'm buoyed a little by the friendly expression until I glance at the man sitting next to her. Beneath pale blonde brows, his cool, blue eyes fix on me and narrow, assessing.

Beneath his intense gaze, I feel like a bug smashed under a shoe, and I think Wes can tell. He shifts the bag in his hand to his shoulder and presses his fingertips into the base of my spine, gently pushing me forward. His touch is gentle yet possessive, an anchor.

"Hey, everyone," Wes says. "This is Lo." He points to the man and woman sitting at the island. "Lo, this is Brandon, my manager, and Emily, my publicist." Wes gestures to the other woman. "This is my agent, Kate."

I give them an anxious wave, uncomfortable with all the eyes on me. Before I can respond, Wes starts talking again, and I sigh inwardly, grateful I don't have to try to make small talk. On instinct, my body sags into him a little more, and although I tell myself to put some space between us, I can't.

"I see you're all here. Lo and I are happy to answer any questions you may have," he says, and when I stiffen, his thumb swipes in a lazy pattern against my back, and my breath hitches. If Wes notices, he thankfully doesn't comment.

"It's been a long day and we're both exhausted. We're going to put our things in the bedroom and freshen up, and then we'll come back out here for thirty minutes. Everything else can wait until tomorrow."

Although his team doesn't bother to hide their annoyance, an immense weight has been lifted off my shoulders.

"The master is through that door," Emily says, gesturing to the closed door off the living room. "Take your time, guys. We will see you in a bit."

"Great," Wes responds and pushes me toward the bedroom.

The door shuts behind me, and Wes slumps against it, his head thumping on the wood as he drops the bags at his feet. I move around the room, running my fingers across the various decor objects, a flurry of butterflies taking flight in my stomach.

It hasn't occurred to me until now that, while we may have separate bedrooms at home, Weston's team would find that a little odd. My eyes catch on the massive bed in the middle of the room, and the thought of sharing it with him both thrills and terrifies me. Either way, it's sure to be a disaster.

When I look back at Wes, his gaze is fixed on me. He pushes off the door, cracking his neck before he settles on the edge of the bed. One blond brow cocks, a dare.

I mirror his movements, settling next to him on the edge of the bed.

He falls back against the covers, staring at the ceiling. "I'm exhausted."

I stare at him for a moment, watching the way his broad chest rises and falls beneath his white shirt, before lowering next to him. We lie side by side, the only sounds in the room that of our breathing and the faint whirring of the ceiling fan.

He radiates warmth, and I must shiver because Wes turns his head, his green eyes locking on me. "Cold?"

"A little," I respond.

"I'll ask them to turn up the AC a few degrees. Did you bring a sweatshirt?"

I smile drowsily. "I never leave for a trip without at least three."

"No wonder your bag was so heavy."

I turn back to face the ceiling, watching as the wicker fan spins above us. It's hypnotic, and it takes everything in me to not fall asleep at that very second.

"After they leave, I'll move my stuff to the guest room we passed on the way in," he says, lowering his voice so they don't hear us.

"They seem ready for business. I have a feeling there's no chance they're leaving here any time soon," I reply.

When he responds, there's teasing in his voice. "I'll tell them we've only been married for two days and we really need to—"

I elbow him in the side, and his laughter rumbles against my arm. His laugh, deep and melodic, is the last thing I remember before I fall asleep.

AN INCESSANT KNOCKING SOUND breaks through my consciousness. I ignore it, loving the cozy cocoon I'm in. I snuggle deeper, reveling in the warmth and softness beneath me.

The knocking persists, though, and I finally pry my eyes open. I'm in a bright room, early morning sunlight peeking through the windows. A ceiling fan spins above me, reminding me where I am.

California. Newport Beach. The rental home.

I sit up, the lightweight white duvet falling around my waist as I look around, trying to find where the knocking is coming from.

There's a deeper knock, but also a quieter, higher-pitch tapping that I can't place.

"Wes, Lo, do you mind if I come in?" The voice is soft, female, and chipper.

I look around madly, trying to find Wes. The bed is empty, the side next to me unrumpled, and I remember him mentioning the guest room last night before we must have fallen asleep.

If this were a movie, we would have woken up wrapped in each other's arms, having been drawn inexplicably to one another in the night, embarrassed yet acutely aware of one another.

Why is my life a bad version of a rom-com?

"Um," I say, my voice scratchy. "Hold on just a minute. Weston's in the bathroom," I call out.

"Oh, good, you're awake," The woman yells back. "Can I come in?"

"No!" I yell so forcefully she must surely think I'm standing at the door stark naked. "We'll be out in a minute," I say, trying to sound more calm. I tiptoe out of bed, hoping to find my phone in my bag on the floor. When I round the bed, I look out the window and see a face there staring back at me. I barely keep myself from squealing when I realize it's Wes, shirtless and looking panicked.

I slide the window open. "*What is going on?*" I whisper.

"Are you going to let me in?"

I back up and allow Wes to climb through the window. "What the heck is going on?"

Wes drags his hands over his face and settles on the edge of the bed before responding. "I woke up at like two and everyone was gone. They must have found us asleep and left. Then a few minutes ago I heard them letting themselves back in. They can't know I slept in the guest room the rest of the night, so I snuck around here and knocked on the window." He pauses, looking chagrined. "You are not a light sleeper."

I sit next to Wes on the bed, putting my hands over my face. "I may have overreacted to whoever was asking to come in, and now they're going to think they were interrupting *something*," I mumble through my fingers, face heating.

Chuckling, Wes wraps an arm around my shoulders. "I can assure them there was absolutely nothing going on in here."

I press my hands to his chest and give him a gentle shove. "Oh, no. Then they will definitely think something was happening."

Wes waggles his brows. "Could you explain what they think was going on? Slowly, so I can take some mental notes."

Shrugging off his arm, I push at his chest again. He falls back against the bed, laughing. With my hand still pressed against his heart, I realize how close we are. It thumps rhythmically beneath his tan, smooth skin. I yank my hand back like it was burned, and Wes gives me a confused look.

Standing hastily, I avoid his gaze. If I thought this man was a temptation clothed, having him shirtless in my bed is a recipe for disaster. "I'm going to change."

Nineteen

WESTON

Lo retreats to the bathroom to change into clean clothes, and I slip a T-shirt over my head, thankful I was too tired to drag my bag to the guest room last night. When she opens the door a minute later, I can't help but smile at her shirt. It says *Readers Gonna Read* in chunky letters.

She catches my look and peers down at her shirt. "What?" Lo asks.

I shake my head, the grin still stuck on my face. "Nothing. You look cute," I say, and her cheeks turn dusty pink.

With a tilt of my chin in the direction of the door, I ask, "You ready?" Lo takes a deep breath before nodding.

To say I'm shocked when I open the door is an understatement. My management team has taken over the open kitchen and living room area. No less than three laptops and five tablets are scattered across the counter and tabletops. Kate types madly on her phone, and Emily is scrolling through what I'm almost positive is a press release. Brandon leans against the counter with crossed arms, his face hard as granite.

So much for hoping he would be happy for me.

"Morning," I say, and three heads snap to me.

Except for the sound of the news playing quietly in the living room, it's silent and charged. The moment is broken when Emily picks up a flimsy white box from the counter and extends it in our direction. "Donuts?"

A pent up breath releases from my lungs, and I'm thankful the tension has been broken for at least a little while.

After Lo and I pick our donuts, Brandon asks us to take a seat at the dining table, where the majority of their stuff is laid out. Lo and I bump shoulders as we sit down on the long bench taking up one side of the table.

The donut is a thick lump in my throat under the weight of their stares. Beside me, Lo is stiff as a board, her hands clasped in a tight knot in her lap. I look up into the faces of my management team. Kate raises her eyebrows, as if waiting for me to explain, and Emily smiles warmly at us. The stormy look on Brandon's face makes my stomach contract, and I swallow thickly.

His arms are crossed over his chest. He leans back in his chair. "So, what's the story here?" He looks back and forth between Lo and me. I know Lo's cheeks are heating as her hands fidget more under the table.

Any lingering feelings of guilt or intimidation instantly evaporate. Lo did nothing wrong, and they're not going to make her feel like she did.

"Okay," I start, pinning Brandon with my gaze. "First, let me start by saying that I'm sorry I didn't let you guys know before getting married." I look at each of them in turn. "You're my management team, but above that, you're my friends. You've been with me through all the ups and downs in my career the past few years, and you deserved to know that I was getting married."

Kate isn't much for showing emotion, but I can see that she's pleased with my apology. And although Emily's smile hasn't faltered, neither has Brandon's stony expression.

I speak directly to him. "This is, however, my personal life, not my professional life. I understand that the two are connected, but they're not the same. I made a decision to get married, and while that may affect my professional life, it is not something I needed to run by you first." As I speak, Brandon's eyes narrow into slits, and by the time I'm done, he's clenching his jaw so hard I'm sure to get a personal bill sent to me by his dentist.

"I don't see why me getting married has made you so mad. I—"

"I'm not mad you did it," Brandon says, and there are underpaid interns out there with less pent-up aggression than he is exuding right now. "I'm mad that you made this decision with the same care that you make all the rest of your life and career choices, without thinking and without preparing."

His words are a stinging slap to the face, mostly because I know it's kind of true. I haven't always thought before making decisions. God knows I didn't think much before I showed up at Lo's house and proposed to her. But in the last year, I've been working so hard to come up with a way to change my image, to change the course of my career, and he's been against it this whole time. The fact that he's now blaming that on me has my hands tightening into fists at my sides, feeling not just annoyed but also hurt.

Before I can respond, Lo interrupts, her voice quiet and timid as she looks between Brandon and me. "Hey, maybe we should take a breather for a minute."

Brandon is a lit fuse, ready to explode. He slams his laptop shut and picks up his phone. "Yeah, maybe I will. I'll be back later." He looks at Kate and Emily. "You guys can try to deal with this colossal—"

"Brandon," Kate warns, her voice stern. "That's enough. Come back when you've cooled down."

He storms off, letting the door slam behind him, and we all sit in silence for a moment.

Emily is the one to finally defuse the tension. She sets one of her hands atop Lo's, which are white knuckled on the table. "I'm really glad you're here," she says.

Lo's smile is a little wobbly, and it punches me in the gut. "Me too."

My palms itch with the need to touch her, to comfort her in some way. Beneath the table, I give her knee a gentle squeeze, hoping that she understands what I'm feeling—guilt that Brandon treated her like that, gratitude that she's here and not on the next flight home, and something else that I can't name, something that feels like liquid pooling in my stomach.

Lo bumps her shoulder with mine, and cocks an eyebrow in silent question. The muscles in my jaw relax as I nod, signaling I'm okay. When she doesn't move away, keeping the bare skin of her arm pressed against the length of mine, the tension eases from my body in degrees.

"As your publicist, I'm thrilled about this marriage," Emily says, drawing my attention from Lo. The keys of Emily's computer clack beneath her fingers as she types. "As you know, you could really use some good press. I don't have anything concrete lined up for you as of this moment, but as soon as we drop the news, I can only imagine the storm that will rain on my head. How do you feel about podcasts?" she asks, looking between the two of us.

"Like being on one?" Lo asks, and I grin.

"Of course," Emily responds. "I'm trying to plan one press event per day, and then nothing on your last day. This is your honeymoon, after all."

Lo and I shoot each other a glance.

"I'm sure at least one celebrity gossip podcast is going to want an interview, hopefully that guy who was on that reality dating show on Netflix last year. You did say you hired a professional photographer for the wedding, right?"

"Yeah," I reply.

Emily flashes me a smile before turning back to her computer, scrolling and making notes. "Perfect. I'll need you to get me in contact with them so they can send me the photos. I'm hoping that a magazine will want to feature the spread, or at least some blogs. We may also want to do a small shoot with Camden as well..."

She trails off, typing something, and when it's clear she's lost in her head and won't be talking again for a few minutes, Kate speaks up. "There are a few brands that I can reach out to now that weren't interested after the bad press with Talia. We would really like to get you guys to collab with that dating scrapbook company, film yourselves doing a few of the dates. They would be really easy TikToks, if not even full YouTube videos. I—" Kate's phone rings, breaking her sentence off. She checks the screen and holds a finger up.

"I've got to take this. Be right back." Kate stands and heads out the back door.

"Lo, I need you to write down all of your social media handles. I already have you on Instagram from when everything happened at your friend's wedding—super cute looking book, by the way—but I'll need to know all of them," Emily says, sliding her iPad toward Lo. It's open to a Notes page with her Apple Pencil resting atop it.

Lo, looking slightly dazed by the tornado that is my publicist and agent, begins to write.

"I bet that meal delivery service would love some videos with you guys making their meals in *Hubby* and *Wifey* shirts..." Emily trails off, getting lost in her work again.

Lo turns to me, looking horrified. I wink at her, and her mouth splits into a grin before she leans her forehead on my shoulder. Her deep breath puffs against my skin.

My chest rumbles with a silent laugh as I wrap my arm around her, tugging her more firmly against my side. My hand slides down her back, my fingers tracing each bump and dip of her spine. The hem of her shirt comes faster than I anticipated, and I'm met with the smooth expanse of skin at her low back.

Lo stiffens against me, and I can feel her quick intake of breath. I'm not sure what compels me to do it, but instead of sliding my hand back up, my thumb makes a lazy circle against the bare skin there. She doesn't move, still rigid against me. I'm about to rip my hand away, embarrassed, when I notice goosebumps raising up along her arms.

Interesting.

The moment is broken when Emily starts talking again, and Lo sits up quickly, not meeting my gaze.

Really interesting.

Twenty

LO

THE MEETING WITH KATE and Emily goes on for another hour, and by the end, I'm completely lost. I handle all the marketing of my book, so I thought I was pretty well versed in Instagram engagement and TikTok analytics, but these people are on a new level.

It doesn't help that I've been zoning in and out for the last hour, unable to think about anything other than Weston's touch on my skin.

Um, what the heck happened?

I'd leaned on him, overwhelmed at the barrage of information being thrown at us. He smiled and rubbed my back, making me feel slightly less anxious. But then he'd touched my skin, and it had felt like a million electrical shocks running up and down my spine. It had been an accident. I could tell by the way he'd stilled, as if unsure about what to do next. But then it wasn't an accident anymore.

And I'm not sure what to make of that.

"Okay," Emily says, snapping me out of my reverie. "I was hoping Brandon would be back when we made the announcement live." She turns to Wes, giving him a meaningful look. "But when I texted him, he said to post it without him."

"With much more colorful language, I assume," Wes deadpans, leaning back in the chair he moved to shortly after *the thumb swipe*. He is stretched out, all long legs and lean lines. If we're calling it what it is, he's hot. Really hot. Which makes this whole thing much more complicated. Why couldn't he have moles and a beer gut and a shiny bald spot on the top of his head? That would make this *so much easier*.

"You would assume correctly," Emily says, grimacing. She looks at both of us in turn, eyebrows raised in question. "Ready?"

Wes gets up from his chair and moves back next to me on the bench. We sit shoulder to shoulder, and his heat seeps through the thin fabric of my T-shirt.

"Rachel Anderson is about to lose her mind," I say, pulling up Instagram on my phone.

"Oh, yeah?" Wes asks, and I can hear the grin in his voice.

I turn to look at him. "You know she was obsessed with you in college."

"Maybe I should give her a call…" he muses. I shove an elbow in his ribs, and he grunts out a laugh.

Emily helped us both craft posts earlier, similar yet different enough to not be identical, so when I open the app, I only have to click on drafts. I swipe through the images one more time, rechecking. Purely for science.

"We look hot," Wes says, and I smile down into my phone. "We look like we're about to have s—"

I shove him again, and he laughs. I know he's messing with me, trying to ease my nerves, and I'm not surprised that it's working. When I peer up at him, a smile tugs at the corner of his lips and the dimples in his cheeks wink at me. He leans a little heavier into my shoulder.

"You ready?" he asks, and although his voice is tinged with amusement, it's also a little deeper and softer than before. His eyes search mine, and I know he's asking, once and for all, if I really want to do this.

I wish I didn't second-guess myself so much. I wish I could say that after I deliberate for ridiculous amounts of time over a decision, that when I make my mind up, it's firm and confident. But it's not. And all the doubts that we're making a mistake run through my mind again. All the what-ifs—everything that could possibly go wrong.

But in the end, it's the way Wes' face softens, as if sensing my hesitation—his willingness to stop all of this if it's what I want, his ability to read my indecision and trust me to make the right decision. That's what does it for me.

I press *share*.

"THE INTERNET LITERALLY BROKE my phone," I say, still stunned as I look down at the blank phone in my lap.

"To be fair, it was an iPhone 7."

My phone is dead. Not dead as in, put it on a charger. Dead as in, it got so overheated last night trying to keep up with all the notifications that it turned off out of self-preservation. I was hoping this was just a hibernating-for-the-winter kind of situation, but even after putting it in the fridge to cool down for a few minutes, charging it all night, and asking it very nicely to turn back on, it did no such thing. I even tried puppy dog eyes at it, which Weston found endlessly hilarious.

I glare at him, which causes him to laugh more. "We'll get you the newest iPhone out there, honey," he says impishly.

Crossing my arms, I grumble, "Don't call me *honey*."

His grin still flirts with the edges of his mouth, and he seems to be enjoying this way too much. "I need a disgusting nickname to call you in front of the adoring fans."

Ignoring him, I turn and scowl out the window. It's ridiculously hard to keep my face set in this sour expression with the gorgeous view of the ocean to my right, but I do my best.

"Babe?" he asks. "Pumpkin?" With every guess, I hear the smirk in his voice. "Poopsie? Lover? Princess? My Old Lady? Mommy?"

"Oh my gosh."

"Sugar Butt? Big Booty H—"

"That's enough," I yell, shoving his arm, unable to contain my laughter.

He dimples at me, eyes shining. "I'm sorry about your phone," he says finally.

"It's fine," I say and pause. "Sugar Daddy." He bursts out laughing, and I can't help but join in with him.

Two hours later, we exit the cell phone store, and I'm grinning widely at my new phone.

"It's so fancy," I say, and Weston smiles down at me as he opens the door to the rental car Brandon left at the house for us. "Thank you again for the case and the screen protector and the pop socket too."

"Anything for you," he says, shutting the door. He runs around the front and climbs in.

"If I had known that I would have gotten a fully-paid for phone and all the accessories out of this, I wouldn't have needed so much time to deliberate. I'll pay you back with my next royalty check. I haven't looked at my publishing platform in a while, but I think I've had a lot of sales since the wedding."

"You don't need to pay me back, Lo," Wes says as he looks up directions on his phone. "This was all a part of the deal."

I swipe through the apps on my phone and log in to my publishing platform. "I mean, not really. You agreed to pay for my insurance. I'm grateful, though."

Wes puts the car in reverse and starts to back out. "I don't mind—"

"Oh my gosh!" I exclaim, interrupting him.

I jolt forward in my seat as Wes slams the breaks. "What?"

My eyes dart across the screen, scanning the information over and over again to make sure I'm not mistaken. This is *unbelievable.* With shaking hands, I shove the phone in his direction.

He puts the car in park and takes my phone, staring down with a crinkle between his eyebrows. "What am I looking at?"

"The sales since yesterday are almost as many as I've sold since I published the book."

He looks back up at me, dimples popping. "That's amazing, Lo."

I can't believe *my book* is in the hands of that many people. A tidal wave of emotions washes over me—pride, anxiety, joy, excitement, disbelief, and even self-doubt. But most of all, I feel an intense desire to write something new. And after months of struggling to come up with a story or find the inspiration to write it, this feels *good.*

"You look happy," Wes says, his voice a low rasp in the enclosed car.

"I am. This is good," I tell him. "All of it." The words are out of my mouth before I can think better of them. But it's true. Two weeks ago my life was falling apart at the seams, but now I'm here, and despite the circumstances, I'm happy about it.

The moment stretches between us, delicate and fragile yet charged and electric. There's a buzzing in my ears and a swirling sensation in my stomach. Weston's gaze is heavy. A blond curl falls across his forehead, landing right above those intense green eyes, and my fingers tingle with the desire to push it back.

"Let's take a picture," I blurt. Wes blinks, looking like I just snapped him out of the same trance I was in. He nods and hands my phone back to me.

I take it from him and angle myself toward the passenger window, holding the phone out in front of me. Weston's breath is warm against my cheek as he leans against the console, and I have to fight against the desire to lean back into him. I paste a smile on my face and glance up at my reflection in the camera. Wes isn't looking at it though, and even if I couldn't see us mirrored on my screen, I would still be able to feel the way his gaze rests heavily upon me, making the whole left side of my body break out in goosebumps.

"Smile," I say, and click the circular button to take the picture.

Instead of smiling, Wes presses his lips to my cheek. My stomach bottoms out at the contact, and I almost forget to take the photo. I won't be surprised if they turn out blurry from the shaking of my hands.

My whole body shudders as he backs away, and I lower the phone, trying to focus on the screen. Wes watches over my shoulder, and when my hands shake too badly to click the photo at the bottom of the screen, he reaches around and presses it for me.

"Thanks," I say, and my voice comes out a whisper.

He doesn't say anything, but I feel the stubble on his chin skim my bare shoulder as he nods. If my body prickles any more, I think it will shut down completely. Cease to function properly ever again.

I'm smiling in the photo, and although no one else would be able to tell, I notice how forced it looks.

Wes looks—I don't even know how else to say it—sexy. Weston looks sexy. In the first few photos, he presses his mouth softly to my cheek. But as I continue to swipe, I can see where he backed up, removing his lips from my skin, but only far enough to give me what I can only describe as bedroom eyes.

If my last phone overheated, this one just caught fire.

"Looks good," I finally manage to squeak out.

He still hasn't backed away, and his breath on my neck is warm as he says, "Yeah, it really does."

I turn my head slightly, and our gazes connect. Earlier, his eyes sparkled with excitement, but they're dark now, the deep green of a forest you almost want to get lost in. There's no amusement on his face, no smile playing at his lips, and I want to ask what he's thinking, but I'm scared of his answer.

My phone buzzes in my lap, saving me from starting a conversation I'm not sure would be wise to have. Camilla's photo lights up my screen, and I sigh as Wes sits back, shattering the moment like broken glass.

"Hey," I say, my voice scratchy. If Wes notices, he doesn't give any indication as he backs out of our parking spot. I clear my throat and speak again. "Hey, Camilla. Can you hear me?"

"Hey, hon," she says, slightly out of breath, and I know instantly that she's calling me from her stationary bike.

"How is California?" Camilla asks as I dig through my bag for some pain medicine, noticing a twinge in my back. The stress of the past few weeks is finally catching up with me. "Is it everything you dreamed of?"

"And more," I say, smiling. "Guess what just happened?"

Camilla is ecstatic as I tell her the news of my book sales.

"I miss you," she says a few minutes later.

"I miss you too, fried." I've barely spoken to her or spent any time with her since a week before her wedding, and even then, with all the craziness that is last-minute wedding details, we've barely talked in weeks. "Let's hang out when I get home."

"Oh, my word, yes," she says between huffs of breath. "Let's watch a movie in that fancy home theater of yours."

"We don't have a home theater," I say, but I glance at Wes to make sure there's not a movie room he's kept hidden from me. He shakes his head, a smile playing on his lips.

I'm glad to see it back on his face. No more sexy looks or tingling skin. Back to normal. Exactly what I want.

"Are you sure? Nowhere in that big new house of yours?"

"Positive," I say back. "And it's not my house."

"Semantics," she replies. I look out the window as she starts making plans for us the Sunday after we get home. I'm only half-listening, staring out the window as we merge onto the highway, heading toward Los Angeles. I would feel bad zoning out, but by the time I focus back on the conversation, she will have already come up with a new, better plan. Camilla is like that—changing directions too quickly for even herself to keep up with.

It's a good thing we became best friends twenty years ago, back before I carried anxiety around with me like a backpack—before I got sick, and before I dropped out of college and forgot how to properly socialize—because I think if Camilla and I met today, I would never be able to work up the courage to be her friend.

"So," she says, drawing me back into the conversation, "double date at the taco place by the duplex, and then we can go back to your house, and the boys can watch whatever sportball game is on. We can plan on doing face masks or watching a movie, but then end up laying in your bed eating brownie mix instead."

Then again, maybe we would still be friends if we met today. "That sounds perfect."

"Yay! Love you, boo." She hangs up before I have a chance to respond, and I smile down at my phone, feeling all the warm fuzzies that I've missed over the past few weeks while keeping secrets from her.

"So what's the plan for today?" I ask Weston, watching as the scenery out the window changes from coastal to suburban.

"We're meeting Hazel and Cam downtown. We're going to take you sightseeing."

"Fun!"

"And make some TikToks," he finishes.

"Fun," I repeat, although my tone of voice does very little to hide how miserable that sounds to me.

Wes chuckle fills the car. "It will be, really." He glances at me fleetingly before turning back to the road. "And if you hate it, we don't have to do it."

"Really?" The point of this arrangement is to show off how committed and, well, *married* he is.

"Yeah, of course. I know this isn't really your thing," Wes replies easily.

"But that's the whole reason we got married." I stare at him incredulously, and I can't help but notice how good he looks with one hand propped on the steering wheel, the California sun making his skin seem even more golden. Two days of stubble covers his chiseled jaw, and his shoulders look cut from granite.

He slows to a stop behind a line of traffic and turns to face me. I try to seem like I wasn't just ogling him. "I'm not going to ask you to do anything that makes you uncomfortable."

My heart races in my chest because I don't know what he's getting from this marriage if he's not making me hold up my side of the deal. I search his face, trying to decipher the answer hidden behind his eyes. A car honks, snapping his attention back to the road, and I clasp my hands in my lap to keep them from shaking.

I grasp for something to say—something to defuse the tension and extinguish the reaction he always sets off inside of me. "You live to make me uncomfortable. You based your whole career on it," I finally choke out, remembering all the crazy antics he talked me into in college.

"I don't live to make you uncomfortable. I just want you to actually live your life—to enjoy it. If being on camera in front of thousands of people isn't something you want to do, then don't do it. Not because it makes you scared, but because it doesn't make you feel alive. There's a difference."

His words pull the rug out from underneath me as I realize I *don't* know the difference, or at least, I haven't been living like it. Blood rushes in my ears as the traffic lets up, and Wes turns back to the road, unaware that he just flipped my entire world upside down.

Twenty-One

WESTON

"I'll film this first one," Lo says as I unpack four zip-up onesies and a Bluetooth speaker from my backpack.

I catch her eye. "Are you scared?"

Lo shakes her head. "Not at all. Just doesn't make me feel *alive*," she says, making jazz hands at me.

"Is that so?"

"Absolutely." With a furrowed brow, she examines the stash I pull from my backpack. "Where did you get all this?"

"Brandon," I say simply as I set my camera up on the tripod. He never came back to the house last night, but when I texted him a list of stuff I would need for filming, it showed up on the porch this morning before I woke up.

I turn to Cam and Hazel. "Well then, Cam, you're off camera duty for this one."

"Joy," he responds dryly, taking the dinosaur onesie from my hand.

"You in?" I ask Hazel.

"Definitely." She makes a grab for the chicken onesie, but I switch it out for the unicorn one.

"That one is for you, Lo, if you change your mind." I look pointedly at the chicken onesie before I push it back into my backpack.

"You picked that one out especially for me, didn't you?"

"Absolutely," I say, parroting her earlier words back at her. I smack a kiss on her cheek and wink at her. "Just in case anyone's filming."

"I was," Hazel exclaims excitedly.

I can't help but smile as I tug the onesie over my clothes. Already, people are starting to look on curiously. I mean, this is Rodeo Drive. Even without the pajamas, we're already the most simply dressed people here.

I feel the stares of people around me as Cam, Hazel, and I take our positions.

"What are you guys going to do?" Lo asks loudly, and from the flush of her cheeks, I can tell she's already embarrassed by the attention.

"Chicken dance!" I yell back.

Her nose wrinkles as she counts down from three. I press a button on my phone in my pocket simultaneously, and the Chicken Dance blares through the Bluetooth speaker.

Cam, Hazel, and I don't miss a beat as we execute the dance perfectly. It's not the camera I'm staring at this time, though. I can't keep the stupid grin off my face as I watch Lo filming us. She shakes her head, but a smile lifts her lips.

As soon as the song comes to an end, Lo presses a button, and the flashing red light on the camera stills. Despite the camera turning off, I can see strangers' phones trained on us. I know I need to give them something good.

I stride over to Lo with quick steps. Her face is creased in confusion as I get close.

"What are you—"

My hand finds her waist, settling on the curve of her hip before I push her into a dip. Her hair falls back from her face, revealing a surprised glint in her eyes."Cameras," I whisper before my mouth lands on hers.

The kiss sets off a fire in my veins, consuming me, and despite it being all for show, I want to fall headlong into it. The claps and cheers of the crowd of people gathered around us snap me back to the moment, and I pull Lo back to her feet. Her chest brushes my own with each deep inhale.

"You guys ready to go?" Cam asks, smiling smugly as he sidles up to us.

I ignore his knowing gaze. "Yeah, let's get out of here." I see some people breaking off from the crowd, obviously recognizing us, but I lead us down the street before they have a chance to approach.

We round the corner and strip off our onesies. I stuff them and the camera gear back into the backpack. "Fun, huh?" I ask, moving next to Lo as we start back down the street.

A flicker of wariness crosses her face, and color darkens her cheeks. I realize she thinks I'm talking about this kiss, and this seems like too good of an opportunity to pass up. "I mean, I get a lot of practice, so I just keep getting better and better every time."

Her jaw tightens and she stares forward, not meeting my gaze. "That so?"

"Yeah, everyone always has nice things to say."

"Mm." She seems agitated, and I hold back a grin, picking up my pace to keep up with her quickening strides.

"Women are always begging for it."

"I bet," Lo mutters, drumming her fingers on her thigh.

"I mean, I don't really get the fascination. It's only the Chicken Dance. But give the people what they want, you know?"

Lo's steps falter before she keeps moving. I don't miss the way her lips curve up in the barest of smiles.

"Oh, you didn't think...?" I say, unable to hold back my own grin now.

Lo tilts her chin to look at me. "No, no. The Chicken Dance. Of course. What a rave."

The wind blows her hair back from her face, allowing me a clear view of her sparkling eyes and rosy cheeks. The long line of her neck. My gaze drops lower of its own accord, focusing on all the parts of her I usually don't allow myself to.

"Where to next?" Cam asks, drawing my attention away from Lo.

"Sunset Boulevard."

THE REST OF THE day passes in a blur. We mostly sightsee, but we film at a few locations along the way. Lo stays behind the camera, but I have one last location up my sleeve.

We pull into the parking lot of the Griffith Observatory at sunset. I hop out and rummage through the trunk. By the time Lo walks around to the back, I already have the yellow dress in my hands.

"No." She shakes her head forcefully, turning back toward the passenger side.

I grab her arm, and she spins around to face me. "Come on, Lo. You know you want to."

"I don't think so."

"You love *La La Land*," I say and her brow wrinkles in confusion. "You played the soundtrack on repeat the whole day you moved into my house." I lean forward until we're almost nose to nose. "Come on, just go with it."

Lo rolls her eyes, exhaling deeply through her nose. "Fine." She snatches the dress from my hands and tugs it over her tank top before wiggling her pants down underneath. When she catches me staring, a pink blush stains her cheeks. "Change your clothes."

I pull my shirt over my head before tossing it in the trunk. Lo's gaze drops to my chest. I push my arms through the sleeves of the collared shirt and slowly button it, feeling the heat of her stare like a touch on my skin. When I roll the sleeves, she swallows hard.

I can't help messing with her. "You okay?"

"Dandy," Lo squeaks.

When I drape the tie around my neck, I ask, "Could you help me out?" I have no problem tying my own tie, but despite knowing it's a bad idea, I want her close.

Lo's trembling fingers grasp the tie, and her earthy, floral scent envelops me. Her knuckles graze my throat as she makes quick work of the knot. She doesn't look up at me, but I want to look in her eyes, try to decipher what's going on in that head of hers. "Lo?"

Cam pulls into the parking spot next to us with a little honk. Lo meets my gaze questioningly, but I wave it off. "Never mind. It was nothing," I say as Cam and Hazel climb out of the car.

Hazel's grin is infectious as she sidles up next to us. "You look exactly like Sebastian and Mia."

She's right, and that's partly why I want to do this. My fans will eat it up. But more than that, Lo will love it. She will be hesitant at first, but recreating a moment from one of her favorite movies will make her heart race and make that beautiful smile light up her face. She'll feel alive and carefree, something I'm getting the sense she hasn't experienced much of in the last six years. It's strange, but despite my career, I haven't really either.

We make our way across the parking lot and toward the observatory. Cam and Hazel walk in front of us, talking to each other, but Lo chews her lip and follows my lead. The anxiety coming off her is visceral.

I stop walking, tugging Lo's arm so she does too. "Cam, Hazel, you guys go ahead. We'll meet you there in a minute."

"Back of the observatory?" Camden asks.

"Yeah."

Cam nods and juts a thumb over his shoulder. "I'll go ahead and get the camera set up."

"We don't have to do this," I tell Lo once Cam and Hazel are out of earshot.

I can feel the stares of people as they pass us, and I know Lo can too. She watches them warily. My hands settle on her shoulders, squaring her to face me. "We don't have to do this," I repeat.

She searches my face for a moment, uncertain. I expect her to let out a sigh of relief. What I don't expect is the steely resolve that crosses her features. The muscles in her shoulders shift as she stands taller. "Let's do it."

One corner of my mouth curves in a smile. "Yeah?"

Lo nods, tucking a lock of hair behind her ear. "Yeah."

"Okay them, come on!" I yell and grab her hand, tugging her along with me. "We're running out of daylight."

"Is this where the dance was filmed?" Lo asks when we get to the back side of the observatory. Her hand is still clasped in mine, but her steps have slowed as she curiously takes in her surroundings.

"It was in the park, but it's a two-mile hike from here. I figured you wouldn't want to walk that far back after dark."

"Thank you," she says, her voice genuine.

The tail end of the sunset has just dipped behind the horizon, bathing the world in a deep blue glow. We weed through the hordes of people who are leaving with the last bit of daylight. There's only a small crowd left, but I feel Lo tense beside me.

"Still want to do it?"

"Yes," Lo says.

I head over to where Cam has set up the tripod. He's adjusting some settings on the camera as we approach. "All set?" I ask him.

"All set."

In the waning blue light, I pull Lo over to the edge. We're separated from the drop-off by a white wall. Beyond that is a view that, no matter how many times I see it, never fails to impress me. As I take in the view now, Lo silhouetted against the backdrop of Los Angeles coming alive for another night, I'm breathless.

She turns around, and my heart stops in my chest. "You know what you're doing?" Lo asks, and I just stare at her, still speechless. "Do you know the dance?" she clarifies.

I clear my throat, pulling myself together. "Right. Uh, no. I figured we'd wing it. And do the little thing at the end." I spread my arms out wide and stand on one leg.

Lo laughs at my moves.

"I'm no Ryan Gosling."

"Don't I know it," she says, a twinkle in her eye.

Reaching for her hand, I tug her close. "Start the music," I yell to Cam, never looking away from Lo.

"This isn't part of it," she whispers as Cam counts down in the background.

"No?"

"They mostly dance separately."

"We're not them," I say as Cam shouts, "One!"

Lo's laugh catches on the breeze as I spin her away from me. She twirls and taps her feet similarly to how they do in the movie, but I stand transfixed, unable to look away. Her hair is an even more vibrant red against the blue sky. The yellow dress bounces and sways against her thighs with every step, contrasting with the creamy paleness of her skin.

She's absolutely beautiful.

When she turns back to me, I realize it's time for the iconic move. We perform it together, so perfectly in unison it looks like we rehearsed it a million times. Her mouth splits in a smile, and I reach for her without thinking. My hand settles on the curve of her waist, tugging her toward me, and the breath wrenches out of her as she falls against my chest. Our gazes lock and hold for one long moment. I don't know who moves first, but we only have heartbeats before the camera stops rolling, and I want to taste her while I still have the chance. Her lips brush against mine in the softest of kisses before Cam yells, "Time!"

We break apart as quickly as we came together, as if zapped by lightning. "We get it?" I ask Cam, although I don't let my gaze drift from Lo.

"Got it!"

"That was perfect!" Hazel screams and launches herself at us, wrapping us both in a tight hug.

It was perfect.

Twenty-Two

LO

My head swims as I stare at the ceiling. It's been a very long, very exhausting day. Hanging out with Hazel and Camden was a lot of fun, but also draining. Not to mention all the strange moments with Wes. My skin still feels like it's on fire, and my lips are prickling. *What happened out there today?*

I drag a hand down my face, annoyed at myself. Wes played his part, and he played it *well*. Much better than I can handle. I knew when I agreed to marry a guy I had a crush on for two years in college that it would be hard to fight my attraction to him. I didn't realize it would be like lighting a match in the forest and trying to extinguish the flames with a watering can.

I pick up my phone from the nightstand and check the time—12:02 AM. I've been lying here for two hours, unable to sleep. If I'm lucky, I might be able to catch my sister awake feeding Kara.

I send off a text telling Alexa to call me if she's up. As I reach to set my phone down, it buzzes in my hand. "Hey, Penny. How's the honeymoon?" Alexa asks when I answer her call.

"I'm screwed." I let out a breath as I fall back onto my pillows.

"Ooh, juicy. I want details."

I scrunch up my face. "More accurately. I'm not screwed, but I want to be."

Alexa tuts. "That sucks, honey."

"I know." My cuticles burn from my nervous picking, but I can't stop. I hiss under my breath when I hit a particularly sensitive piece of skin.

"What happened?"

Ignoring the pain in my finger, I roll over to my side and catch a view of the moon peering in through my thin curtains. "Nothing. Everything. I don't know."

"Hm, when you put it like that..."

I let out a small laugh. "Nothing actually happened. There was just a lot of fake stuff happening that I don't think I was prepared for. I thought we would kiss casually in public a couple of times and maybe hold hands when we go to the grocery store or something."

"You got more than you bargained for," Alexa concludes.

"Way more."

"Is that so bad?" she asks, and I hear Kara mewl quietly in the background. "Can you really get too much of that man?"

I put Alexa on speaker and click on Instagram. Immediately, I see I've been tagged in photos people took of us today. Wes dipping me in the street. Wes holding my hand as we crossed Sunset Boulevard. Wes sneaking me onto the Santa Monica Pier, since he's apparently been banned for life. And finally, Wes kissing me at twilight on top of the world.

"No, but it's very possible I won't get enough," I tell her.

WEDNESDAY IS TURNING OUT to be much less eventful than the previous day. We spend most of the morning with Kate and Emily, plotting out the rest of our time in California and strategizing things for the next few months.

"You guys are doing a podcast tomorrow," Emily tells us, not looking up from her computer.

I stiffen, and Wes squeezes my knee under the table. *Why, oh why, can this man not keep his hands to himself?* If he knew the way it sent my heart racing, he wouldn't do it. Actually, he probably would, but just because he loves to mess with me.

We get the afternoon off, and after much prodding, Wes convinces me to try surfing. The beach house has two surfboards stored in the garage, and he lets me choose which one I want. Mine is heavy and orange, and it reminds me of something you'd see in an old beach movie.

Wes is, to absolutely no one's surprise, a great surfer. My arms give out before I even make it past the breaking waves.

I'm laid out on my board on the sand when I feel droplets of cold water sprinkled across my drying skin. I squeal, my eyes popping open to find Wes grinning down at me, silhouetted by the sun. My eyes follow his movements, watching the way his muscles move and flex and the saltwater glistens on his skin as he lays his board on the ground and stretches out next to me. I am a greedy addict, desperate for a hit of him.

The rich, huskiness of his voice makes my every cell prickle with awareness. "This is nice."

I close my eyes, cutting off my view of him as my own way of practicing self-care. The testosterone radiating off of him has no effect on me. "Mm," is my only response.

"I can see why you'd spend your day like this. Why enjoy the ocean when you could lie here in the gritty sand all day?"

A dark shadow blocks the sun, and I peep open one eye. Wes is standing above me, a wicked grin on his face. I know immediately what he's about to do. "Oh, no, you don't!"

Sun-warmed hands clasp around my wrists, tugging me to my feet. My toes don't have time to sink into the sand before I'm swung over his shoulder. The world is upside down and jostling as he sprints toward the waves. I scream and pound his back, but it's broken up by my laughter. Saltwater sprays me as he splashes into the water, slowing only slightly as he moves farther and farther in. My hair is a bright red contrast against turquoise blue as the ends dip into the waves.

An instant later, Wes heaves me over his shoulder, and I sink below the surface. Cool water surrounds me, but I'm pulled up just as quickly by warm, firm hands around my middle.

Wes looks like a little kid on Christmas—like he's got everything he's ever wanted. His blond curls are plastered to his head, looking almost white against his tan skin. Pink dots his cheeks as his face splits into a heart-stopping smile. "Lo—"

A wave crashes hard against us, knocking us apart and dragging me under the water. I come up spluttering, and Wes finds my hand again. He tugs me close. "Are you okay?"

I'm still coughing, having swallowed a mouthful of seawater, but I manage to nod.

"Let's go back to shore."

We're both covered in sand when we collapse on our boards a moment later. Weston's brow is furrowed as I wring the water from my dripping hair.

"Are you sure you're okay?"

"Yeah, I'm fine," I say, although my voice is scratchy from ingesting seawater and coughing it back up. Wes searches in the beach bag and produces a bottle of water. I gratefully take a sip.

"Do you want to go back?" His gaze is tender and laced with concern as he looks me over, searching for injuries. His fingers graze a blue-green bruise forming on my knee, and his troubled eyes meet mine.

"It's from earlier," I say softly, feeling my skin heat beneath his touch. "I bumped my knee on the bed frame earlier. I'm fine, really."

His hand lingers for another moment before he snatches it back, taking all my breath with him. I lean back on my board, carefully avoiding the fins. I shut my eyes against the sun, and after a moment, I hear Wes mirroring my movements, his board shorts swishing as he stretches out on his board. A silence stretches between us, and I desperately think of something to fill it.

"Have you talked to Brandon?" I cringe inwardly at myself. *Literally any other topic would have been better.*

Wes is quiet for a moment, and I think maybe I've upset him. "No," he says finally. "He's been CC'd on all the emails between Kate, Emily, and me. And he's sent me a few personally, but he hasn't texted or called."

"Is that normal?"

"Eh," Wes replies. "It depends on his mood." I'm getting the sense that much of Wes and his manager's relationship depends on Brandon's mood.

It's as if Wes hears my thoughts. "Brandon's not a bad guy. I know he was rude the other night, but he's not normally like that. He let me stay with him when I first moved out here until I got on my feet. He celebrated all the holidays with me when I couldn't afford to go home during those early years. He was there for me when I had no one else."

I know what he means. Despite staying in Tennessee and having my family and friends around, a lot of times, Camilla was the one there for me when I had no one else.

"I get it," I say quietly.

"Yeah?"

"Yeah." I'm silent for a moment, unsure of how much I want to say. Wes doesn't press, and I find myself wanting to open up to him—share with him this part of my life he missed.

"Camilla was that for me. Our friends weren't all going to cancel their plans just because I had another flare-up that no one could see or understand. My family wasn't going to skip vacation just because I couldn't afford to take time off after all my sick days."

He rolls his head and looks at me, his expression pinched in sadness. "That sucks, Lo."

"It's okay. I'm sorry you were lonely when you moved. I guess I always thought you were out here living your best life." I never thought that while I was going through all that back home, Wes might also be going through it here, although in different ways. I'm not Brandon's biggest fan, but I'm glad Weston has had him over the past few years.

"It was really hard for a while. And then it was really fun. And then it was hard again," he says cryptically.

I'm about to ask what he means when he changes the subject. "Enough about me. How's the next book coming?"

I throw an arm over my face and let out a frustrated breath. "Any topic but that, please."

"That bad, huh?" he asks, a faint hint of amusement in his voice.

"Worse."

"I don't see how. *The Lake House* was amazing." I'm grateful my arm hides the blush that creeps into my cheeks at the title coming from his lips. My book is not based on our time at the lake six years ago. It is not. But it may have inspired certain elements of it. And had a much happier ending than the one we had.

I definitely never thought he'd read it. If I had, I would have published it under a pen name and never told a soul that I was the one who wrote it. But it's definitely not based on any real events. Let's be clear about that once and for all.

"What's so bad about this next one?" Wes asks, and I can tell from his nearness that he's turned to face me.

"There's not a next one."

"Ah," Wes says. "No new ideas?"

"No new ideas," I confirm, finally moving my arm and threading my fingers into the sand at my sides.

When I meet his gaze, he says, "I'm sure something will come to you."

I think about how easily Axel's character took shape in my mind—a tall, tanned hero with curly blond hair, glimmering green eyes, and a wide, carefree smile. No, I think I'm a washup. I'm only able to write one perfect man, and I can't duplicate him.

Twenty-Three

WESTON

"Are you nervous?"

"Not at all," Lo says, worrying her lip as she looks around the podcast studio waiting area. The space is bright and colorful, with red leather couches the squeak as Lo shifts anxiously for the millionth time.

I lean back and put my hands behind my head. "That so?"

"Cool as a cucumber."

"Because if you're nervous, I bet I could think of a few ways to get your mind off it," I say, grinning wolfishly at her.

Lo pins me with a flat stare just as the receptionist calls our names. "They're ready for you. Would you follow me back this way?"

My arm is seized in a death grip, Lo's fingers tightening like a boa constrictor around my bicep. She tugs me down so her lips are pressed against the shell of my ear. "Are there any dirty secrets I should know before we go in there?"

I pat her hand, my mouth quirking in a smile. "Other than the tattoo on my butt cheek, I can't think of anything."

"I really hope you're kidding."

"Wanna find out?" I ask with a wink. She lets go of my arm and rolls her eyes so hard I'm sure she can see another dimension. "Anything I should know?"

"The only wild things I've ever done were with you," she replies seriously before entering through the door the receptionist opened for us.

Our host stands as we walk in, extending a hand in our direction to shake. "Noah Goodson. So nice to meet you both."

"Weston King," I tell him and gesture to Lo. "My wife, Lo Summers."

It's the first time I've referred to Lo as my wife, and the words send an illicit thrill through my system.

"Why don't we take a seat?" Noah sits on one side of the large table and motions for us to sit in the chairs across from him. Lo looks warily at the microphones in front of us.

Noah tracks Lo's movements as she sits down. Something primal trips in my brain as his stare lingers, and without thinking, I slip an arm around her chair, letting my hand smooth across the sheet of hair falling over her back. I expect her to shoot me a questioning glance at my random show of affection, but to my surprise, she leans ever so slightly into my touch.

"Why don't we go ahead and get started," Noah says, dragging my attention back to the task at hand.

Los shifts in her seat, anxiety rolling off her in palpable waves. Slipping my hand beneath her hair, I give her neck a comforting squeeze. The smile she gives me is pure sunshine, radiating warmth like a summer day.

"Ready?" Noah asks, and I turn to find him watching us curiously, a slight crease between his brows.

"Let's do it," I say, letting my hand slide down to rest on the back of Lo's chair.

"Well, guys," Noah says into the microphone in front of him. "I'm here today with Weston King, YouTube star, and his new wife, Lo Summers. I gotta say, when I first heard the news that you'd gotten hitched—I didn't believe it." My stomach clenches at his words, and I feel Lo tense up beside me. "I wish you all could be here to see them today, though. Any doubts I had vanished just watching them."

Lo and I relax simultaneously, our bodies mirrored movements of one another.

"You guys are the real deal, huh?" Noah asks, giving us warm smiles. I can't speak, still coming down from thinking the whole charade was up. Lo must notice my distress because her hand lands on my thigh beneath the table. Her touch is a balm to my nerves, calming me instantly.

"The real deal," Lo confirms, giving me a small smile. "I'm just glad we found our way back to each other after all these years."

I thought, out of the two of us, I was going to have to be the one to do all the convincing. Lo is a terrible liar, but she's surprising me now. Her acting skills are much better than I expected.

"Tell us about that," Noah prompts.

I pull myself together and take this next question. When I sit up taller in my seat, Lo pulls her hand back into her lap. I want to snatch it back and hold on tight. *I'm so royally screwed.*

"Lo and I have been good friends for almost eight years now. We met in college." I face Lo, hoping that when I say this next part, she thinks I'm as good an actor as she is. She can't know it's all the truth. "I remember the first time I met Lo."

Her gaze is heavy on mine, a thick blanket tucked around your shoulders in the winter to keep out the cold. The memories flip through my mind like an old movie reel, a comfort film you haven't watched in ages, but you still remember every line.

"Her best friend and my best friend had hit it off earlier that week. They wanted to go for coffee and brought Lo and me along. Lo walked in that day wearing these dark jeans that made her legs go on for miles. Her hair was pulled up, and she had the most amazing smile I'd ever seen. She had a book peeking out of her bag—*Pride and Prejudice*."

Lo watches me, knowing none of this is fake. It all happened just like I said. I hope she doesn't read into it, see more than I want her to.

"That very first night, I tried to get her to let me order a surprise drink for her." I smile at the memory. "She turned me down, and from then on, my mission was to push Lo out of her comfort zone. That's right where I lived—just outside her comfort zone."

I turn back to Noah. "That's where 'Just Go With It' came from."

When Lo speaks, her voice is a little shaky. "He said that to me at least once a day for two years."

Noah leans back in his seat, watching us carefully, a stunned look on his face. "Wes, have you ever shared that publicly? That your catchphrase was something you used to say to Lo?"

I shake my head before remembering that the audience can't see me. "No," I answer. "Some of my early fans from Vine will probably remember seeing me trying to get Lo to join in my shenanigans and telling her to just go with it." I fold my hands in my lap. "But no, I don't think I ever specifically shared it."

"So what you're saying is that your entire career—the videos, the merch, the whole idea—was basically a love letter to Lo?" Noah asks.

I swallow hard and don't dare allow myself to look at Lo, sure I won't be able to convince her it was all for show if she sees the look in my eyes. "Yeah, I guess you could put it that way."

"Wow," Noah says, grinning from ear to ear. "That's good stuff. So, not to bring up a painful topic, but do you think that's why you couldn't commit to Talia?"

Even though I knew this would come up, it still hits me like a freight train. Everything Talia did to me flashes through my mind—using me to further her career, lying to the press about me, writing an album that trashed me—all because she felt more for me than I did for her.

Lo clears her throat, and my gaze snaps to her. "I can't speak for Wes' actions with Talia, but I know that Wes and I have always had something special—something that's lasted almost a decade. We may have been apart from each other for a while, working on our own things, but we always stayed friends." She pauses and looks at me. "I think we always knew we'd find our way back to each other."

When we climb into the car late that afternoon, having just finished recording the podcast, Lo and I are both quiet. She stares out the window pensively as we inch through the traffic from Los Angeles back to Newport Beach. Instead of taking the fastest route, I maneuver onto the highway that hugs the coast.

I try to keep my eyes on the road, but my attention keeps drifting back to her. The sun sets to her right, and she watches with rapt curiosity. She's bathed in a warm light that brings out all the golden highlights in her red hair. It's tucked behind her shoulder, giving me a view of her silky skin and enticing curves.

"This isn't the way we came, is it?" she asks.

I clear my throat, hoping she didn't notice my wandering gaze. "No, uh, this way has a better view, though. I thought you'd like it more."

"Oh," she says quietly. "Thank you." She turns back toward the window before I can see her expression.

I turn on the radio, no longer able to take the silence. When a song from Talia's new album—the one about me—comes through the speakers, I immediately switch the station.

Lo's stare burns the side of my face. She's silent as she watches, no doubt noticing my white-knuckled grip on the wheel and the tense line of my shoulders. I know she wants to ask me about it, but my breath releases on a relieved exhale when she doesn't.

My stomach growls loudly, breaking the companionable silence as we pull up to the beach house a little over an hour later. "Want me to order a pizza?"

"That sounds good," Lo replies.

"Supreme?"

She hesitates for a moment before responding. "Yeah, that's my favorite."

A small smile tilts my lips. "I know." After placing the order, I ask Lo if she wants to go for a walk on the beach while we wait.

Our shoes thud softly in the sand as we drop them at our feet. A cool breeze plasters my shirt to my chest and sends Lo's hair flying in every direction. Despite how warm summer in the city is, I always forget how chilly it can get on the coast at night.

Lo shivers next to me. I shrug out of my zip-up hoodie and hold it out to her, the fabric smooth and warm against my fingers. She looks at it hesitantly for a moment before slipping it on. It hangs on her frame, the sleeves dipping well past her hands. I reach for them, rolling each one back. Lo watches silently, not moving.

When I drop her hands and start walking down the beach, she follows beside me. The tension rolls of her in waves as palpable as the ones crashing against the shore. She has something on her mind, and I'm really hoping it's not what I said back at the studio. I don't think I'll be able to lie to her again if she asks about my feelings for her in college. It was hard enough to do it back then when she said it had all been a mistake.

"Can I ask you about Talia?" Lo asks finally, catching me off guard.

Even though Talia is my least favorite topic, I'd much rather talk about her than what I was expecting Lo to ask about. I let out a breath. "What do you want to know?"

"Whatever you're willing to tell me," Lo says, her voice soft. It's something I've always appreciated about her—one of the few things we have in common. Neither of us is prone to sharing our feelings the way Rod and Camilla are. Lo has never pressed me for more than I want to share, even though I've rarely paid her the same courtesy—always pushing her to give me more of herself.

I need to be more like Lo.

"Talia and I never really dated," I confess, and Lo peers up at me with a furrowed brow. "Well, I guess we dated some, but we weren't really in a relationship. We met at some party and hit it off. Some fans saw it, and we got some really good press from it. Both our management teams suggested we play it up, be seen together in public more."

I remember it now—the reactions I'd gotten from fans—and how good it felt to gain a bigger audience. Thousands of people who loved Talia and now loved me. I'd give it all back now, that fame I gained in the early days with her if only to not have to deal with everything that came after.

"I thought we were just friends," I continue. "I mean, it was our managers who encouraged it. It wasn't as if either of us had asked each other out. I was blindsided when Talia asked me to commit to her. I didn't realize she thought any of it had been real. I told her I couldn't, and she hated me for it."

"Why couldn't you commit?" Lo asks, and her quiet voice seems almost shaky.

"I wasn't in love with her," I say simply.

Lo is quiet for a moment. "But she's so beautiful."

"Beauty isn't everything."

She kicks at the cold surf that reaches her toes. "That's something only beautiful people say."

"You think I'm beautiful, huh?" I ask, my lips curving in a smile. I step in front of her, blocking her path so she has to stare up at me. The heavy weight of the conversation lifts, and I'm much more comfortable now that we're back to teasing each other.

"Yes, Wes, you're beautiful," she says with a roll of her eyes, but when she looks back at me again, there's something undefinable in her expression—something softer, more vulnerable.

I take a small step forward, wanting to test a theory. When she doesn't move away, I lean a little farther. She exhales against my skin, and a soft pink colors her neck. I want to press my lips there and drag them up the slope, see if that blush is as warm as it looks.

My body sways another inch.

The loud ding of my phone shatters the moment, echoing on the breeze. Lo stares at me with wide, unblinking eyes. "Pizza's here."

Twenty-Four

LO

"I don't have anything else for you today," Emily says, glancing over the notes on her iPad one more time. "Go enjoy your last day."

"Are you sure?" I ask desperately, and Wes flashes me a narrow-eyed glance. There's a reason I don't play poker, and this is it—I'm more transparent than a window.

I can't spend a whole afternoon *alone* with Wes. My head is spinning enough already. It's been one thing after another—the TikToks and kissing, the surfing, the lies mixed with reality during the podcast. Not to mention the walk on the beach last night. If his phone hadn't dinged, I would have made out with him right then and there. And worse, I think he would have let me.

It would have been a disaster because there's no running away if we screw this thing up again. We absolutely cannot make the same mistake twice.

"Not a thing," Emily replies. She's taken over a lot of Brandon's duties this week since Brandon still hasn't come back to the beach house. "I blocked the rest of today off for you to enjoy your honeymoon." She wiggles her eyebrows at us, and my face catches fire.

"Oh, we have been," Wes says suggestively, and I pinch his leg under the table.

Emily notices the movement, and she stands up hurriedly. "Wait for me to leave!" she exclaims, obviously misinterpreting the gesture. I wish more than anything that I could melt into the floor right now. Living out the rest of my days as gelatinous goo on the beach house floor wouldn't be so bad.

Emily rounds the table and wraps her thin arms around our necks. "It was so nice meeting you, Lo. Wes, as always, I love you and stay out of trouble." Before we can respond, she scurries down the hall. The clack of the screen door slamming against the frame reverberates through the house.

I fix Wes with what I hope is a withering glare. His head falls back, and he laughs loudly.

I need to work on it, I guess.

"What are we going to do today?" I ask tentatively.

"Oh, I've got plans."

My breath hitches. Wes catches my expression and laughs again. "Calm down, Lo, nothing like that." His chair squeals against the floorboards as he stands and heads into the kitchen. "You don't have to look so horrified."

I don't correct him and tell him that I could think of literally nothing better. Memories of his kisses haunt my dreams, and I swear if I checked in the mirror, I'd find a brand on my skin where he dragged his hand across my back.

"I thought we'd go to Balboa Island," Wes says as he fills up a glass of water. He leans against the counter, crossing one leg over the other, and takes a sip.

I watch in fascination, finally able to take my fill since he's not focused on me. He's all long, lean lines. Tight muscles that flex even when he's doing something this simple. Wes is so perfect he's hard to look at.

"See something you like?" Wes asks, catching me staring. His voice is deeper, a gravelly murmur that sounds like pure temptation.

"Thought you had a stain on your shirt. Just a fuzz," I say hastily and rise from my seat. "I'm going to get ready."

My legs are wet noodles, barely able to hold my weight as I retreat to my room. As soon as the door shuts behind me, I collapse against it, letting out a shaky exhale. I have to get a hold of myself. He's just one man. So what if he could convince a nun to leave the convent? I'm stronger than this. I resisted him for *two whole years*. Why am I having such a hard time now?

Pushing off the door, I head into the bathroom. My reflection in the mirror is frazzled—eyes bright and wide, hair wild, face tinged pink. I need to get myself together.

My brush snags on the knots in my hair, salty and air-dried after swimming in the ocean this morning. Freckles cover every available square inch on my face, and my slight tan means my tinted moisturizer is now too light. This means I have to go out in only colored lip balm and mascara with the subject of God's best handiwork as my date.

I spend another five minutes trying to primp before finally giving up. This is as good as it's going to get.

When I return to the living area, Wes is stretched out on the couch, scrolling through his phone. My footsteps grab his attention, and a slow smile crooks one corner of his mouth. Oh, be still my disloyal heart. My brain is going to give it a firm lecture later when I'm not held captive by that bewitching grin.

"What?" I ask, tugging at the hem of my shirt.

His feet hit the floor, and he stands in a fluid motion. "You look nice."

If I were wearing a corset, my bosom would be heaving. "Thanks," I manage to squeak out.

Wes stops in front of me, close enough that I have to look up to meet his eyes. One of his hands curls around a lock of my hair, rubbing it between his fingers. "I like your hair like this."

"It's wild," I breathe.

His shoulder lifts in a shrug that mirrors his lips. "I like wild." He holds my gaze for a heartbeat before stepping back, putting much needed space between us. "Ready to go?"

I nod, not trusting myself to form coherent words.

It's not until we're in the car, the salty, balmy air whipping through the open windows, that I attempt speaking. "What's on Balboa Island?"

A mischievous grin slashes across his face. "A surprise."

If I'm going to be able to handle myself around Weston, there can be no surprises. I chew my lip and stare out the passenger window. Despite Weston having me tightened up like a jack-in-the-box ready to spring open, the warm sunshine and the distant sound of the crashing surf finally begins to loosen the tension in my body.

When we get down to the end of Balboa Peninsula, Wes follows the signs for the ferry. "We're taking a ferry?" I ask, finally feeling something other than trepidation and actually getting a little excited.

"Yeah, it's all part of the experience." He darts a glance my way before making the final turn. "Is that okay?"

I prop my elbow on the door and let my hand dangle out the open window, a smile tilting my lips. "Just go with it, huh?"

I hear the delight in his voice as he parks the car. "Yeah, just go with it."

We're the last passengers ushered onto the packed ferry, and there's only one seat left. Wes sits and pulls me onto his lap. His nose nuzzles beneath my hair, brushing against the sensitive skin on my neck. "In case anyone is watching," he says.

I jostle unsteadily on his legs as the ferry takes off, and his hands slip around my waist, stabilizing me. "Thanks," I breathe. Shifting, I brace my hand on the railing behind us.

Wes watches my movements. "What are you doing?"

"Trying to move." I shimmy again, attempting to maneuver some of my weight off his lap. "Am I crushing you?"

"No, Lo," he says, his fingers pressing more firmly into my hips. His voice has dropped, rasping pleasantly in my ear. "You're not crushing me."

When I meet his eyes, they're unbelievably dark and heavy lidded, the color of fresh-cut grass in spring.

The ferry bumps up against the dock, jarring me again. This time, I stand before Wes can help me. But the crowd is thick as we maneuver off the ferry and into the streets, so when Wes offers his hand, I take it.

The island is picturesque, the harbor dotted with white boats, their sails peppered against the backdrop of the azure sky, the streets lined with pastel beach homes. Salty air kisses my skin and sunshine catches in Weston's hair, turning it to golden silk.

Wes stops, gesturing in front of him with his free hand. "We're here."

We're standing in front of a vintage storefront. A weathered sign in the shape of a peeled banana hangs over a royal blue portico that reads, "The Original Frozen Banana."

I look back at him. "Frozen bananas?"

He's grinning like he's a kid in a candy shop, or rather, like he's the parent of a kid in a candy shop. I'm the kid in this scenario. Except I'm not exactly sure what I'm looking at here. Bananas?

He urges me forward to a line that's forming on the other side of the stand. "This place is known for their frozen bananas dipped in chocolate. I know you're allergic to bananas, but—"

"How do you know that?"

His eyebrows pinch together. "You always have been, right?"

I have. And for some reason, the fact that he remembered that makes my heart turn to mush in my chest. So instead of responding, I nod.

He points at the menu ahead of us. "But, they also serve something I believe to be even better—the Balboa Bar. It's a bar of ice cream dipped in chocolate and whatever toppings you want. And while that may not sound like anything life-changing, there's something about—"

"It does sound life-changing," I interrupt, excitement pulsing through my veins at stuffing my face with this treat.

His smile widens. "Yeah?"

"Absolutely." I nod vigorously.

His arm comes around my shoulder, wrapping me in a hug, and laughter rumbles in his chest. I want to lay my head there and let it be my own personal sound machine as I fall asleep at night. He releases me, and I have to remind myself *again* to calm down.

We are friends.

Friends who are married.

But not friends who are married who also get freaky.

It's complicated.

A few minutes later, Balboa Bars in hand, we round the corner of the shop and lean against the brick wall. Tall bushes scratch against my back and tangle in my hair.

"Cheers," Wes says, holding his bar up to clink with mine. Mine is dipped in dark chocolate and coated with coconut and peanuts. Weston's is covered in a colorful array of sprinkles, and both are starting to melt and drip down our fingers beneath the warm sunshine.

I tap it against his, and the chocolate coating cracks a little, so I take my first bite from that corner. It's sweet and salty, smooth and creamy. Literal heaven in my mouth. "Oh my gosh," I moan. "This *is* life changing."

He smiles around his bite. "I thought you'd think so."

My tongue darts out, catching a melting bit of ice cream sliding down the stick. Weston's smile is gone when I meet his eyes again. His expression is serious—thoughtful and determined. My stomach bottoms out as his gaze dips to my mouth and holds.

His eyes slowly track up my face and meet mine. In my periphery, I see him lick his lips.

"I think I should kiss you now, just in case anyone is watching."

Twenty-Five

WESTON

I DON'T KNOW WHAT made me say it except that it's all I've been thinking about this entire trip. Memories of that kiss from six years ago play on an endless loop in my brain, awake and asleep, so there is no reprieve. I remember how she tasted—sweet, like marshmallows and chocolate from the s'mores we'd been eating. I remember how she felt against me, the way she leaned in, searching and exploring, finally diving headlong into something for the first time in her life. I remember that kissing her felt like stardust, like finally surrendering to a wave threatening to pull you under, like losing yourself in a bit of magic.

All the kisses between us the past week have been for show—passionless and quick.

But I want to kiss Lo now, to feel her melt into me like she did that first time. My mind has been on fire this week, unable to think about anything but the velvety feel of her lips, a texture that's been branded so thoroughly in my mind that I couldn't forget it if I tried.

I'm desperate and wanting. I think I'll explode into the darkness like a dying star if she doesn't let me kiss her.

Lo's eyes widen as she registers what I said. But she doesn't say no. Or even really look like she wants to. In fact, she looks like she wants to say—

"Okay," she says, and my whole body catches flame. "Let me toss this," she says, nodding down at her mostly finished Balboa Bar. Her voice is low and smooth as silk.

Her body stretches in a lean line, drawing my gaze to each swell of her curves as she leans over, throwing her trash into the garbage can. My feet move of their own volition, drawing me closer until I can smell the earthy aroma of the essential oils she rolled on her skin. I want to press my nose to her neck where the scent is strongest and breathe her in.

Unreadable emotions flicker across her face, and I don't know if it's nervousness or excitement. Every one of my muscles jump to attention as her hand slides up my stomach before coming to rest over my wildly beating heart.

"For the cameras," she whispers, and I nod, moving closer. There's no space between us now, and I can feel every single bit of her softness pressed against my hard planes.

Her dark lashes flutter, a stark contrast against her creamy cheekbones. The color of her eyes is the blue-green of the open ocean, wild and beautiful and utterly dangerous. My exhalation flutters the fine russet hairs framing her face. The soft Cupid's bow of her lip begs for my attention, and my every atom yearns to pay their respects, to shower her mouth with the reverence it deserves.

"We should try to make it really convincing."

She nods, and it snaps the last vestiges of my restraint. My kiss is bruising, devouring, and Lo surprises me by matching my intensity. Her hands tunnel into my hair, scraping against my scalp, and her teeth nip at my bottom lip.

My body has been an electric wire, humming for the past week, but now it's like sticking my finger in an outlet. I feel the static all the way to my toes. Her lips open, causing me to lose any ounce of self-control I had left. She tastes of chocolate and vanilla. Her tongue is cold from the ice cream as it meets mine, although her body is warm pressed up against me. The contrast in sensations makes my heart race and blurs my vision until all I can see is *her*. Lo. *My* Lo.

Lo gasps against my mouth as one of my hands slides around her back, dipping below the hem to graze the delicate skin I accidentally touched that first day we were here. It's taken every bit of my willpower to keep from doing it again, but given her response, I don't think I should have bothered.

She arches into my touch, somehow managing to press closer. The feel of her like this will be branded on my skin, marked all the way down to my bones.

And yet, it's not enough. I need *more*.

Instinctively, I push forward, pressing her into the wall at her back. Her hands are desperate, grasping and tugging, holding tight to me like a buoy in a tempest.

Lo breaks the kiss with a shocked gasp, and it's only then that I realize she's falling. The wall behind her isn't a wall at all, but bushes.

My palm, still tucked beneath her shirt, splays against her back, hauling her into me. She lands with a thud against my chest, her giggle muffled in the fabric of my shirt. The sound unlocks my own laughter. My head falls, buried in her hair, until we can finally regain our composure.

Lo tucks her lip between her teeth to hold back a grin. "I think we were pretty convincing, huh?"

Oh.

The pleasure of kissing Lo is stripped away in an instant, replaced with the icy emptiness of a barren landscape. It shouldn't bother me, that I thought we'd taken the first exit out of the land of make-believe and ended up somewhere real.

We have an arrangement, and Lo was only holding up her end of the deal. It wasn't excitement that lit her eyes. I bet it wasn't even nervousness about kissing me that made her hands tremble. We did that plenty already. She was worried she wouldn't be able to sell it if anyone was watching.

Lo shouldn't have been concerned; she managed to convince the one person who knew the truth.

"Yeah, we did alright." I say, and the words taste sour in my mouth. Her skin is hot beneath my touch, scalding me enough to realize my hand is still trapped beneath her shirt. I let go like she's a hot coal, stepping back to put some space between us. "We should probably start heading back if you want to stop in some of those shops along the way." My voice is ragged, a piece of fabric roughly shorn along the edges.

Lo nods, tugging loose a leaf that got lodged in her mass of hair.

My feet pound against the pavement, eating up the distance to the shops. Lo falls in line next to me. I don't take her hand like I did before. The distance between us is a tangible thing, wrapping around our lungs to cut off our oxygen. Moments ago she clung to me like I was the tether keeping her tied to this realm, and now she walks stiffly beside me, leaving enough room for the Holy Spirit.

A bright arrangement of souvenirs in a shop window grabs my attention, and I stop. "Want to go in here? It looks nice."

"Sure." Lo murmurs, brushing past me to walk through the narrow open door.

The shop is small and brightly lit, with pastel trinkets lining the white shiplapped walls and shelves. It smells of sea salt and citrus, like eating an orange creamsicle on the beach. A soft breeze blows through, setting wind chimes that hang from the ceiling pleasantly tinkling.

Lo's long fingers trail over the stacks of kitchen towels and throw pillows with the same light touch she pressed against my skin a few minutes ago. With every graze against the fabric, my muscles clench involuntarily, tightening until I'm a bowstring ready to snap.

She continues perusing, completely unaware of my inner turmoil. Her hand drops to her side as she crosses the shop, stopping in front of a small shelf of candles. I'm pulled behind her by an invisible string, a puppy who still follows its owner even when the leash is off.

Her gaze flicks over the display before she moves on, her back brushing against my chest as she moves. The contact sends my heart skittering against my sternum once more, and I force my feet to stay planted so I can gather my wits.

Something on the shelf catches my eye, and I reach for it with a trembling hand. My thumb swipes over the label. Without giving it another thought, I spin on my heel and head for the register. Lo sidles up next to me after the cashier has already wrapped it in brown paper.

"Find something?" Lo asks as the cashier carefully stuffs it in a plastic bag.

"Just something for my mom," I lie.

"Nice. I found something too." She places a small canvas print on the counter. It reads *Newport Beach* and looks like the artist sat on the stretch of beach along our vacation house to paint it.

"I like it," I say and hand it to the cashier to ring up.

"So we won't forget." Lo's voice is soft and wistful, like she's telling a story.

I won't need a memento to remember this day. It will be burned in my brain forever.

Twenty-Six

LO

SILENCE HANGS HEAVY IN the car on the way back to the beach house, and although I know the reason for my discomfort, I don't know what's bugging Wes.

I'm not really feeling like myself. After falling into the bushes and being jerked back into place, an ache has made its way up my back. What started as a twinge earlier has, after walking and sitting in traffic, turned into a sharp pain that, no matter how much I adjust, will not allow me to get comfortable.

Not to mention the headache crawling up the back of my neck to settle right between my eyes. I dig through my purse and find a pill bottle.

Wes glances at me out of the corner of his eye as I swallow the medicine. "Are you feeling okay?" he asks, concerned.

"Just in a little pain."

"Did we overdo it this week?"

"No, no," I assure him, throwing the bottle back in my bag and zipping it closed. "It's okay, really."

"Have you been in pain all day?"

My immediate answer is no, but as I think about it, maybe I have been. I shrug. "I don't know." I pause for a moment, not sure how much I want to open up. "Sometimes I don't know if I've really gotten that much better in the past few years or if

I've just gotten so used to the pain that I can't remember how it feels to be without it."

Weston's face crumples, and it makes my heart tug painfully in my chest. He sounds broken when he speaks. "That's terrible, Lo. I'm sorry. I don't know what to say."

"It's okay."

"No, it's not," Wes says, turning down the street the beach house is on.

I shrug again. "I'm used to it. It's a daily part of my life, and it won't ever go away. If I let myself dwell on it..." Despite my confident words, my voice hitches. "If I let myself dwell on it, it will destroy me."

Wes pulls into the driveway and turns to face me. His steady gaze is my undoing. A tear slips out, tracking down my cheek. Before I know what's happening, Wes is out of the car. The passenger door groans on its hinges as he yanks it open. Strong arms envelop me, pulling me tight to his chest.

What's meant to be comforting breaks me.

I wish I could attribute it to my aches and pains, but that's not it. That's all normal. What's not normal is the way my skin is on fire. The way my stomach is clenched in knots and I can't stop myself from remembering that kiss.

It was earth-shattering. Life-changing. It was as if his hands were branding the small of my back, burning his fingertips into the skin so I would never forget he was there. My lips are still tingling, and my nerve endings are still humming.

Standing here now, clinging to him, I know he has ruined me. I'm gone for him, yet I can't erase the image of him in front of me at the ice cream shop looking completely unaffected by our kiss.

Wes kissed me like the world was ending, but the moment it was over, his face had gone completely blank. He may have enjoyed that kiss, but it wrecked me.

The realization hits me like a freight train, I pull back, no longer able to handle being this close to him.

His face is creased with concern. "What's wrong? Are you okay?"

"Yeah, I'm fine."

He's still holding me, his thumbs tracing circles on my arms. I'm sure he doesn't even realize he's doing it, but I'll feel the lingering ghost of his touch all night. I shrug off his hands, and he releases me like I'm a hot burner he accidentally touched.

Wes grabs at the back of his neck, his eyes glancing over my shoulder at the beach house. "Want to go for a walk on the beach?" He sounds timid and vulnerable, and it almost cracks my resolve, but my mind draws back to the moment yesterday, right before the pizza was delivered. If I'm ever going to make it through this sham of a marriage, I need to start setting boundaries.

"No," I say quickly before I allow myself to change my answer. "I think I just need to rest."

Weston gaze is searching, and I'm terrified he can read every emotion written on my face. "Yeah, okay," he says finally, nodding.

Instead of heading to the beach, he follows me to the front door. His presence is like a weighted blanket at my back as my trembling hands try to fit the key in the lock. I don't risk looking at him before making a beeline straight for my room.

Despite the early hour, I change and climb into bed, hoping the whir of the ceiling fan will lull me to sleep again like it did the first night I was here. But it's no use. My mind races, playing back every single moment Wes and I have shared this week. I see Wes closing in on me and pressing a kiss to my lips, Los Angeles drenched in twilight behind us. I feel his hands smoothing against my skin beneath my shirt, making me shiver. I can smell his spicy aftershave as he wraps his arms around me.

It's all just too much. We've been married for a week, and I'm already drowning. I don't know how I'm going to make it.

I must have finally drifted off because when I'm awoken by the soft knock on my door, the room is bathed in shades of sunset.

"Come in," I say, sitting up and hugging the blankets to my chest.

The door squeaks open, and Wes's broad shoulders fill the frame. An In-N-Out bag crinkles in his hand as he holds it in front of him. "You up for some company?"

I stare at him for a moment, my heart constricting. His hair is wild from the sea breeze, curls standing at odd angles that shouldn't look this charming. His eyes are soft and crinkled at the edges in concern. His empty hand fidgets at his side, and I wonder if he's *nervous*. Weston King, nervous.

It's that hand, curling and uncurling at his side that, against my better judgment, makes me say yes. "Yeah, thank you."

I push my legs out from under the covers, starting to get up, but Wes motions for me to stay.

"You're hurting. Let's just hang in here."

Abort. Abort. Abort, my brain screams at me, but I just scoot over, making room for him. He sets the drink carrier down on the nightstand and settles atop the blankets next to me. The tightness is gone from his expression when he gives me a warm smile. The butterflies that took up residence in my stomach the day we met take flight once again.

The bag crinkles as Wes opens it and pulls out two burgers and two baskets of fries. He hands me a meal before grabbing the remote. "Want to watch a movie?"

"Yeah, sure."

He goes straight for the On Demand, and I watch as he types *Pride & Prejudice* into the search bar. My heart hammers in my chest as he fills in his card info and purchases it.

"Um, Wes? Why are we watching this?"

He squints at me, confused. "Isn't this your favorite movie?"

"Yeah…"

Wes grins. "Good. Let's eat." He hits my burger with his own like he's giving it a cheers before taking a bite. A pleased, humming noise comes from the back of his throat.

My eyes drift between Wes and the TV screen, trying to make sense of this situation. If you would have told me eight years ago, even a *month* ago, that I would be married to Weston King and watching *Pride & Prejudice* in bed with him while we ate dinner, I would have thrown my back out from laughing so hard.

Wes catches my gaze. "Aren't you going to eat?"

Oh, yeah. I take a bite, savoring the flavor, but I'm still unable to concentrate.

Wes must notice because he pauses the movie and turns to face me. "What's up?"

"Why did you get dinner and turn this movie on?"

Wes looks almost sheepish as he puts his food down and clasps his hands between his knees. It's so endearing that I want to snap a picture and post it on my Instagram for all the Talia fans that call him heartless.

"I, uh, I called Camilla." Be still my heart, he's *blushing*. I may expire. "I didn't know what to do. I was so worried about you. Camilla said this is all normal and the best thing to do would be to get you some food and turn on a movie and just make sure you're not alone."

My vision blurs with unshed tears, and a tight knot forms in my throat at his words. Weston King called my best friend because he was worried about me. Instead of spending his last night of vacation doing something fun and spontaneous with his friends, he got me greasy fast food and crawled into bed with me to watch my favorite movie since I couldn't go out.

"Lo?" Wes asks, concerned. "Are you okay?" His touch is light against my arms, fingers smoothing in mindless circles.

My hands tremble as I wipe away my tears, but my smile is genuine. "Yeah, I'm okay. This is just really nice. Thanks for doing all this."

His lips quirk in a relieved grin. "I wouldn't want to be anywhere else."

And wonder of all wonders, I think he's telling the truth.

Twenty-Seven

LO

"Are you ready to make your first vlog?" Weston asks me, looking way more excited than this event calls for.

It's Saturday, and we got back from California late last night. We slept in today, and while it did wonders for my tired and aching body, I still feel like death. Which is not how I want to feel when making a video that hundreds of thousands of people will see, but I don't tell Wes that.

Brandon never came back to the beach house, but he did send a few emails with ideas on how to keep the public interested in our relationship. In one of the emails, he listed several things he thought Wes needed to do over the next few weeks—vlogs, social media posts with specific hashtags to use, and some ads to film. I don't like to admit it since I personally wish Brandon's lint trap would catch on fire, but he's good at his job.

And so, although I feel absolutely terrible today, I don't tell Weston. I know he would be the one to get flack from Brandon over not putting out any content, not me. So I ignore the aching feeling in my muscles, the throbbing in my head, and say, "Absolutely."

Wes grins. "You may want to make your smile look more realistic if you're meant to be looking madly in love with me.

Plus, you're getting fake laid, and if it were real, you would be positively beaming."

I roll my eyes, and he says, "Unable to contain the joy you feel." I prop my hands on my hips, knowing he's got plenty more to say. "Desperate for me."

That one isn't entirely untrue. I pin him with an exasperated look. "Can we film now?"

His smile is contagious, and I can't help but mirror it. Weston's shoulder brushes against mine as he moves to my side, holding the camera out in front of us. I can see us reflected back in the small screen sticking out the side, and my eyes are wide and unmoving. I look like a deer in the headlights.

Wes lowers the camera onto the counter and turns to face me. "You're nervous," he says. It's not a question, just a statement, and it's kind of scary how easily he can read me.

I can't handle the concern in his eyes. The color changes with his mood, and right now they've turned from their usual bright green to hazel with a crinkle between the brows. That worry is trying to convince me to forget the way he looked after our kiss on Balboa Island. I turn away from their intensity, staring at my mismatched socks.

"Not nervous," I say, my voice muffled behind the curtain of my hair. "Just not feeling the best today."

Weston's fingertips brush under my chin, tipping my face up to him. His voice is soft and gentle, the tone a mother uses to soothe her child in the night. "You're nervous."

I tug my bottom lip between my teeth and his eyes flicker at the movement. "Maybe." Despite all the exposure I had in California, the camera still sets my heart racing.

"We don't have to do this. You don't have to be on camera if it makes you uncomfortable."

"But Brandon—"

"Screw Brandon," he says. "We're not doing this right now if you're not comfortable with it."

Unexpectedly, warmth blooms in my chest and spreads through my stomach, like caramel drizzle running down the sides of a cake. Wes is getting much, much less from this marriage than I am. Sure, he's getting people off his back and getting some good press, but he probably could have made that happen a much easier way. And without dealing with Brandon's anger. And now he's basically offering to let me back out of my side of the deal.

Without thinking, I wrap my arms around his muscled middle, and my head nestles into the solidness of his chest. His heart beat is steady against my ear as he folds his arms around my shoulders, the beat of a drum that anchors an entire orchestra.

His hand smooths down my back, fingers bumping along each notch of my spine. He stops right above the hem of my shirt, and I know by the way his breath comes a little faster that he's remembering it too, the way his hands felt on my skin.

I don't know if I consciously move against him, arching my back so his hand slips that extra half inch, but the touch sends a lightning bolt through me, jarring me back to reality. I jerk back like I've been burned, stepping out of his embrace. Weston's gaze is heavy on my back as I walk around the kitchen island and fill a glass of water.

Wes scrubs a hand over the back of his neck and clears his throat. "Let's just blow off our plans for the day and go sit by the pool."

The idea is so tempting, it's surely from the serpent himself. But I can't do it. Wes has been more kind to me than I deserve, and I want to do something nice for him in return. Plus, if I sit out there next to him all day, my resolve is going to melt under the scorching sun.

My hands are still trembling as I set the glass of water on the counter. "No, let's film."

"No," he says, and I'm a little shocked by the firmness in his voice.

I cross my arms over my chest. "I want to do it."

Wes gives me a hard look, as if trying to determine if I'm telling the truth. I school my features to not reflect any of the lingering anxiety I'm feeling.

Finally, Wes nods and reaches for the camera sitting on the counter. He rests his hand on it but doesn't lift it up. After a moment, he disregards the camera and turns back to me, a glint in his eye. I don't have any time to contemplate what he's doing before he picks me up and tosses me over his shoulder.

"Oh, no you don't!" I scream.

His shoulder is firm beneath my stomach, his hands warm against my bare thighs below my shorts. Laughter rolls through him, jostling me even more as he runs out the back door. The day is stifling, the humidity so thick you can almost see it in the air, but a few seconds later, Wes jumps into the pool and the heat evaporates. In its place is cool, invigorating water, rising to meet me on all sides. When I break the surface, he's there in the water with me, grinning like a kid on Christmas.

We don't end up filming. We change into our bathing suits and spend the rest of the day lounging by the pool and drinking fruity drinks that Wes makes in the blender. Wes snaps a picture of us sitting side by side, cheesy grins plastered on our faces and posts it with the caption, "My favorite girl."

As the sun beats down on us, drying the water droplets pebbled on our skin, I end up pulling out my laptop and writing. It's the first time I've felt inspired in a long time. I'm not sure exactly what the story is or where it's going, but I do know that the love interest has green eyes that change color with his mood.

LATE IN THE AFTERNOON, I head into the house to get ready for our double date with Camilla and Rod. After sitting by the pool all day, my skin is tight and a little pink, and my freckles are out of control, covering every available square inch on my face.

With my hair wrapped in a towel after my shower, I rifle through my closet. The *college* box catches my eye again, and for a moment, I consider opening it. My fingers slide against a linen sundress, and I push thoughts of the box from my mind.

I'm putting the finishing touches on my hair, a copper strand still wrapped around my curling iron, when Camilla's voice booms up the stairs. I slip my feet into sandals, and give my reflection a final once over in the mirror before following her voice downstairs. I have no idea how she speaks so loudly. You wouldn't be able to hear me over the sound of a fan set on the middle speed, but I could hear Camilla whispering next to a lawn mower.

When I hit the final step, Camilla notices me. Her scream is loud enough to move a mountain range as she launches herself into my arms. From over her shoulder, I see Wes staring at us. Rodrigo is still talking, used to Camilla's loud outbursts, but it doesn't appear that Wes is listening to him. His lips part and his chest expands as it fills with air.

My brows draw together as he meets my gaze. It seems to snap him out of whatever trance he's in, and he shakes his head as if to clear it before focusing on Rod once more.

I have no idea what *that* is about.

Camilla's arms tighten around me, cutting off the oxygen to my brain as she prattles nonstop in my ear. "I've just missed you so much. We barely saw each other before the wedding. Not to mention that every interaction we had the week before was cloaked in your deceit and so, therefore, our bond was severed. And then we went on our honeymoons. And I had to move in with Rod, and I love him. Of course I do. But he's not as good a roommate as you, and he leaves socks on the floor, which is something you would never do because you're a perfect saint of a roommate." She takes a deep breath. "All that to say, I really miss you, fried."

"Camilla," I gasp. "I'm seeing spots."

She backs up immediately, and I suck in deep lungfuls of air. Her small, cool hands clasp my cheeks. "Are you alive? Do you need medical attention? Rod, Wes, hurry! Lo is *dying*."

"I'm fine," I say, letting out a breathy laugh. "I've missed you too. I'm glad we're back in the same city and that there is not, as you so delicately put it, any deceit to sever our bond."

"Don't think that your brush with death is going to get you out of a lecture later."

"I would never even consider it."

"So everyone is okay?" Wes asks, looking between me and Camilla. He looks like he wants to get out a stethoscope and check to make sure my lungs are working properly. It makes warmth spread through my chest.

I give him a reassuring smile. "Yeah, I'm fine, I promise." My elbow prods Camilla's ribs. "Camilla doesn't know her own strength."

"Oh, I know," Rod intones gravely.

I clap my hands together loudly. "*That* is our cue to leave."

Thirty minutes later, Wes and I slide into a sparkly red vinyl booth at our favorite taco shop. Camilla and Rod are still in line, figuring out what they want to order.

Queso drips off my chip, splattering on the table as I take a bite.

Wes drags his finger through the drip, and before I realize what he's doing, he wipes it on the tip of my nose. I stare at him, wiping the mess off with my napkin. "You did not just do that."

He grins, crunching on a chip of his own. "I think I did."

I dunk my pointer finger in the queso and brandish it like a sword. Weston's hand closes around my wrist. "Oh no, you don't."

I don't fight his hold because he's stronger and I know this cheese is about to drip any second. When it does, it's going to land with a satisfying splat in his lap. My eyes dart to my finger then back to his, and I realize my mistake when Wes follows my gaze, zeroing in on the queso forming a teardrop on the tip of my finger.

"Smart strategy, Summers."

My lips quirk in a satisfied grin. "I thought so."

The smile falls away, however, when Weston's mouth closes around my finger, sucking the queso clean off. My breath hitches in my throat as his tongue brushes against my skin. Someone get the smelling salts because I'm a goner.

"Hey," Camilla says, sliding into the booth, Rod following behind her.

Wes drops my shaking hand, and I stuff it beneath my thighs. A muscle flickers in his jaw as he turns to face our friends. I've rarely seen him look so...irritated, and I can't help but wonder what caused it.

As quickly as it appeared, his irritation disappears beneath a practiced smile. It's the one he gave fans when they were watching us in California, and although Rod and Camilla don't seem to notice, I immediately recognize it as fake. He's a much better actor than I thought.

Which leaves me wondering, what's fake and what's real?

Twenty-Eight

WESTON

"I'D SELL MY SOUL for another Meg Ryan and Tom Hanks movie," Camilla mumbles through tight lips, the peel-off mask hardening on her face.

"When does she go to Seattle?" Rod asks before stuffing a handful of popcorn in his mouth.

"Rodrigo," Camilla grumbles. "This is *You've Got Mail*. You'd think I never forced you through a nineties rom-com movie marathon before."

"Yes, for I do pay close attention during those," Rod deadpans.

Camilla smacks him with a throw pillow. "You men should take note of these perfect male specimens. They can do no wrong. Right, Lo?"

Lo jumps as my foot accidentally brushes against hers under our shared blanket. She's been flustered since dinner, and I can't say I'm entirely unaffected either. I think Lo knows it, too.

"Right," Lo stammers. Her own mask has grown shiny on her somewhat red face.

"You should throw a pool party," Camilla says, changing the subject as quickly as only she can.

"*What?*"

"I think you should throw a pool party—make good use of that giant pool in your backyard," Camilla repeats.

"We should do it for your birthday next weekend," I announce before Lo has a chance to shoot the idea down.

Camilla squeals, cracking the mask on her face. A clear, shiny bit falls down in front of her eye and she swipes it away. "Yes! Let's do it!"

Rod places a hand on Camilla's arm, stalling her. "LoLo hates parties."

Lo nods, looking relieved.

"I don't know, Lo. A party could be fun." I purposefully tap her foot under the blanket, and she jerks again. I have to hold back a smile. I should have known messing with her would be the thing to get me out of this funk.

"Parties are fun!" Camilla nods enthusiastically.

"Lo hates people," Rod reminds her. "And parties."

"That's true. I do," Lo mumbles through her own tight lips.

I lean back on the couch, stretching so my legs are pressed firmly against Lo's. Her smooth skin drives me to distraction, almost making me forget my mission to push her to do something fun. "You know what I always say…"

"Just go with it," the three of them say in unison, and a smile splits across my face.

Lo leans her head back against the couch cushion, looking defeated. "Fine," she grumbles through her barely open mouth. "We'll have a birthday party."

She kicks my legs out from under the blanket and tries to smile smugly at me but can't accomplish it with the face mask.

"When are you supposed to take those off?" I ask, unable to hide my amusement at the way her face looks.

"Sixty minutes," Camilla announces from where she's sprawled out on the loveseat.

"That just doesn't seem right," Lo mutters. "It's only been forty minutes, and it's so tight. It's starting to burn. Is yours burning?" Lo reaches for the packaging she left on the coffee table.

"It's been burning for the last twenty minutes."

"Mine too."

"Then why did you leave—"

"Oh my gosh," Lo exclaims, interrupting me. "This says *six* minutes, Camilla!" Her eyes move quickly over the directions on the back of the packaging. "It says it can leave a chemical burn if you leave it on longer than instructed."

The color drains from Camilla's face. She turns to Rod. "Get it off! Get it off!"

"Okay, okay!" Rod stands up hastily and drags Camilla to the downstairs guest bathroom. Lo's eyes are wide as I pull her up off the couch and into my bathroom. As I shut the door behind us, I hear Camilla screaming that she's going to die.

"She's so dramatic," I say, but when I look at Lo, I can see the same fear.

"Please help me," she whispers, and if she weren't so scared, it would be comical with her tight, expressionless face.

"Okay, hold on." Hot water burns my hands as I wet a washcloth in the sink.

"It stings, Wes!" Lo cries.

She claws at the mask like a kitten on the side of a brand new couch. Her nails scratch against the smoothness, unable to find a vulnerable spot to dig into. "It's burned onto my face! It's going to melt my skin off!"

The washcloth lands with a wet thump in the bottom of the sink as I drop it and grab onto her shoulders instead. Her wide, terrified eyes meet mine. "Lo, I need you to calm down."

Lo nods and her throat works with a gulp. My hands flex on her shoulders, moving to position her against the counter. Taking the warm washcloth from under the stream of water, I work to dissolve the mask. The rag glides right over the tight, shiny skin.

"It's not working, is it?"

"It's working," I lie and press on the washcloth with a little more pressure.

A tear runs down the smooth surface of the mask. "No, it's not."

My thumb sweeps against her cheek, wiping it away. "Okay, let's try a different approach. It's a peel-off mask, right?"

"Yes."

"Let me try to peel it." I find the edge and try to slip my fingernail beneath it. "This is probably going to hurt. I'm sorry, Lo," I say, catching her eye.

"It's okay."

When I get enough hold to lift up the corner of the mask, she hisses and grabs on to the hem of my shirt, balling it in her fist. My stomach clenches at the contact, but I try to stay focused on the matter at hand.

"You okay?"

She nods, but sucks in a breath between her teeth when I tug again. Without thinking, I blow on the skin, hoping it will ease the stinging.

Her breath hitches, whether from pain or surprise, I don't know.

I keep pulling on the mask and blowing on her skin until almost half her face is uncovered. Being this close to her, in such an intimate position, strings my body tighter and tighter. With every bit of her red face exposed, and every accidental swipe of her knuckles against my stomach, I feel like I'm a bomb waiting to detonate.

"Does it hurt?" I ask, trying desperately not to think about how easy it would be to press my lips to hers right now.

Lo hisses as I pull on another piece. "Yes, but the parts you got off are starting to feel a little better."

"Good," I say, blowing on another inch of exposed skin. Goosebumps prickle up along her arms. I wish I could look into her eyes, try to decipher what she's thinking, but they're squeezed shut.

I'm almost finished. Just another few tugs and she'll be free. I should make it quick, but I'm in a bad way. With her so close, desire clouds my better judgment. I decide to test a theory. We're already almost chest to chest, but I press forward a little more, and Lo's eyes snap open, connecting with mine.

I pull the last piece off her chin and toss it onto the counter behind her. My breath fans against her jaw, and when she leans forward ever so slightly, my lips brush against her delicate skin.

The door bangs open, and I back away quickly. Lo moves from the counter, her chest heaving.

If Rod or Camilla notice anything, they don't mention it. Camilla launches herself at Lo. "You're alive! I thought for sure we were goners."

"Me too," Lo murmurs. "I think we should put some aloe or something on our faces. Mine still burns. I have some in my bathroom."

Camilla follows her out of the room. I sag against my closet door, sucking in the first full breath I've taken in the last fifteen minutes.

When I open my eyes, Rod stands there with his arms crossed, a smug expression on his face. "What exactly did Camilla and I walk in on, buddy?"

I drag a hand down my face. "I'm losing my mind."

"Why don't you just do something about it?" Rod chuckles quietly.

I pin him with a glare. "You know what happened last time."

"You mean six years ago when you were twenty-two and about to move across the country?" He rolls his eyes. "Yeah, I'm positively *shocked* it didn't work out then."

"It didn't work out because Lo said it was a mistake," I say through gritted teeth.

I make to move past him, but his next comment stops me in my tracks. "I would try again. Camilla seems to think there's something going on between you two."

I hover in the doorway, trying to calm my racing heart. "She does?"

"Yeah, when she saw your posts from California, her exact words were that Lo looked 'besotted.'" Rod uses air quotes around the last word.

"Hmm," I say, thinking over everything that's happened the last few weeks—the moments with Lo, the way she's responded to me more and more, the matching desire I've seen reflected in her eyes.

I pat Rod on the shoulder. "You might be right."

He grins at me. "Could you say that again? I'm not sure I heard you."

"You might be right," I repeat. "Now I just need to figure out what to do about it."

My plan to seduce Lo into loving me gets off to a rocky start the next morning after Camilla and Rod leave.

Lo is acting weird. Like, weirder than normal. She's always somewhere on the weird scale. I mean, she wears book themed T-shirts almost constantly and has seen more rom-coms than can be healthy, but this is different.

This morning, I asked Lo if she wanted to go get some breakfast. To which she replied, "I don't eat breakfast," before scurrying back up the stairs in her bunny slippers.

It confused me because I know for a fact that breakfast is her favorite meal and that she would gladly eat breakfast food for every meal if she could.

It's past lunchtime now, and Lo's been sitting outside by the pool for the last three hours, working on her laptop. She has AirPods in and her hands haven't stopped flying over the keyboard.

I wonder if she's working on her next book. If so, I'm excited for her. She mentioned in California that she hasn't had an idea for another book yet and that it's been bothering her. With all the recent book sales, she's terrified she's not going to be able to live up to the success of her first book.

But her laser focus must mean she had an idea. I know that feeling well, even if I haven't been inspired like that in a long time. But being back here with Lo and my friends feels like a step in the right direction.

Sighing, I debate with myself. If I'm going to convince Lo to give us another chance, I can't do that from here. I fill two glasses of lemonade, the condensation wetting my fingers, and head out back.

Lo is so wrapped up in writing she doesn't notice me approaching. I stop directly behind her and lean over her shoulder. "Whatcha doing?"

A little yip escapes her throat, and she spins around, slamming her laptop closed with such force that I'm surprised it doesn't shatter. Her eyes are wild, and she looks almost...caught.

A grin tugs at my lips. "What are you doing on the computer, Lo?"

"I was writing," she stammers.

I reach for her laptop, and she twists away, holding it tightly against her flushed chest.

"What were you writing?"

Lo doesn't say anything, so I slowly inch my hand toward the computer. She yanks it away again. "Your new book?" When she doesn't look like she's going to respond, I press on. "Let me read it."

She splutters. "Oh my gosh, no."

"Why not? Is there something you don't want me to see?"

She shakes her head swiftly. If she's not careful, she'll end up with whiplash. "No, no, that's not it." Her words are drawn out as if she's looking for what to say as she says it. She's a dog, digging for a bone she thinks she left hidden somewhere. "I just don't let anyone read my first draft."

Lo looks so pleased with her excuse that I know it's not the truth. That may be the case, but that's not why she's hiding it from me now.

I round the lounge chair and lift her feet, settling them in my lap as I sit down at the foot of her chair. Her skin is smooth as silk beneath my fingertips and warm from baking in the sun, almost distracting me from my thoughts.

"You don't let anyone see your first drafts, huh?" I ask, my voice dropping an octave.

Lo's loose bun quivers as she shakes her head, making wisps fall down around her face. She's stopped breathing all together.

I lean a fraction closer, close enough now that I can see the white and golden flecks in her irises. "Not even your husband?"

"N-no," she stammers.

When I sit back, she releases a shallow breath. "Okay," I say, letting her think I've dropped it. Lo eases back in her seat, losing her death grip on the laptop.

"Are you writing something scandalous?"

She rolls her eyes, her body relaxing more. "No, Wes."

"So why can't I read it?" I ask again.

"I already told you. I don't let anyone read my first draft. It's poorly written and all over the place. I don't even have a name for my male character yet."

"What are you calling him, then?"

Lo's eyes blow wide, and she looks away quickly, her gaze darting everywhere but my face. "Oh, um…Uh."

As I watch her struggle, something clicks in my mind, and a slow grin curves my lips. "You don't remember what you're calling your character?"

Lo opens her mouth twice and shuts it. "He's um—"

"He's not…" I trail off, unable to stop smirking as I let my gaze travel her face. "He's not named Weston, right?"

Lo shakes her head, absolutely mute, a criminal going to the grave with her secrets. "You're not writing about me on there?" I tap the laptop she has crushed to her chest. She doesn't answer. "I wouldn't blame you if you did. I'm, like, really hot," I say. The ghost of a smile tugs at her lips, encouraging me to go on. "I have a winning personality. And, I mean, you've seemed to really enjoy making out with—" Her foot digs into my side, cutting me off.

"You're so full of it," she says.

My fingers close around her ankle and set it in my lap. Instead of letting go, I rest my hand on her shin. My heart races faster the longer she doesn't pull away.

I know I should say something, break the silence. Or maybe she should. But either way, neither of us are speaking. The moment stretches, a tightrope we're in danger of falling off of.

The air between us is charged, the instant before a tornado. I can almost hear the crackling as our gazes lock, waiting for one of us to make a move—to close the distance between us.

"I think we probably need to plan the party," she says, her voice coming out whisper soft.

For a long moment, I stay quiet, although not sure what I'm waiting on. "Yeah, okay,"

I know I should feel embarrassed since it seems like she turned me down. But underneath the nervousness coloring her cheeks and vulnerability hiding behind her eyes, I saw something that gives me hope—a longing exactly like my own. Rod wasn't wrong last night. Lo wants this just as much as I do.

Twenty-Nine

LO

THE NEXT WEEK PASSES quickly. Wes spends most of his time working on content by himself, and I get lost in writing. When I wrote my last novel, I spent every free minute I had writing. I was working full time and was only able to catch an hour or two to write each day while Maddox napped and when I got home from work. Although it was rewarding, it was also exhausting and stressful.

Getting to write all day every day next to the pool is paradise. Except for when Wes is around—then it's pure torture. He hasn't been his normal teasing, flirty self.

Instead, I'll look up to find him staring at me with dark eyes. Just last night, I was making dinner when I felt him brush up against my back. I tensed, my heart racing, my pulse skyrocketing. His breath was warm on my neck as he opened the drawer next to me, looking for a specific spice.

I shiver at the memory. It's almost like he's doing it on purpose.

I'm not sure when or where or how, but I think Wes is as dissatisfied with our current arrangement as I am. Yet instead of trying to ignore whatever is happening between us like I am, he keeps pressing it like a button he was told not to touch.

We've been there before, and I can't let us go there again. Wes may have been fine when he moved across the country, but I definitely was not. It took months for me to put myself back together, and then right about the time I started feeling okay again, I got sick.

Weston's bedroom door opens, pulling my attention from the scene I was writing. It's not lost on me that it was his eyes and smile I was picturing as I wrote this hero—just like last time.

It's raining for the first time in weeks, meaning I can't retreat to my pool chair outside if things get too steamy in here. I hope against all hope that Wes will return to his room and not start a flame inside me that I'm not sure I can extinguish much longer.

Wes retreats to the kitchen, and I hold my breath. Each step he takes ratchets my nerves up a degree. I try to focus on my computer, but I just stare at the screen until Weston's shadow falls over it a minute later.

In his hand, he holds out an orange prescription bottle. The rattle of the pills echoes through the quiet house. "Did you take your medicine today?"

My teeth catch on my bottom lip. I forgot, and now that he's mentioned it, I realize I've forgotten pretty much since we've been back from California. This is most definitely not good. While I haven't noticed too much of a difference in my pain levels yet, it's sure to come.

I wrap my fingers around the bottle, and he squats in front of me. His brow is furrowed in concern as the pills scrape down my suddenly tight throat.

"Lo, you need to take care of yourself," Wes says, reaching up to push a lock of hair off my face.

The air seizes in my lungs at his touch, at how *badly* I want to lean into it. I know I need to defuse this moment, to be strong. But under the intensity of his gaze, my resolve crumbles like ancient ruins battered by time and the elements. Despite knowing how bad this idea is, I want to explore this feeling. Get lost in it. Give up all hope of being rescued and stay there forever.

The sway of Weston's body toward mine breaks me from my trance. I can't do this. When I press back into the couch cushions, Wes sits back on his heels. "Thanks for reminding me to take my meds."

A resigned sigh escapes Wes' lips. One large hand pushes through his hair, making the curls stand in disarray. He looks so *defeated*, so unlike himself that I feel as though my world has tilted on its axis. Up is down, hot is cold, and Weston King is melancholy.

I hesitate to ask what's bothering him. I don't know if I'll like the answer. Finally, I ask, "What's wrong?"

His smile is tight, more artificial than the one he gives to fans who interrupt at the worst possible moment. When he stands, his body is smooth, tamed grace, and I want to grab his hand and haul him back down here with me, regardless of the consequences.

"Nothing. I'll leave you to write," he says.

When he leaves, all my inspiration goes with him. I spend the next few hours writing scene after scene, only to hate them and delete them immediately.

Wes exits his room again just as I slam my laptop shut, releasing a frustrated breath.

"I'm heading out," he says, slipping on his shoes by the back door. "Be back in a bit."

The door slaps against the frame, the sound echoing through the too-quiet house, before I even have a chance to ask if he wants company. Rain patters against the window, making his taillights a pixelated red blur against the panes as he backs out of the driveway.

The house feels so big and empty without his larger-than-life presence here with me. This is the first time I've been here alone, and I hate the way it now feels foreign. The couch is no longer comfortable, sending a sharp pain up my back. The ceiling fan is too fast, and my skin breaks out in a cold sweat. The ticking of the wall clock pounds in my head like a drum.

A realization hits me, a freight train to my chest. Without Wes, this doesn't feel like home. And that's *terrifying*.

I push off the couch, no longer able to sit there with my heart racing and my skin crawling. I need to do something—anything.

My gaze is drawn to Weston's open bedroom door. He's told me lots of times that I'm free to come and go as I please, but I haven't been able to step foot in there. The rooms we keep separately are the only places that don't feel like *ours*. They're mine and his, and I think crossing that threshold would feel too much like erasing that final boundary.

I can't look at his sheets and imagine what they would feel like against my skin. I can't see the indentation in his pillow and picture waking up next to him. I can't smell his aftershave and think about it being the last thing I smell at night and the first thing I smell in the morning.

His room is *his*, and I am not.

But here alone, with this desperate clawing sensation in my chest, I want to be as close to him as I can get. If only this once.

I look over my shoulder once, just to make sure he's really gone. The house is just as empty as it was moments before.

Tentatively I walk through the door. His room is darker than the rest of the house, which is decorated in various neutral shades. His bed is large, and the wood stained a deep walnut. The linens are a bright white that contrasts with the black accent wall behind the headboard. It's surprisingly tidy, although he has a pair of gym shorts and a T-shirt draped over a leather arm chair in the corner.

I drag my fingers over the dresser, loving the way the smooth wood feels to the touch. The surface is mostly bare, decorated only with several gold picture frames that catch my attention.

There's one of Wes, Camden, and Hazel standing in front of the Hollywood sign. Next to it, there's another of Rod, Camilla, Wes, and me at Rod and Weston's graduation. When I see the third photo, my heart stops. It's the picture from the lake house—the same one tucked away in the box in my closet.

My shaking hand knocks it over in an attempt to pick it up. I drop to the ground quickly, praying the glass didn't shatter. I don't know how I would explain my actions to Wes without giving away more than I want him to know.

When I flip it over and see everything is intact, my heart rate returns to normal. The photo did slip out of the back of the frame, though. My breath hitches in my throat when I flip the worn photo over. Written on the back in Weston's sloppy handwriting are the words *best day ever*.

I swallow hard, eagerly eating up the words like they might change if I don't commit them to memory.

What does this mean?

My mind flashes back to that morning six years ago—the way Weston's face was flushed with excitement as he ran into the kitchen. I'd thought it was because of Brandon's call, because of his big break. It couldn't have been because of...us. The possibility that I might have ruined *everything* steals the breath from my lungs.

Headlights slash through the window, sending shadows across the walls. My hands are useless, trembling as I try to shove the picture back in the frame before Weston comes inside. I've just landed on the couch, my heart beating wildly, when Wes steps through the back door. Raindrops cling to his hair like iridescent beads, and the way his white shirt is almost translucent as it spreads across his chest is almost obscene. A convenience store bag dangles from one hand.

"Hey," Wes says, and I'm petrified he'll be able to see what I've done written clearly on my face. "You okay?"

"Y-yeah. I'm fine."

The weight of it all—the endless possibilities of what could have been—threaten to swallow me whole. There were so many years, so much distance, so little communication between us. Wes could have been *mine* all this time.

The bag crinkles in Wes's hand as he moves around the couch to stand in front of me. A raindrop falls from his hair and lands with a wet *splat* against my thigh. He digs in the bag and produces a Klondike bar. "It's no Balboa Bar, but I figure it's the best we can get at home."

I swallow thickly, trying to hide the wave of emotions coursing through me. The ice cream bar is cold against my fingers as I take it from him.

"Want a Weston Special?"

"Sure," I say, my voice coming out as a breathy whisper.

Wes retreats to the kitchen, and the espresso machine whirs to life, spitting and hissing as he makes our drinks.

The past few weeks play through my head, and I see them through a new lens. The lingering touches, the meaningful looks, the drugging kisses. His immediate willingness to marry me to help me out. His mounting frustration this week every time I pulled away from him. His kindness now.

What have I done?

The couch dips beneath Weston's weight as he settles next to me, two mugs in hand. He hands me my favorite, the speckled ceramic one that looks like it belongs to a lonely widow living in a cottage in the woods. I've used it almost every day since I moved into this house, and my heart melts a little more in my chest knowing he's noticed.

His lips pucker as he blows on the steam rising from his cup, and my eyes fix there. I want those lips on mine. I want them everywhere.

He meets my gaze, and my heart jerks to stop. "Are you sure you're okay?"

"Yeah, I'm fine," I lie. I'm anything but fine. I'm desperate and wanting and heartbroken and nostalgic and so utterly hopeful it scares me.

"Want to watch a movie?" Wes asks.

"Okay."

Wes flashes me another confused glance before turning the TV on. "Anything you want to watch?"

"No, I'm good with whatever."

I can't look away as he clicks through the movie selection, the blue light coloring his features. I want to trace a fingertip down the slope of his nose, over his cheekbones, and map out the shape of his lips.

"How about *La La Land*?" he asks, and I blink, snapped from my reverie.

I flash back to that moment at Griffith Observatory. I was spinning around, dancing as well as I could remember, when I turned to see the look on Weston's face. He was frozen, a heart-melting look in his eyes. I motioned for him to meet me in the middle for the iconic move. He did, but instead of finishing the dance, he'd grabbed me. I smacked into his chest just before he'd kissed me.

There, under the waning twilight, on top of the world, time had stopped.

And now, as he turns on one of my favorite movies, I can't even concentrate. All I can think about is the feeling of his lips on mine, the beating of his heart under my fingertips, and how much I want to experience it all again.

LATER, AFTER THE MOVIE is finished, I slip into bed and open my laptop. I know exactly how I want my novel to end. It's early, early morning before I finish the final scene. The book isn't done—I still have a lot in the middle to write, but the ending is perfect.

I set the laptop on my nightstand and tug the blanket up to my chin. Sleep claims me like a lost lover, and I dream of a green-eyed hero with a crooked smile.

Thirty

WESTON

My heart beats an unsteady rhythm as I stand outside Lo's room, gift bag in one hand, the other fisted and hovering an inch from her door. I don't think I imagined the change in her last night, and I'm nervous to knock. In the dim living room, nestled in the couch cushions with a Klondike bar and a steaming latte, she'd been softer, like she'd finally let her guard slip.

I don't know why, but dangerous hope stirs in my chest. It's only been a month since our wedding, and every day it's been harder and harder to remind myself that the vows we made were no more substantial than early morning mist that dissipates in the sun. I don't know how much longer I can do this, how much longer I can hide my feelings and not get on my knees and beg her to give me a second chance, to make this marriage *real*.

My hand raps on the door, and it swings open a moment later, knocking the breath from my lungs.

Lo stands in the doorway, the morning sunshine peering through the windows behind her forming a golden aura around her like a Victorian angel painting. Her hair is luminous in this light—brilliant russet, burnished gold, gleaming copper—and hangs around her shoulders in loose waves that look softer than satin. Tiny shorts expose her long, pale, freckled legs, and my mouth goes dry.

My eyes trail slowly up her form, lingering in all my favorite places, despite my better judgment, before finally settling on her face. Her cheeks flame, bright red rubies that tell me my thorough examination was much more obvious than I'd hoped.

I prop my arm on the door frame, and her eyes dip to my bicep before fixing on my face once more. "Happy birthday, Lo."

"Th-thanks," Lo stammers, her breath releasing on a shaky exhale.

The tension weighing down my shoulders dissolves in the wake of that blush. It reminds me that no matter the state of our relationship, we always have *this*. This easy, comfortable teasing that feels as natural as breathing.

"Are you hot? Your face is kind of red."

Her gaze darts everywhere but my face. "Um, yes. Really warm. I should turn the temperature down."

Goosebumps pebble along her arms, and I reach out, tracing them with a fingertip, leaning into the opportunity to get beneath her skin the way she's burrowed beneath mine. "Hm, why do you have goosebumps then?"

She blinks rapidly, watching my fingers glide along her skin, but doesn't tell me to stop. It's the smallest of signals, but I latch onto it like a flotation device in the middle of the ocean.

I keep going, the tips of my fingers taking a lazy path across the expanse of her forearms before trailing down the ridges of her knuckles. She surprises me by turning her hand so we're palm to palm. Her breath comes out in a shallow gasp when our palms slide against one another, an oddly sensual movement that leaves me just as breathless.

"Is that for me?" she asks, her words skating against the recesses of my brain, but I'm too lost in the sensation of her skin on mine to process what she asked. When I don't answer, she says, "Wes?"

My name snaps me out of the trance, and I draw back, standing to my full height. I lift my hand with the gift bag, holding it between us.

Lo gently takes it from me. "You didn't have to get me anything."

"What kind of husband would I be then?" I mean to sound teasing, but my voice is deep and low, like a whisper in the night.

She raises her eyes, peering at me through her eyelashes, before pulling the tissue paper from the bag. Inside rests a small Mason jar candle. Carefully, she pulls it out, and I take the bag so she can examine the gift.

"Balboa Bar," Lo says, reading the label. Twin creases form between her brows as she looks back up at me. "Is this what you got at the souvenir shop on Balboa Island?"

"Mm-hmm."

"I thought it was for your mom." She glances at me, tracing the gold lid with a fingertip.

"No."

Lo unscrews the metal lid and the sound reverberates loudly in the space between us. The scent is strong, immediately drawing me back to that moment at the frozen banana stand. If there was something that smelled the exact way her lips tasted in that moment, this is it. That same memory is reflected in her eyes, like an old time movie playing on a reel.

"Thank you," she says, her voice coming out a whisper. Her gaze catches on mine and holds.

I think I could kiss her right now. I think she would let me. And I want to. Desperately. I need her lips on mine like a man wandering the desert needs water. But if I want to win her over, I need to make our next kiss count. It won't be here in her doorway. It will be life-changing, earth-shattering, and it will show her just how serious I am about all of this.

I back up, my footsteps heavy against the wood floors, and disappointment crosses Lo's features. The seed of hope that's been planted in my chest blooms into a garden that quickly outgrows its boundaries, taking up every square inch of available space. "Whenever you're ready, I have birthday donuts for you downstairs."

"I'm ready now," Lo answers, and I swear she sways toward me ever so slightly.

A smile curves my lips, slow and dangerous. She better stay in her doorway or my resolve will shatter like broken pottery. "You're still in your mermaid PJ shorts."

Lo looks down, cherry pink coloring her cheeks. "It's a new look," she says.

"I like it. Mind spinning around for me?"

Lo eyes narrow, the blush disappearing. A laugh rumbles from my chest, and I back toward the stairs, never looking away from her.

"I saw it in Vogue," Lo tells me.

"Mm-hmm."

"I think Kim wore them."

"Seems like something she would do."

"Oh my gosh, do you know Kim Kardashian?"

I tip my head back, unable to hold in my laughter, before spinning around and heading down the steps. Once in my room, I dig through my drawers for my swimming trunks. A photo on my dresser catches my attention. It's the one of Lo and I that day at the lake house. The memory of that day—of that kiss—is as fresh in my mind as if it happened yesterday. I can still feel the silkiness of her skin sliding against mine under the water, still remember how beautiful she looked drenched in moonlight, still hear the little moans she made in the back of her throat. It gives me a wild, risky idea.

My phone buzzes, dragging me from my thoughts, and Brandon's name flashes across the screen.

I answer the call, unable to hide the surprise in my voice. "Hey, what's up?" We haven't communicated other than emails since that morning in California.

"Hey, I just got a call from my friend who works for that online gossip magazine." I know immediately who he's referring to since he calls Brandon to give him a heads-up any time they run a story about me.

"What'd he say?"

"He interviewed Talia. Apparently, she had some things to say about you, but he wouldn't tell me what."

Dread pools in my stomach. I thought we were past this. I thought marrying Lo was going to prevent these kinds of things from happening. What more could Talia really have to say?

"Is there anything you need to tell me?" Brandon asks.

My mind instantly flashes to Lo. He still doesn't know that this marriage is fake—or at least started that way. But no, there's no reason to mention it now. This is about Talia.

"No, I swear."

"There's nothing new she could have to say to the press about you?"

There's no way she found out. The only people who know are our most trusted friends and family. Yet, on the off-chance she did, Brandon needs to know.

I swallow hard, anxiety fluttering in my gut. He's not going to be happy, but I *need* to tell him the truth now. "The marriage is fake."

Silence hangs heavy over the line for a long moment before Brandon asks, "What?"

"Well, it was." I run a hand down my face, my scruff scraping against my palms. "I don't know anymore. I—"

"What did you do?" His voice is terse.

I blow out a breath. "I was losing my audience. Everyone thought I was a joke. Talia wouldn't quit trashing me for not committing to her. So I proposed to Lo. It was all fake. But now—"

"It was fake?" Brandon repeats.

"It was. I mean, legally, we are married. But it just started off as an arrangement." I pause. Now I'm not so sure."

"Why would you do this?" He sounds one wrong comment away from exploding, sending shrapnel far enough to injure me two-thousand miles away.

"I was just trying to fix things."

"That's my job, Weston."

"Right, but it's my career." My voice rises before I can think better of it. For the first time in years, I'm saying *exactly* what I think, regardless of the consequences. "I didn't like how you were doing things, so I did it myself."

It's so quiet I can hear my watch ticking on the dresser. Regret closes around me in a vise grip, suffocating me. I shouldn't have said that. "Brandon, listen, I'm s—"

"I gotta go," Brandon says, his voice hard and unyielding. "I need to figure out what to do about this."

Before I can respond, the line goes dead.

Thirty-One

LO

Wes hovers in my periphery all day. He is a flame, and I am the moth hopelessly drawn to him. His laugh is a musical melody I can't get enough of. His smile is pure sunshine. His eyes are the meadow you frolic through on a perfect spring day.

I am so utterly gone for him, I can't think straight. I want his soul imprinted on mine like a glitter bomb, brilliant and explosive and everlasting.

"Whatcha lookin' at?" Alexa sing-songs in my ear, snapping my attention from where Wes is grilling shirtless, pool water gleaming on his sun-bronzed skin. She snags a grape off the fruit plate I've been snacking on and waggles her eyebrows. "You hitting that yet?"

I roll my eyes. "Gosh, Alexa. Shut up."

Camilla sidles up next to us, tying her dark braids up in a bun atop her head. She nudges me with her shoulder, her white teeth gleaming when she smiles. "She asked if you're fooling around with Wes?"

My mouth falls open. "Not you too."

"You could burn this house down with the heat between you guys today," she says, fanning herself with her hand.

"That's not true," I splutter, my cheeks turning into two ripe cherries.

Alexa talks around another mouthful of fruit. "It's absolutely true. If Matt were to look at me like that right now, we would be—"

"Please, for the love of God, do not finish that sentence," I interrupt.

"I'd like to know," Camilla says, brown eyes twinkling.

My breath releases on a weary exhale and I stand taller, squaring my shoulders. "I hate you both. I'm getting a drink."

A kaleidoscope of butterflies takes flight in my stomach as I near the cooler next to where Wes is grilling. He looks up and catches sight of me, a smile curving his lips. "Hey, birthday girl."

Despite his smile, the light behind those vibrant green eyes has dimmed and the broad expanse of his shoulders are tense.

My brows draw together. "Are you okay?"

I think surprise flickers across his features for an instant, but the smoke from the grill clouds his expression, and when it clears again, the grin is back. "Yeah, of course."

Reaching into the cooler, I pull out a can. It pops as I open it, fizz hissing. Wes turns off the grill, loading the burgers onto a plate. His muscles bunch and flex with the movement, momentarily mesmerizing me, but when I allow my gaze to drift upward, I notice the clenched jaw and pursed lips.

Wes is most decidedly *not* okay.

"You're lying," I say, a little shocked at my own boldness.

His brows arch, green eyes intensely focused on me as he roughly wipes his hands on a rag. "Maybe a little." Grinning, he holds two fingers in front of my face, leaving a sliver of space between them.

I see that smile as the diversion tactic it is, but I don't take the bait. He's been a soft place for me to land the past few weeks, and I want him to know I can be the same for him—that I *want* to be the same for him. "What's up?"

Wes holds my gaze for a long moment, as if gauging my sincerity. Finally, he blows out a breath, and says, "It's just Brandon. But it's not a big deal. Nothing that can't be dealt with tomorrow."

I want to press for more, to squeeze into the soft, vulnerable place he shields the world from, but I can't tell from the way his eyes dart away from me that he isn't ready to talk about it yet. "You sure?"

"Absolutely. It's your birthday. Have you had a good day so far?" The smile he gives me this time is genuine and blindingly bright. It's the same smile he wore in that photo he keeps on his dresser. I wonder if his lips were curved just like this when he wrote *Best day ever* on the back. I want to know whether he was smiling or frowning when he put it up on that dark wooden dresser, if he was full of hope for the future or nostalgic about a past he would never revisit again.

That smile makes me bold. I move forward, so close I have to tip my chin up to catch his gaze. "It's been incandescently perfect." My voice is a husky whisper, full of promise.

His hands are restless, flexing at his sides, and I don't know what he plans to do with them, but I know I want them on my body. My own arms slide around his middle, and he responds immediately, fingertips trailing across my bare shoulders and down the bumps of my spine.

His heart beats against my cheek and he feels like a trapped panther, energy coiling beneath his skin. I want to burrow beneath it and trip his wires.

"Incandescently perfect?" he asks on an exhale, hands still moving restlessly against me.

I nuzzle a little closer, my nose brushing right over where his heart beats. "Best day ever."

"I saw that," Alexa whispers later that evening as she squeezes me in a hug. The sun has long since disappeared behind the horizon, blanketing the world in stars and moonlight.

"What?"

She gives me the Mom Look that she's already perfected, the one that sends a shiver down my spine. "I saw you and Wes earlier." She pats my cheek, her voice taking on a syrupy sweet quality. "Have fun tonight."

Wes comes up beside me, his shoulder brushing up against mine and sending goosebumps racing along my skin. "You guys heading out?" he asks Alexa.

"Yeah," Alexa says, almost managing to sound contrite. "We would *love* to stay and hang out, but we need to put Kara to bed." She winks at me, and my face flames.

Wes cocks a brow, looking between the two of us questioningly.

"We're heading out too," Camilla says.

My throat bobs in a dry swallow. All I've wanted all day is to be alone with Wes. Now that it's here, my stomach is in knots and my skin feels stretched too tight.

Camilla looks around the backyard. "Do you need help? Rod just took the trash out."

"No, we're good. Thanks," Wes says, just as I'm about to make up a task so they can't leave. They can't go or I'll drag Wes into my cottage in the woods and force-feed him a love potion so he will never leave me again.

I grasp at straws. "You sure there's nothing?"

"No, can't think of anything," Wes says, forehead wrinkled in puzzlement at the wild, desperate quality of my voice.

Alexa smirks like she knows exactly what I was trying to do. "Love you, Penny. I'll call you later." She joins her husband, Matt, at the car, where he's buckling Kara in her car seat. Even from here I can see the wink she flashes me before shutting her door.

Thick arms wrap around my shoulders. "Happy birthday, LoLo. We'll see you later," Rod says before smacking a kiss on my cheek.

Camilla does the same before following after him. As the wrought iron gate shuts behind her, she yells, "Love you, fried!"

Their taillights disappear down the driveway, leaving Wes and me completely *alone*. I turn to face him, but find his intense gaze already settled firmly on me. The flames burning in the firepit sending shadows dancing across his skin, and the stars above us twinkle in his eyes. A lock of golden blonde hair shines pale in the moonlight, like a black and white version of him.

The breath steals from my lungs and my pulse beats in the tips of my fingers, the hollow of my throat, and the unsteady pit in my stomach. I can hear it echoing like a bass drum, like a chant urging me to close the distance between us and try to capture the magic of a long ago night just like this one.

"Wanna get back in the pool?" Wes asks. The words are almost from that night at the lake house, like second chance, an opportunity to rewrite history.

So I grasp onto them like a lifeline and repeat my line from the script I now know neither of us has forgotten. "Okay."

His lips curve in a slow smile, hitching on one side first and then the other. It's a smile full of promise, of hope, and it feels like rain after a long drought, like a sip of sugary, sweet lemonade on a summer afternoon.

Wes reaches for the collar of his shirt he threw on earlier, pulling it over his head and revealing his skin inch by torturous inch. His eyes leave mine only for the split second it takes too tug the garment free of his head. The shirt lands in a heap at his feet, and it's the single most erotic thing I've ever seen in my life.

One brow arches as his gaze drifts across my body. My thin, white coverup hangs from shoulders, and I know what he wants. Six years ago, I felt too vulnerable to strip down to my bathing suit under his watchful stare. This is the first crossroad—the first moment I can decide to change the course of what happened then.

My heart pounds so loudly in my chest, he's sure to hear it. Every single nerve ending feels electrified, like sticking my finger in a light socket or being struck by lightning. My hands tremble as I lift the coverup off, the fabric sliding against my skin.

Weston's eyelids are heavy as he watches me, but his eyes are sharp and bright, a glint of sunlight on a mirror, signaling me to go on. I feel bolder as I drop the dress on the ground beside me. My bathing suit is a modest one piece, the same one I've been wearing in front of him all summer, but we both know things are different now.

I took a leap to change the past. Now it's his turn to decide the next step in our future.

Weston's hand finds mine, threading our fingers together. His tumb swipes a reassuring path across my palm as he pulls me gently toward the still glowingly blue surface of the water.

He drops my hand to sit on the edge of the pool and lower himself in, the muscle in his arms flexing distractingly as he does. Even the crickets hold their breath as he sinks his whole body into the water before popping up again.

Fat rivulets of water drip down his skin as he turns to face me. He watches with rapt attention as I slowly descend onto the pool edge and dip my feet beneath the surface. He doesn't move from his spot a few feet away as his eyes trail up the expanse of my leg, over my quivering stomach, and past the pulse jumping in my throat before meeting my eyes. "Are you going to come any closer?" he asks, his words still mirroring that night. His voice is barely a rasp, full of such desperation and longing that I think I might crumble.

Six years ago, I told him no, too scared to do anything but let him play my piece. Tonight, I want to be an active participant.

Nodding, I inch over the edge, submerging my body into the water. Weston doesn't make me do it alone—he meets me halfway. He closes the distance between us and his hands find my waist, sliding right below my ribs like they were made to be there. My fingers slick over his shoulders and slide into the hair at the nape of his neck, relishing the way the curls feel, soft and smooth, like spun silk. Usually, I can just barely reach those curls, but I'm above him now, slowly sliding down the length of his body and cataloging every eyelash, freckle, and wrinkle to dream about later.

My feet finally land against the gritty floor of the pool, but Wes doesn't release me. His thumbs trace small circles on my stomach, and now that I've noticed, my every bit of concentration is focused on that exact movement.

Back and forth.

Back and forth.

It's like a match striking on a box, the way my skin catches flame under his touch.

My own hands slide down the slope of his arms, goosebumps pricking in the wake of my touch. His breath is warm against my skin, his eyes a black hole I want to be devoured by.

"Do you trust me, Lo?"

I know what he's asking. They're the same words as before, but they carry a different meaning tonight. I was the one who rushed to conclusions last time, who called it off before we even tried to see where it would go.

And now, he wants to know if I trust him enough to give us a chance this time.

"I trust you."

The distance between us shrinks in slow increments, like he wants to savor it—the first lick of an ice cream cone, the last rays of sunset, the crescendo of a symphony. One of his hands leaves my waist and comes to trace my lips. My mouth parts beneath his touch, but the fingertip slides lower, curving over my chin, dipping into the hollow of my throat, outlining my collarbone.

I think I might combust from the anticipation.

Wes stops a breath away from my lips, so close I can feel them brush against my own as he whispers, "Just go with it, okay?"

I don't wait any longer. My mouth crashes against him, hungry, wanting, and insistent. He meets me stroke for stroke, just like I knew he would. That's the thing about Wes—he's always pushed me to my limits, but he's never left me to do it alone.

His kiss is burning, a fire set ablaze in a forest that hasn't seen rain in *so long*. He tastes like the coconut cake we had earlier, a hit of sugar to my bloodstream that's going to keep me buzzing for hours. He smells of sunshine and chlorine, of a summer day I never want to end.

My hands are no longer content to stay at my sides. They slide up his arms, over the divots in his shoulders, and into those curls. I apply pressure there, opening my lips to give him more, to *take* more. I want all of him, and even that will never be enough. His low growl rumbles through me, and I know that exact sound will haunt my dreams.

We've kissed for show a handful of times since starting this whole charade, but I can say, with absolute certainty, that Weston was holding back. I knew he was. I knew the kisses we shared recently were nothing compared to our kiss in college. And even that pales in comparison to this one.

Kissing Weston is like getting swept up by a wave in the ocean. For a moment, you don't know if you're drowning or careening toward safety. At any second, you could break through the surface and catch your breath, or you could be caught up in it so completely that you don't realize you're without oxygen until it's too late.

His mouth leaves mine and a little whimper escapes me. His scruff scrapes against me as he trails his lips over my jaw and down my neck. "How have we not been doing this the last month?" he murmurs into the valley of my throat, his words getting muffled against my skin. "We should be doing nothing but this."

"I agree," I say, hooking my legs around his hips.

He doesn't need any further invitation.

I DON'T KNOW HOW much time passes, but when we finally get out of the pool, my skin is wrinkled like laundry left in the dryer too long. I shiver against the chill in the air as we make our way across the yard and to the back door.

Warm, kiss-swollen lips press against the back of my neck as my trembling hands struggle to open the door. Finally, I give up, spinning on my heel to face Wes. His mouth crashes against mine, and he easily opens the door, guiding me through it.

The door slaps against the frame as he kicks it shut, his hands back on my waist, lifting me to sit on the counter. The granite is cool as ice against my flushed skin.

Wes steps back, bare chest heaving. "Lo, six years ago I—"

He's interrupted by a knock at the front door, the sound echoing through the house. I look down at my bathing suit, clinging to my every curve. Motioning toward the stairs, I say, "I'm going to change."

Wes catches his bottom lip between his teeth, his gaze searing as it trails down my body. I don't think I can breathe. Leaning forward, he presses another kiss to my mouth as the knock comes again. He lifts me off the counter, and I scurry upstairs. I hear Wes opening the front door just as I lock myself inside the bathroom.

My reflection is almost unrecognizable in my bathroom mirror. The tips of my hair are wet, while the rest air-dried in a thick, tangled mess earlier in the day. My cheeks are rosy pink, ripe apples ready for the plucking, and dotted with freckles. I brush my fingers across my sensitive, kiss-swollen lips.

As I stare at myself a moment longer, I can't help but think I look really, really happy. The kind of happiness that makes anything seem possible. The kind of happiness that feels sweet as custard and bright as a sunrise.

I decide to shower quickly, washing the chlorine and sunscreen off my body before changing into a pair of pajama pants covered in tiny unicorns—they're much cuter than the mermaid shorts I was wearing this morning—and a T-shirt that says "What Excellent Boiled Potatoes." It's a look. I am, quite frankly, shocked that Weston has been able to resist me this long when I dress in such a provocative manner.

Wes is stretched out on the couch when I descend the stairs, his long legs propped on the coffee table and one arm shoved behind his head. The lights are dimmed, casting the room in shadows. When he sees me, his smile is slow, crooking up one side of his mouth and the other.

"You know exactly how to seduce a man, Lo Summers," he says.

"Don't I know it," I reply, sinking into the cushions on the opposite side of the couch. "Who was at the door?"

"Rod. Camilla left her phone out back. She said she tried calling first, but neither of us were picking up…"

"Hm, that's odd. Was something distracting you?" I sound casual, but my heart is racing faster than I care to admit. That kiss in the pool felt like an appetizer, and I want the whole meal, but I don't know how to tell him that. I shift slightly, trying to scoot closer without him noticing.

"What are you doing, Lo?" His voice is slow and amused, and his grin is devilish. He knows exactly what I'm doing.

"Oh, just trying to get comfy," I say breezily.

"Mm-hmm. No hidden agenda?" he asks as I snuggle deeper into the couch and, consequently, closer into his side.

"Hidden agenda? That doesn't sound like me."

I'm still squishing my body into the couch (read: Weston) when his fingers start digging into my sides, tickling me mercilessly.

"No, no, no!" I shout, trying to slap his hands away. That's certainly not something I pictured having to do tonight.

His hands keep roaming, finding all the places I'm most ticklish, until my back is pressed into the couch cushions. He hovers above me, eyes wild and playful. I'm suddenly very, very aware that his body is stretched out over mine. I think this was his plan all along.

Thank God he's a quick thinker.

His eyes slowly lose some of their amusement, replaced with a longing so stark it robs me of breath. His lips are still quirked in a smile, but it looks different now, soft and tender. He's looking at me as if there's nowhere he'd rather be. I can't help but agree.

"You look beautiful tonight, Lo."

He must be delusional because I absolutely do not. My hair, which he is now winding around his finger, is splayed, wet and lifeless, around me. My skin is free of any makeup, and I know the day in the sun has left my cheeks pink and freckled. I'm wearing a *Pride & Prejudice* T-shirt and unicorn pajama pants, for heaven's sake. But Wes is looking at me like I'm the buried treasure he's been in search of for years.

I wish I had a camera because I'd like to snap a picture of that look and pull it out whenever I'm feeling self-conscious. I could never feel anything but perfect with him looking at me like that.

So instead of making a self-deprecating remark, I trail my hands up from where they were resting on his biceps and thread them into the thick hair at the nape of his neck. It takes no effort at all to coax his lips to mine.

This kiss isn't hungry like the one in the pool. It's slow and languid. The kiss in the pool was desperate, two people unsure of what would happen when they climbed out. But this kiss is different, two friends who have realized that nothing and everything can change at the same time.

His lips are reverent as they caress my mouth. He's taking his time, savoring every taste like I am a piece of dark chocolate melting on his tongue. It's so unlike him that it makes me smile against his mouth. I like that I bring out this side of him.

He pulls back, trailing kisses across my jaw and down my throat, his scruff creating a pleasant burn against my sensitive skin. "What are you smiling for?"

"I just really like kissing you," I whisper.

The look he gives me is so full of tenderness I want to cry. "Same."

This time his kiss is exploring, an archeologist searching for long-forgotten artifacts. With every secret he unearths—the way my heartbeat quickens when he tugs at my bottom lip with his teeth, the way goosebumps prickle along my skin when he whispers in my ear—he gives me one in return. He likes it when I scrape my nails against his scalp, and he sighs with pleasure when I press my lips to the pulse point at his throat.

This kiss goes on and on, devouring me whole, and I love every single second of it.

Eventually, Wes pulls back, groaning as he digs his face into my neck. "You're really good at this," he says, and I laugh against his shoulder. No one has ever said that before, and it sends a jolt of pleasure through me. I'm on cloud nine. Cloud ten, if there is one.

His fists press into the cushions beside my head as he pushes himself up. He grips my hand and tugs me up with him. Our knees press into each other as we sit facing each other, and Wes chews his bottom lip, looking like he's debating something in his mind.

"I want to show you something," he says finally, his voice more serious than I've ever heard it, and it makes my stomach flutter. He extends a hand palm-up in my direction, and twines our fingers together when I grab hold of it. My pulse beats in my ears as he leads me into his bedroom.

"Sit right here," Wes says, motioning to the edge of his bed. The mattress sinks beneath me as he crosses the space to his dresser. I think his hands are trembling as he picks up the photo of us at the lake house and gives it to me.

"Do you remember taking this?" he asks.

I meet his gaze, so intensely green right now, the color of grass covered in morning dew. "Of course."

Wes opens the top drawer of his dresser and pulls out a small stack of photos, though these are not in frames. Some are Polaroids, with thick white edges, but some are glossy prints, soft and crinkled with age.

He hands them to me, and I sift through them. Some I recognize, and others I don't, but it's like watching an old film reel of home videos, replaying a thousand memories. One is from that night we went downtown in college, a picture he must have had printed from an old phone. Another is a Polaroid of us the day he dunked me at the carnival. There's a selfie of the four of us—Rod, Camilla, Wes, and me—watching a movie under a pillow fort in Rod and Weston's off-campus apartment.

The last few make my breath hitch. They're not group photos. They're just pictures of me. Some must be still shots from his early videos, but others are just candid pictures I didn't know he'd taken.

I look up at Wes, words stuck in my throat. He's leaning against the dresser, thick arms crossed over his chest, his bottom lip tucked between his teeth. "I didn't think it was a mistake, Lo."

My heart stops. Time has ended and the rest of the world has fallen away. There is nothing but *this* moment. Wes and me and whatever cataclysmic shift is going to happen between us. I'm ready for us to rip down a fault line and have to rebuild our lives, together this time.

His footsteps echo the blood rushing through my veins as he comes closer, squatting in front of me so we're eye to eye. His hand reaches out, slowly tracing a line across my jaw and down the slope of my neck. "I wanted to kiss you—had been wanting to for two years. I was in love with you then."

He searches my face, and I feel my heart crumbling in my chest. *What did I do to us?*

"I never stopped," he says, and I can't get a full breath. "It's okay if you thought we made a mistake back then, but I need to know if you think we're making one now."

I want to commit every single moment of this to memory—the way his thumb feels tracing circles on my collarbone, the way his hair curls over his ears, the way his eyes look steady yet fragile, like he really doesn't know how I'm going to respond. I can't believe he even has to ask. "I didn't think it was a mistake either."

"And now?" he asks, his voice a breathy whisper but so full of unrestrained hope.

"No."

I don't have to tell him twice. The word unlocks something in him, a desperation that I'll never be able to forget. It will be branded in my memory when the world ends and all that's left is dust.

Wes covers my mouth with his own, and I drown in him. In us. His hands burn everywhere they touch—a line up my spine, a caress over my shoulders, and brand on the back of my neck. I gasp when his lips leave mine and trail across my throat, his stubble scraping against the sensitive skin.

Weston's boldness fuels my own, and I slip my hands beneath his shirt, feeling the hot silkiness of taut skin over sinewy muscle. He stops moving, his breath rasping my ear as I continue my exploration. I can't count how many times I've imagined this—wanted this.

I push up the hem of his shirt, revealing him inch by inch, and he lifts his arms to accommodate me. When he's free of the garment, he stands there, bathed in lamplight. I've seen him shirtless hundreds of times, but it's different now. He's not sluiced in water from the pool or shimmering in sweat from working out. He's bare. For me.

My hand reaches out, almost against my will, and trails along his chest, sliding through the blonde hair there, bleached and barely visible from being in the sun so often. It slips lower, along the ridges of his abdomen that twitch beneath my touch, until I get to the waistband of his pants. I hook my fingers in the band, tugging him toward me.

I think I'll die if he doesn't put his hands on me again.

Wes follows my urging, pressing his body to mine. We line up perfectly, and I can see the pulse jumping in his throat. The sharpness of his stubble scrapes against my cheek as he leans closer, and I suddenly want to feel that *everywhere.*

"What do you want, Lo?" Wes asks, his voice breathless and almost pained.

I can tell he's holding back, his muscles taut as a bow string, his skin feverish. That simply won't do.

I slide my hand up the hard planes of his body and his neck, threading my fingers through the thick curls at his nape.

My whole body shivers in anticipation. Slowly, I bring my lips to his ear. "Everything."

Thirty-Two

WESTON

I WAKE TO MORNING sunlight filtering through the curtains and the sound of Lo breathing softly beside me. Her hair is spread across the pillows, a russet and bronze contrast to the stark white of my sheets. She's breathtaking like this, one of my old T-shirts slipping off her shoulder, revealing constellations of freckles dotting across her skin.

Lo stirs, one of her arms sliding against my bare chest to wrap around my middle. I pull her closer, my nose nuzzling into that soft spot where her shoulder meets her neck. When she snuggles closer, my mouth stretches into a smile. I could get used to this.

"Morning," I say, and my voice is husky. I'm drugged by the presence of this woman in my bed—my *wife*.

"Morning."

My phone buzzes on the nightstand, and Lo starts to back up, but I tighten my arms around her.

"Aren't you going to answer that?"

"No," I say, smoothing my lips over the long slope of her neck, trying my best to distract her.

It doesn't work. "What if it's something important? Rod or your parents or—"

Groaning, I roll over and pick up my phone before pushing up so I'm leaning against the headboard. "You're going to pay for this," I tell Lo, and she laughs.

It is not, in fact, Rod or my parents calling. It's Brandon, and he makes all my cozy, lovey feelings disappear like a cloud of dust.

I swipe open the phone to answer the call. "Yes, Brandon?"

"You're grumpy."

"Now isn't a good time," I say, and Lo bites back a smile.

"Sorry to interrupt." He definitely does not sound sorry. "The article came out. Have you even looked?"

His words sink like a weight in my stomach. I rub a hand over my face and press my palm into my eye until I see spots. Lo sits up, concern etched across her features.

"What did it say?" I ask, dreading the answer. Whatever it is, it can't be good.

"You seriously haven't looked?"

"No, Brandon," I answer, exasperated. "I just woke up."

"Talia told them your marriage is fake."

My breath catches, and the sound of a vinyl scratching echoes through my head. *Not again.* I've gotten this call before, the one where I find out Talia has ruined me. I'm back in the grocery store, hearing her songs about me playing through the speakers. I'm on Brandon's couch, scrolling through the article where she told everyone I'd been leading her on for months, playing with her like she was a game.

Lo's hand on my knee brings me back to the present. Her brows are drawn together in worry.

"How did she find out?" I ask Brandon, though my mind is still spinning in every direction, the world around me a hazy blur.

"I don't know. But we need to get you to LA to sort this out."

For the first time in a long time, I'm grateful that Brandon is my manager. There's no way I'd be able to handle all this on my own. He's always been there for me, and he will know what to do; he will fix this.

Breathing deeply through my nose, I nod before I remember he can't see me. "Okay, yeah. I'll get there as soon as possible."

"I'll book the flights and send you the information."

"Okay." I start mentally packing and making a to-do list. It's calming me down, thinking through all the practical things that need to be done. I can pack my toothbrush and get on a plane. Brandon will handle the rest.

"Wes?" Brandon asks.

"Yeah?"

"We'll figure this out." He's been saying this for months, but I finally believe him. We'll figure this out together. As long as Brandon and Lo are by my side, everything will be okay.

"See you tonight," I tell him and the line clicks off. I turn to Lo, her bottom lip caught between her teeth. She must have pulled her hand from my thigh at some point because it's in her lap, clasped tightly with the other.

"What's going on?"

I lean my head back against the headboard and stare at the ceiling. "Talia somehow found out our marriage was fake, and she went to the press about it."

"Oh," she breathes.

My hands drag over my face, going over my to-do list again. We're going to be gone for a few days, so I'll need to see if Rod and Camilla will keep an eye on the house. I need to pack my vlogging equipment in case Brandon wants us to make a video addressing the rumor. I should text Cam and Hazel to tell them what's going on.

"So you're going back to LA?" Lo asks, pulling me out of my thoughts.

"Yeah, Brandon will book us the next flights out. We'll probably be there for a few days."

"I can't go with you," she says, sounding shocked at the idea.

My eyes snap to her, and I sit up straighter, my shoulders tensing at her tone. "What? Why not?"

"I have a doctor's appointment."

I stare at her, uncomprehending. My thoughts are a jumbled mess, laundry on tumble dry, rolling though mind. I can't think straight, but the one thing I can focus on is that Lo isn't coming. My career is possibly over, and she isn't going with me while I try to sort through the wreckage?

"You can't reschedule?" I ask, almost wincing at the hard tone of my voice. I didn't mean to sound like that, but I also can't stop. I feel like an earthquake is rippling through me, and I'm doing my best to hold on for dear life.

Annoyance crosses her features. "No, Wes, I can't reschedule. She's booked months out. They only squeezed me in because they need to sort out my new insurance."

"And you can't do that another time or over the phone?" Her mouth is parted, like *I'm* the one being ridiculous. It's the same look Brandon gives me when he thinks I'm being unreasonable, and the last vestiges of my sanity snap. "God, Lo. My whole career is blowing up in my face, and you're not even going to be there for me?"

"The whole reason we got married was so I could get this insurance!" she spits. I rear back at her words, feeling like she slapped me across the face.

After everything we've gone through, it all really comes back to that. Why did I think it would be any different? She practically avoided me like the plague when I came back until I offered her insurance.

Last night flashes through my mind—showing her the photos, telling her I'd loved her for the last eight years, everything that came after. But she never said it back.

I can't do this anymore. Maybe I'm being irrational, but it's all just *too much* right now. I need to be alone to think. Lo has a way of muddling my mind, of making me see what I so desperately want instead of what's actually true.

Throwing off the blankets, I stand and pull a shirt from my drawer.

"Wes—"

"I can't do this right now, Lo," I say, tugging the shirt over my head.

"Wes, I didn't—"

"No!" My voice reverberates through the room, louder than I intended, and Lo withers like a deflated balloon. The breath is stolen from my lungs as she slips quietly from the bed, my T-shirt sliding down the smooth slope of her shoulder that I had my face buried in only minutes ago. Her footsteps echo as she leaves, all the way up the stairs, followed by the soft snick of her door shutting.

I should call her back and apologize, try to make this right, but I'm worried nothing will put our world back on its axis. We tried and failed. *Again.* I was honest with her last night, and I thought she'd finally been brave enough to be honest with me, but she wasn't. It was just like last time. Lo will always be too scared to tell me how she really feels.

My heart hammers as I stand at the base of the stairs, my hand clenched on the railing. Lo hasn't come back down after retreating to her room this morning. Despite everything, I want to see her, to hold her close as I tell her goodbye before I leave, to promise her we will sort everything out when I get back. But there's a niggling fear in the back of my mind that she won't *want* to try and fix things when I get back. It's what's keeping me here, sixteen stairs between us.

Casting one last glance at her door at the top of the stairs, I retreat to the kitchen. I pull a legal pad from the drawer. My hand shakes slightly, poised above the paper, trying to figure out what to say—how vulnerable I want to be.

The pen scrapes loudly against the paper as I scrawl a quick message on the top sheet.

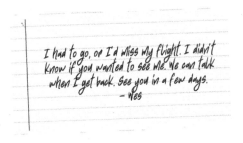

I rip the note off and leave it on the counter. Before I can second-guess myself, I hastily write something on the next slip of paper. Tearing it from the pad, I fold it twice and walk into my room. *The picture* stares back at me in its frame, a memento of a happy time, of when we had our first start. I hope it won't be our last.

I place the folded sheet on the dresser, right next to the picture of us at the lake house. She'll only find it if she comes in here. If it's still here when I get back, I'll have my answer about what she wants.

Thirty-Three

LO

The sound of the garage door rouses me. I climb out of the bed, my body screaming in protest. An ache formed deep in my bones the moment I walked away from Wes this morning and has continued to worsen all day.

The curtains part beneath my touch, and I watch through the window as Weston's Range Rover backs down the driveway. Something cracks in my chest at the sight of those tail lights disappearing down our street, leaving me *again*.

Time quivers and stands still as I make my way downstairs, my clammy palms sticking to the hand rail. There's a splash of yellow standing out amidst the neutrals in the kitchen, a slip of paper resting on the counter. My hands shake as I pick it up, and with every one of his unfeeling words, a piece of me shrivels.

So this is how it's going to be, then. He said it wasn't a mistake back then. He said he still loves me. But his career comes first. It always will. It did then. It did when he proposed. It does now.

I try to make it back to the stairs, but my strength ebbs, and I end up falling onto the couch instead. Everything hurts—my muscles, my bones, my head, and most of all, my heart. I thought it hurt last time Weston left, but this time I'm left shattered, a broken piece of pottery that can never be mended.

I don't know how long I lie curled on the couch, but sometime, long after the sun has disappeared behind the horizon, the back door opens. I don't sit up. Whoever it is can do what they please. Nothing can make me hurt more than I do right now.

Camilla lowers herself gently next to me on the sofa. Her smooth, cool hand pushes the hair off my face. She swipes at my eyes, and I realize I must be crying. "Lo, what happened?"

I don't move or speak, just keep my gaze fixed on Weston's closed door.

"Lo, where's Wes?"

When I speak, my voice comes out as a croak. "Gone."

Rod sits down next to Camilla and hands her the slip of paper from the counter. Camilla scans it. "I don't get it."

"He left," I say simply.

"Because of the article?"

I nod, still curled in on myself.

"Why didn't you go with him?" Rod asks. "Wes told us he was on his way to the airport and to come check on you, but when I asked why, he never responded."

"It was a mistake," I whisper.

"What was a mistake?" Rod asks, confused. Camilla murmurs something to him. I could probably hear if I tried, but I don't care. Let them say what they want.

"Hey, hon, let's get you into bed," Camilla says, rising. She pulls me to my feet, and I groan in pain. Hot tears track down my face, and I don't know if it's from the pain or the *fear*. It hasn't been this bad in a long time, and I'm terrified I'm going to slip back into a state where I can't take care of myself, where I have to rely on everyone to help me fulfill my most basic needs.

That fear is cold and slick and suffocating.

My teeth chatter, and I'm shaking so hard that Camilla has to help lower me into my bed. She doesn't say anything as she tucks the blankets up to my chin and digs in my nightstand drawer for my heating pad. I shiver harder when she puts it behind me and the warmth starts to seep into my back.

My vision is so blurred from tears that I almost can't see Camilla's hand extended in front of me, two of my prescription pain pills in her palm. I take them and the glass of water she hands me, swallowing against the lump in my throat.

"Thank you," I tell her and my voice is small and choked.

She climbs into bed next to me and reaches for my hand, threading her fingers through mine. "You don't need to thank me."

"I don't know what I'd do without you."

"You won't have to find out," she promises, and it's the last thing I remember before drifting off into a fitful sleep.

WHEN I WAKE UP later, my room is bathed in moonlight. Every inch of my body aches, though nothing hurts worse than the pounding in my head and the hollowness in my chest.

Camilla stirs next to me. "Are you okay? Do you need more medicine?"

"I'm fine. I think I just need to move to the couch."

"Want me to come?" Her voice is drowsy as she tries to sit up.

"No, I'm okay. Go back to sleep."

She rolls over, falling back into her slumber easily. The floor is cool beneath my feet as I climb out of the bed, using my phone flashlight to make my way through the darkened room. I grab my laptop and hold it to my chest as I head downstairs, using the banister for support.

The sofa mocks me, lit up in patches of moonbeams. Last night I'd been on that couch with Wes, wrapped in his arms and thinking this was just the start for us. And then today I laid there, feeling like everything was crashing down around me.

I decide to avoid the couch and quietly tiptoe out the back door. I don't know if Rod is asleep in the guest room, but I don't want him coming out and seeing me slip out into the darkness.

The night air is balmy and warm, with humidity thick enough to slice through. My computer screen fogs over as I open it, staring at the first draft I'm halfway finished with.

I had an idea after we left California—a second chance romance between two people who never quite got the timing right. The story wrote itself. It was Weston's green eyes I pictured and his quick wit that made the hero utterly loveable. It was my insecurities and fear that held the main character back from admitting her feelings. If she did, he may still leave her again anyway.

A photo on a dresser changed everything. It broke down my world and rebuilt it. And after finding it two nights ago, my hands itched with the need to write an ending for these characters where everything worked out. Their ending was perfect, and I wanted it so desperately for myself that I decided to drop my death-grip on fear and reach for it.

That ending feels like a stab to my gut right now, a happily-ever-after that will inevitably end in heartbreak.

My pointer finger presses against the delete button before I can think better of it, the letters disappearing into nothingness. With each one, my chest gets tighter and tighter until I think it might snap, leaving a gaping hole.

I accidentally go too far, erasing more than I mean to, but I keep pressing the button, watching hours and hours of work disappear before my eyes. This story isn't worth telling anyway.

The back door opens and closes as I erase the last letter, leaving a blank white screen glaring in front of me. Camilla sits in the pool chair next to me, wrapped in the quilt from my bed. "I heard the back door and thought maybe you could use some company."

I close the laptop and hug my knees, feeling chilly despite the heat. "You should go back to sleep."

Camilla is quiet for a moment, the silence interrupted only by the chirping of crickets. She shifts in her seat, pulling the blanket tighter around her shoulders. "What happened, Lo?"

My eyes are fixed on the pale blue-green water of the pool, the way it glows from the lights below the surface and ripples in the light breeze. I remember how that water felt against my skin last night, how it looked running down Weston's body in rivulets. I remember *everything*.

"He left."

"I know," she whispers. "Why did he leave?"

"The article."

"Lo, I'm going to need more than two-word answers."

I turn to her, and her skin looks even darker in the moonlight. Her eyes are hard and glinting. "What do you want me to say, Camilla?"

Her mouth falls open, shocked. I've never snapped at her before, not in twenty years of friendship, and guilt sinks in my belly. I rest my head on my knees, unable to look at her, scared she will see too much. She always sees too much.

Even though she got married and moved out, she still came here because I needed her. She took care of me like nothing had changed at all, like she didn't have anything she'd rather be doing. I married Wes so Camilla wouldn't need to keep taking care of me, yet here she is.

"I'm sorry," I murmur, my voice ragged.

Camilla scoots closer, her hand smoothing across my back. "It's okay, hon."

My breath comes out in a shaky exhale. "He told me he never thought kissing me in college was a mistake."

"Oh, babe."

"He said he loved me then, and he never stopped. I ruined everything, Camilla. We could have been together this whole time."

Her fingers tangle in my hair, brushing through the strands with heartbreaking gentleness. "Why can't you be together now?"

"He said all that, but then as soon as Brandon told him there was a problem with his career, he took off again. He left. For California. Again. When it comes down to his job or me, he's always going to pick his job first." Camilla doesn't say anything, still rubbing my back, so I continue. "He asked me last night, just like he did at the lake house, if I trusted him."

"Do you trust him?"

"I did," I say, pain rippling through me once more. I feel wrung out, tired all the way down to my bones. "I trusted him, and I shouldn't have."

"He never asked you to go with him?"

I sit up, and Camilla's hand falls from my back. There was something in her tone that made my skin prickle with irritation. "No, he did. But I couldn't go. I have a doctor's appointment."

"You couldn't reschedule?"

"No," I say, frustrated at her question the same way I was when Wes asked me this morning. "My doctor is backed up forever."

"But you don't really need to see her for another couple months, right? She gives you prescriptions for like three months at a time."

"What are you getting at, Camilla?" My voice is loud enough to wake the neighbors, but I don't care. She's picking at a wound that hasn't had a chance to heal yet, and I want to smack her hands away and wrap it with bandages until the skin is brand new.

"Why didn't you go with Wes?"

I snap like a brittle rubber band. "Because I need to go to the doctor!" I yell. "That's the whole reason I married him." The same sick feeling I had in the pit of my stomach when I said that to Wes this morning comes back now.

"Is it?" Camilla asks with a calmness that sets me on edge. "Or did you marry him because you wanted to give him another chance? Give your relationship another chance?"

"No," I say, although the seed of doubt is already taking root. While rekindling things with Wes was a happy accident, it wasn't the *reason* we married. We couldn't possibly be that backward. "I married him because I needed insurance." I hate the way my voice quavers, no longer as self-assured in my answer.

"Why did Weston want to marry you, Lo?"

Her question is a KO, and I'm left sprawling on the mat, grasping for answers. I can still feel those Polaroids in my hands, their edges battered like they had been sifted through often. An image flashes in my mind of Wes, sitting alone in his house in LA, flipping through old photos. It's so lonely it makes my chest hurt, but I can't let myself think like that.

Wes *did not* marry me for a second chance. "He needed some good press," I tell her, but my answer comes out like a question.

"How much content have you filmed together other than the stuff you made that day in California?"

None. We haven't done anything. "He wanted me to go with him today so I could help him fix this, try to make everyone believe this is real," I say, but even to me it sounds like I'm grasping for straws.

"Is that what he said?" Camilla asks.

I think about this morning, ignoring everything I was feeling and focusing on the facts. He'd been upset when I said I couldn't go with him, but he hadn't said why. I'd thought it was because I wasn't holding up my side of the deal, and so I retaliated by telling him he needed to hold up his.

I'd done that. I'd said that after he'd tried to prove to me why he'd married me. After he'd shown me those photos he'd held on to all this time, in his dresser drawer, not in some box in a closet. After he'd told me he loved me.

Did I ever even say it back?

No, I hadn't. I'd been too scared.

My head falls into my hands, tears sliding down my cheeks. "Camilla, what have I done?"

"We'll be back after work," Rod says the next morning. "Do you want me to get you anything other than more IcyHot while I'm out?"

"No, thanks. Thank you for coming last night." I smile gratefully at him from my position on the couch. After my talk with Camilla, she slept in the guest room with Rod, and I spent the rest of the night in the living room, the couch feeling vastly larger without Wes on it with me.

I stared at the ceiling all night, memories playing on an endless loop in my head. My eyelids finally started to flutter closed when Rod and Camilla got up for work.

Rod kisses the top of my head. "Call me or Camilla if you need anything. See you later, LoLo."

The house is eerily silent after he leaves. It feels weird to be in this giant house without Wes. Without the espresso machine sputtering when he makes his third latte of the day. Without his voice drifting through the house while he talks on the phone with his parents or Cam.

Without Wes, it doesn't feel like home.

Shifting on the couch, I try to get comfy. The down feathers I sunk into at the store feel flat and hard beneath my aching back right now, and my hip that's wedged between two cushions throbs.

I let out a heavy sigh and sit up. I don't want to go back upstairs, so I try the recliner, and then the loveseat, but neither feel good. I even try reclining on the floor, but my body screams in protest. I know where I want to go, where I'll be able to rest somewhat comfortably, but I'm scared to go in there.

Weston's door is closed, taunting me as I finally push off the floor and move to stand in front of it.

It shouldn't be a big deal to let myself in and climb into his bed. But I know that I want to go in there to ease more than just the physical ache. I want to wrap myself in his sheets and feel like he's there, holding me through the pain. If he can't be here, this is the closest I'll get.

My hand trembles as I twist the knob and push the door open. The musky, cedar scent of Wes's cologne lingers in here, and I want to stuff my face into his pillow and inhale. That smell clings to him no matter what he's doing, like the company that made it bottled up his scent and sold it on the market. It's so familiar that a knot forms in my throat, making it hard to breathe.

Wes must have made the bed before he left, because it's tidy now, not rumpled like it was when I left yesterday morning. I smooth a hand across the quilt, remembering how it felt against my skin. There's a bag of Hershey kisses on his nightstand that I never noticed, and a smile flirts with my lips as I picture him snacking on them while he watches TV before bed. When I turn around, something on the dresser catches my eye.

There's a folded yellow slip of paper next to the framed lake house photo, exactly like the one I found on the kitchen counter last night. My heart hammers as I stare at it, remembering how hollow I'd felt after reading his words while his tail lights still lingered down the street.

I pick it up before I can talk myself out of it, unfolding the paper quickly, like an impatient kid on Christmas. I can only hope I like what's inside.

That familiar, chicken-scratch handwriting is scrawled across the paper, and my breath hitches as I read the words once, twice, three times, to make sure I read them right.

> Lo, I put this in here, hoping you'd come in and find it. I meant what I said last night. I don't think we made a mistake, not now and not then. I loved you then, and I still do.
> I would have stayed or come back if you'd asked. But you never asked. Not six years ago, and not this morning. I think I need you to, just once. I need you to tell me you want this as much as I do.
> I'll come back for you if you want me to.
> — Wes

Thirty-Four

WESTON

"Door's unlocked," Brandon calls from inside his apartment.

I let myself in and give him a grim, tired smile. We didn't have time to do anything last night after he picked me up from the airport and dropped me off at my hotel, so I know today is going to be a long day.

"Hey," he says from where he's perched at the kitchen counter with his laptop. "There's Gatorade and—"

"Orange juice in the fridge." This isn't the apartment I crashed at when I first moved here—Brandon's since upgraded to a much nicer place—but for as long as I've known him, he's always kept the fridge stocked the same.

I'm filling a glass with orange juice when Kate and Emily arrive. Kate is busy typing something on her phone, but Emily gives me a quick hug, and looks around the kitchen before asking, "Where's Lo?"

Something deep in my chest pinches at the question. "Lo couldn't make it. She has a doctor's appointment tomorrow."

Kate sets her phone on the counter with a thud, her face a hard mask. "I think we need to get the record straight here. Are you or are you not married to Lo?"

Right to the point, I see. I slump onto a barstool, unnerved by the three sets of eyes fastened on me, and push a hand through my hair. "Lo and I are legally married."

"So was it all for show, then?" Emily asks, her face scrunched in confusion.

I chew the inside of my mouth, not sure how much I want to divulge—especially since I'm not sure where Lo and I stand right now. Not knowing is killing me, little by little, and I don't think I have the strength to come up with a lie, so I decide on the truth. "I don't know."

"We're not here to talk about Lo and Wes," Brandon interrupts. "We need to figure out where to go from here."

The next few hours are spent strategizing, but my heart isn't in it. I can't even enjoy the fact that Brandon is in my corner again. While it's like a weight has been lifted off my shoulders by letting him take charge again, the sinking feeling in my gut gets stronger with every hour that passes without hearing from Lo.

At eleven thirty, I can't take it anymore. My senses are dulled and there's a headache throbbing behind my eye. The lights are too bright and my orange juice is warm. The chair legs scrape against the floor as I stand, and they all stop talking, turning to me with matching looks of surprise. "I need some fresh air. Anyone want lunch?"

"Actually," Kate says, pushing up from her chair and shrugging into her blazer, "I need to get back to the office. I'll send you guys an email this afternoon."

Emily starts gathering her things. "I need to head out too. I'm meeting a friend for lunch. I'll be back later today."

After they leave, Brandon and I decide to place a to-go order from a restaurant a few blocks away. "Why don't we just order delivery?" Brandon asks.

"I need to get out of here for a bit."

He goes back to typing on his laptop. "Fine, I'll be here when you get back." I know he's annoyed I'm not working through lunch with him, but I just can't take it anymore.

I'm lost in my own head as I walk the few blocks to the restaurant. I barely notice the shining sun or the pleasant breeze that's not the least bit humid. I'd give anything to be sitting next to Lo by our pool, hair curling in the damp heat, sweat beading on my skin. It would be hot and miserable, but I would be *there*.

When I arrive at the restaurant, I tell the hostess Brandon's name, and she sends someone off to fetch my order. I retreat into the shadows or a large plant, hoping no one notices me. I'm pretty sure the hostess recognized me, but she works for an upscale restaurant in Los Angeles and probably knows to leave people alone. Not everyone feels the same way.

I'm about to check my phone when the front door opens again and warm summer air rushes in. Lead drops in my stomach as Talia Benson's eyes connect with mine. Anger surges through me, hot and swift. I thought time would dull the feeling, but in the wake of everything that's just happened, I'm overwhelmed by it. What did I ever do to this woman other than not feel the same way about her as she did for me?

She doesn't even have the decency to feign remorse as she looks at the person whose reputation she systematically demolished over the last year. Instead, the smile she gives me is practiced, one she's flashed to a thousand paparazzi. That smile used to represent success to me, but now it rubs raw, like a new pair of shoes on a blister.

Her gaze doesn't leave mine as she whispers in the ear of the man with her. He looks familiar, someone I should probably recognize, but don't, and I wonder if he's her new project. If she'll turn on him like she did on me.

The man's lips brush against Talia's temple before he follows the hostess, leaving me and Talia alone.

"Hi, Weston," Talia says, her voice dripping with a sticky sweetness. I used to think her easy affection was genuine, but it turned sour so quickly, there one moment and gone the next.

"Talia."

"You're looking well, all things considered." She glances around the space. "Where's your *wife?*"

My jaw clenches until it aches. "She's back home."

Talia's eyes narrow, and I know she's sniffing out my response like an animal hunting for prey. "Is she having a hard time after the news?"

Exhaustion suddenly grips me. I don't know what I'm doing here, having a cat fight with Talia, when all I want is to be home with Lo, sorting through the events of the past few days. I want this all to be *over*. Only one solution comes to mind, the one I've been too prideful and hurt to consider before now.

Taking a deep breath, I ask, "Can we talk outside for a moment?"

Talia makes a show of checking the gaudy watch on her wrist. "We'll have to keep it short. I don't want to keep my date waiting."

The slight breeze blows my hair in my face as I push the door open, and I grind my teeth together as Talia walks out slowly. She follows me around the corner to a small alley between buildings, where we can hopefully avoid being seen.

My body is tense, stretched to the point of breaking. I want to scream. I want to yell. I want to ask her how she found out about Lo and me. Instead, I take a deep breath and say the last words I want to. "I'm sorry about how I treated you, Talia."

Her mouth falls open.

"I didn't mean to lead you on, and I wish I could go back and redo it." I've never said anything truer. "I handled it all terribly, and I'm sorry for any pain I caused you."

"Thank you," Talia says, kicking at a pebble with her expensive heels.

She doesn't apologize. I don't expect her to, but it still fuels my anger more. I know I should leave, be done with her. But I can't. "How did you find out about me and Lo?"

Her eyes narrow into slits. "So that's what this is about?"

I exhale loudly, my shoulders drooping. "No, Talia. I wanted to apologize to you, regardless of what happened. But now that it's happened, I want to know."

Talia keeps her gaze trained over my shoulder as I talk, not even giving me the courtesy of looking me in the eye.

When I finish, she takes a step closer to me, chewing her bottom lip. The gesture is so like Lo, but the venom in her eyes is unlike any way Lo has ever looked at me. "Tell Brandon thank you for the tip-off." And then she presses her lips to mine.

I stand there for a minute, shocked, before I even realize what's happening. When I try to step back, she grabs my chin with her hand, holding me in place.

That's when I hear it—the unmistakable click of a camera behind me.

BRANDON LOOKS UP FROM his computer when I slam through his front door. "I saw Talia," I say through clenched teeth.

A caught expression flashes across his face quickly before he feigns indifference. "I bet that was—"

I cut him off, not wanting to hear whatever he has to say. "Why did you do it?"

My hands curl into fists at my sides, my heart hammering in my chest. It's taking everything in me not to snap, to throw my phone in the Pacific, go home, and never give this life another thought.

"Why did you marry Lo?" he shoots back, his jaw a hard line.

"Because I love her!"

"Come on, Wes." He rolls his eyes. "You don't love her. You love yourself. You always have. You married her because you thought it would fix your career."

Brandon stands, moving so he's right in front of me. He's eerily calm, like he knows exactly what he's done and doesn't feel an ounce of remorse. "You keep trying to do my job, and you're running your career into the ground. You married Lo, and it got you nowhere. So I took things into my own hands."

"I can't believe you did this."

Stepping back, he spreads his hands out. "I fixed this, Weston. If you try to project yourself as some domestic husband in the suburbs, no one is going to care about you anymore. That's not what people want to see."

I'm fuming. Never before have I wanted to hit someone, but I feel that urge now as I stare at my manager—my friend. His betrayal rockets through me, shrapnel knicking in all my most vulnerable places. "Then I'll do something else."

"You can't do anything else. You have no other skills or talents, Weston. You were barely making it on Vine when I reached out to you. I built your career from the ground up. I made you who you are today. You're nothing without me."

I just stare at him, blood rushing in my ears. I don't know how we got this far off track. When did Brandon start thinking that managing my personal life, or more accurately, running my entire life, became his job? Everything feels twisted, like diseased vines spreading and choking off the life of a plant that was once thriving.

"We're through, Brandon." I don't know where the words come from, but they feel so *right*, puzzle pieces finally snapping into place.

His mouth falls open. "What?"

"You're fired."

The muscle in his jaw ticks as he clenches it, his eyes burning through me. "You can't fire me."

"I can, and I did."

He stares at me silently for a moment, as if racking his mind for another bullet to fire, another punch to land. "No one else is going to work with you."

The words don't have his desired effect. Instead of maiming, they solidify my decision. We can't go on like this. *I* can't go on like this. The people in my corner have to want to be there, have to listen to what I want and respect it.

Surprisingly, a small smile curves my lips. "Then I'll quit. Or I'll do it myself. Regardless, I'm not your problem anymore. Goodbye, Brandon."

I swivel and let myself out of his house. Despite everything, I feel a sense of peace. No matter how much I've screwed up my career, I finally made a decision I know is going to put me on the right path.

My feet have barely hit the sidewalk outside Brandon's building when my phone starts buzzing. My heart races as I pull it from my pocket. There's a text from Emily. It's just a link.

I click it, and the picture of Talia and me kissing in the alley fills my screen. I'm just about to call Emily and explain when my phone vibrates again.

It's Lo.

Thirty-Five

LO

My heart beats wildly as the phone rings. There's a knot in my throat as I wait for Wes to answer. I stared at his note all day, folding and unfolding the edges nervously while I tried to work up the courage to call him—to ask him to come back for me. I know he said he would, but I'm terrified to ask it of him.

Wes answers on the fourth ring. "I'm so sorry, Lo," he says before I even have a chance to speak.

Tears pool in my eyes, and I clutch the note to my chest, the paper crinkling beneath my fingers. "I'm sorry too."

When he doesn't respond, my stomach flutters nervously. The silence on the line is deafening, and I can no longer bear it. "Wes?"

"Um," he pauses. "Did you see the article?"

My brows furrow in confusion. "The one from yesterday?"

"No, it was today," he says on an exhale. "Lo, I'm so sorry. It's not what it looks like. I ran into Talia, and I was talking to her outside. I actually apologized to her. And then she told me it was Brandon who tipped her off. And—"

Wes stops suddenly, and I try to connect the dots of his story. My mind snags on the part about Brandon, and I'm about to ask when he starts again. "Talia kissed me. And paparazzi took a photo. I didn't kiss her, I swear, Lo. I swear."

My brain stops working, doubts creeping in. Talia kissed him, and that hurts like a kick to the gut. But even as I think about it, I feel the frayed edges of the note in my hand, the one I've read and reread so many times today, running my fingers over the words as I try to commit them to memory. His words are a mantra I want to repeat in my head when doubts like this creep in.

I stare at the crisp white bed sheets, smoothing my palms over the glossy photos spread out around me. I've been looking at these too today, and scribbling my own little notes on the back like the one he wrote on our lake house picture. I want to stuff these pictures back in his drawer and see how long it takes him to find my notes, how long he goes before he has to relive our past. I have a feeling he's not going to pull them out as often now, not when we have new memories to make.

That desperate hope for a future and that unwavering assurance I get from staring at all these pieces of time he's stolen and hid away is what squashes the doubts swirling through my mind. It makes my voice firm when I say, "Okay."

"Okay?"

"I believe you."

His sigh is relieved, and I can imagine his broad shoulders drooping with the easing of tension. I trace my finger across our long-ago smiles in the photos, wishing I could see his right now.

"I fired Brandon," Wes says, and I don't know how to respond—good riddance seems kind of harsh. Brandon has been his friend for the last six years, but he also betrayed him.

"How do you feel about that?"

"I feel good," he says and I can hear the smile in his voice. I wish he was here so I could see it, one corner hitching up before the other, that tiny dimple popping in his cheek, his spring day eyes crinkling at the edges. "I feel free."

"I'm glad. What do you think you're going to do next?"

He blows out a breath. "*That* I don't know. I've been fighting Brandon on the direction of my career for months. I've been thinking about changing up the type of videos I make."

"No more pranks?" I ask, unable to keep the incredulity out of my voice. Weston's whole brand has been built on harmless pranks and causing scenes.

"I think I'm done with pranks. It's not making me happy anymore."

I don't know why, but I feel a little pang of sadness at the thought of *Just Go With It* ending. It started as our thing, that little phrase he would always say when he wanted me to trust him, but it belongs to everyone now, and it feels like the end of an era.

"So no more *Just Go With It*?" I ask.

"Oh, no," he says. "It's sticking around. For good," he adds, and I wonder if we're still talking about his brand. "I've been thinking for a while about maybe doing random acts of kindness. I don't know. It just feels right."

My heart melts a little at his words, and I can't help but think of all the things he's done for me the last month—sitting in bed with me when I'm not feeling well, bringing me ice cream bars on rainy days, getting me a candle that smells like my favorite memory, *marrying me*. His kindness is overwhelming, all-consuming, and it needs an outlet. Everyone should get to experience Weston King's goodness.

"I love that, Wes."

"Yeah?" he asks, and I don't miss the way he sounds desperate for my approval, like he was worried I wouldn't think he could do it.

"I think you'll be even better at that than pranks." And because he seems like he needs it, I decide to be a little vulnerable, to break off a piece of my heart and give it to him without knowing if he's going to give it back in return.

"You're good all the way down to your bones, Weston King," I tell him. "The world needs what you have to offer, and anyone who gets to experience you is lucky."

A lump forms in my throat as I wait for his response.

"I...thank you," he says, and his voice is thick with emotion. He's silent for another long moment. "Lo, if you didn't see the article, why did you call?"

My pulse hammers at his question, and nervousness claws at my stomach. I called because I wanted to beg him to come back, to take care of me and make everything better. But now I'm not so sure. He would be on the next flight home if I asked, but he *needs* to be there. He's done so much for me, and this is the one thing I can do for him. I can let him stay and figure things out there and not have to worry about rushing home.

"Lo?" he asks, when I haven't answered.

"I went into your room," I tell him, my hands starting to shake again.

"Yeah?" I'm buoyed by the expectant tone in his voice.

"I saw your note."

He's quiet for a beat. "And?"

"I was going to ask you to come back."

Weston's voice falls. "Was?"

"Yes, *was*." I exhale heavily, making my mind up. "I think you need to stay there, sort everything out with Kate and Emily. Try to find a new manager."

"You don't want me to come back?" he asks, and my heart breaks at his flat tone.

"I want you to come back."

"Lo—"

"I'm messing this all up," I say. "I want you to come back, Wes. I do more than anything. But I'm saying I don't want you to have to choose me or your career. You can have both. You should have both. And right now, you need to be there."

"I don't want to be here," he says with a quiet laugh.

I snuggle down into his sheets, breathing in his musky smell left on them. "I don't want you to be there either. But I don't want to ask you to come back. I don't want to be Brandon, forcing you to choose between your life and your career. They have to go hand-in-hand."

"You're not Brandon," he says. "You're a way better kisser than he is."

My face heats even as I laugh. I miss him terribly, and I'm hovering on the edge of asking him to come back, but I push the urge away.

"I don't know how long Kate and Emily will want me to stay," Wes says, sobering.

"It's okay. Stay out there as long as you need to." Even as I say it, my heart aches at the thought of staying here all alone for days or weeks, in pain and unable to do even the most basic tasks easily. Darkness washes over me, drawing out all the warm feelings from before. The time alone stretches before me like a black hole, threatening to suck me in.

"Maybe you can come out here in a few days? After your appointment?" He sounds so hopeful that I can't tell him that I won't be going anywhere until this flare-up is over. I can't tell him about the flare-up at all. He would come back, and his career would be shoved to the back burner when it needs to be front and center right now.

"Yeah, that would be nice," I tell him, hoping he can't hear the sadness in my voice.

"Hey, Emily is calling me. Can I call you back in a bit?"

"Yeah, of course."

"I love you, Lo," he says, and the line goes dead before I have a chance to respond.

Hot tears fall unchecked down my cheeks, but I don't have the strength to wipe them away. It's like Wes was a balm for the pain, dampening it while we were on the phone, but the minute he hung up, it all came rushing back, devouring me whole.

I feel the pain everywhere, an ache deep in my muscles, a cramping at the base of my spine, a throb between my eyes. Even the blankets feel too heavy, the sheets too rough. I'm having sensory overload, but it's all *pain*.

I don't know how much time passes before the back door opens. Camilla's voice rings through the house. "Lo, hon, I'm back. Where are you?"

Camilla passes Weston's door on her way to the stairs, her eyes zeroing in on me curled up on the bed. She kicks her shoes off and climbs in next to me, sorting through the pictures I left scattered on the blankets.

"This is a good one," she says, holding up a photo of the four of us standing in snow gear the year we had a huge snow storm in college and all our classes were canceled.

I can't even bring myself to smile at it, not with pain overwhelming me.

Camilla frowns at me, her brows etched in concern. "Any word from Wes?"

I nod, not trusting my voice.

"Good or bad?"

I shrug. Camilla drags a hand through my hair, pushing it off my face. Her hands are smooth and cold, and the gesture calms me.

"I called him to tell him to come back."

"Yeah?"

I pick up my phone, squinting at the bright screen as I locate the picture online of Wes and Talia kissing. When I hand it to her, she gasps, her deep brown eyes igniting with fire.

"It was a setup," I say.

"Are you sure?"

I let out a deep breath, overwhelmed by the emotional roller coaster I've been on today. "Yes, but I can't ask him to come home now. Not when he has all this stuff to deal with."

"Hm." Camilla says, her body relaxing as she resumes combing my hair with her fingers.

I sit up, ignoring the protest of my body. "What?"

"Nothing," Camilla murmurs, crossing her arms over her chest.

"Come on, Camilla."

She pins me with a look. "Did you tell him you're having a flare-up?"

"No, of course not. If he knew, he'd be on the first flight back. It's not fair to him to make him choose when this much is at stake."

"But it's fair to withhold information from him? To let him make this decision without knowing all the facts. Do you really think he would be okay with staying there if he knew what you were going through here?"

"No, he wouldn't!" I say, my voice rising. My emotions are too raw to deal with this right now. "But it's not fair for me to ask him to come back either."

"How many more ways does he need to prove to you that he loves you before you'll believe it?" Camilla asks harshly. "Or are you always going to act out of fear that if you ask for too much, he'll leave?"

"How many more ways do *I* need to prove that I don't need people? I may want him to come back, but I don't need him, Camilla."

Camilla waves her arms wildly. "Look around, Lo. You do need people. You're living in Weston's house because you couldn't live on your own."

Her words are like a slap in the face, stinging in their intensity. I've worked so hard to be independent, and she's throwing it in my face. It's like my efforts the last few years are nothing, and I feel like that girl I was six years ago, devastated by her illness with no idea how to handle it.

Camilla must see how her words affect me because she gentles her voice. "Lo, everyone needs people. And you more than most."

"I—"

"It's not because you're not strong enough or independent enough, Lo. You're sick. You can't make yourself not sick. You're going to need people. And that's okay."

Tears blur my vision, and I bite down hard on my lip to hold back the sob that wants to break free. I feel so helpless, so *broken*.

"You push us all away. You kept things from me for weeks before the wedding. It hurt, Lo. And now you're keeping this from Wes, and it's going to devastate him. He wouldn't want you going through this alone."

"You're here," I manage to get out.

Camilla puts her hands over mine. I hadn't realized they were shaking. "And I'm not going anywhere. But I wouldn't have been if Wes hadn't called us. You wouldn't have told me because you wouldn't have wanted to bother me, and you would have stayed here suffering alone."

The truth is a bomb in my chest, tearing me open, exploding all of my excuses into dust. She's right. I would have stayed here alone, and I would have slipped further and further into darkness that would have taken me months to climb out of. I would have become that shell of myself that I hollowed into when I first got sick.

Camilla wraps her arms around me, holding me up like always as I fall apart. For once, I don't resent it. I let her smooth her hands over my aching back and tell me it's going to be okay.

"I'll call him tomorrow, I promise."

Thirty-Six

WESTON

Camilla's photo flashes across my phone, and I almost silence the call, not wanting to be chewed out by her over Talia when she doesn't know what actually happened. Instead, I let it ring, trying to concentrate on all the things Kate and Emily are saying.

"Are you going to answer that?" Emily asks.

I shake my head and tap my fingers across the table. "It's fine."

"Go ahead and answer. I'm going to get more coffee."

"Yeah, don't worry about it. I have a phone call to make," Kate announces.

The phone has already stopped ringing, and a missed call notification hovers at the top of my screen. Snatching it off the table, I head out to the hallway of Emily's apartment building, and I redial Camilla.

She answers on the first ring, and says, "It's Lo."

My heart stops in my chest, a thousand different scenarios playing through my mind. "What's wrong?"

"She's okay," Camilla says, and a strangled breath escapes me. "She's just been having a flare-up since you left. She's in a lot of pain, and she's struggling." She pauses before adding, "She needs you here."

"What? Why didn't she tell me?"

"Only Lo can answer that." She sounds frustrated and a little hurt. "Actually, no. I could. I'm the one who explained it to her. But I'm going to let her tell you."

That answer leaves me with more questions, and I want to force her hand until she tells me everything she knows, but more than that I want to be home *now*, so I can find out for myself.

"I'm booking a flight right now," I tell her, putting her on speaker as I search for flights and find one leaving in three hours. I'll need to leave for the airport immediately to make it on time, but that's good. I'd go crazy waiting hours for a flight.

"Good," Camilla says.

"Are you there with her?"

"Yeah, she's sleeping now. She's barely slept since you left." I can hear the worry in her voice, and I feel strangled by it.

"My flight lands around three."

"Okay, Rod and I will head out soon then."

"Will she be okay there by herself?"

Camilla hesitates, like she's mulling over her words. "Yeah, she'll be okay. She just needs you. You remember what I told you when you called me from California?"

I can practically taste my fear, remember the stark look of pain Lo had been trying desperately to hide. I called Camilla in a panic, needing to know how to make Lo feel better. I would have taken her pain and made it my own if possible, moved heaven and Earth to fix it for her, but Camilla told me to get her some food, turn on a movie, and make sure she wasn't alone.

It felt so inadequate in the face of Lo's pain, but she cried and told me it was nice. I'm glad she thought so, but my heart was still breaking all the same.

Suddenly, I need to move. I'm antsy, my hands itching with the need to pack my things, my mind whirring through my to-do list. Lo needs me, and nothing is more important than that.

"Yeah, I remember," I tell Camilla. "I'm going to get off here so I can get my stuff and head to the airport."

"Wes?" Camilla says, and I pause, my hand resting on Emily's door handle.

"Yeah?"

"I'm really glad you and Lo found your way back to each other," she says, and I don't mistake the emotion in her voice.

"Me too, C." I hang up and lean my head against the wall, fighting tears of my own. I feel so helpless here, and I can't imagine what Lo must be feeling.

Why didn't she tell me? Why didn't she ask me to come home when she called earlier?

I know the answer, though, and it breaks my heart. She didn't want to make me choose. What she doesn't know is that I'd choose her every time.

When I gather myself enough to head back into Emily's apartment, both women look up from where they sit at the counter. Emily must see something in my expression. "Everything all right?"

I start to gather my things. "No. I need to go home."

"You're not serious," Kate says. She gestures at the mess of laptops and tablets covering the kitchen. "We have so much to do. We need to get on top of this and find you a new manager—"

Emily cuts her off, searching my face. "You need to go home and be with Lo, right?"

My hands freeze, and I look her in the eye, needing her to see how serious I am. "Yes."

"Lo comes first," she says simply.

I regard both of them in turn. "Is that going to be a problem?"

Their answers are important to me, something I can't leave without knowing. Brandon was always going to demand that my career come first, and I need to know if Kate and Emily are going to attempt the same thing.

Kate folds her hands on the table and tips her chin. "No, it's what you need to do."

"Go home, Wes," Emily says with a smile.

I don't need to be told twice.

It's the wee hours of the morning when I let myself into the house. Stars pepper the sky like pin holes lit from heaven, and a symphony of crickets drowns out the sound of me opening and closing the back door.

I drop my bag and tiptoe across the living room, pausing in the doorway to my room. Moonlight hangs over the room like a cloak, making Lo's hair look like crimson silk draped across my pillow. Even from here, I can see the grimace painted on her sleeping face, and an ache builds beneath my sternum. I want to wrap her in blankets, tuck her against my chest, and make sure she's never in pain again.

My feet propel me forward, needing to hold her close. As I slip between the sheets, she stirs, those cerulean eyes hazed with sleep.

"Wes?"

"I'm here," I say, the mattress sinking beneath my weight.

Now more awake, she sits up, the blankets pooling around her waist. Fierce possessiveness surges in my chest at the sight of my shirt sliding down her shoulder.

"What are you doing here?"

My hand snakes out, unable to keep from smoothing over the creamy exposed slope of her shoulder. She shivers beneath my touch, her gaze fixing on mine. "Let's talk in the morning," I murmur. "Go back to sleep."

Lo sits back, flipping on the lamp on the nightstand. When she faces me once again, her expression is torn, and she has exhausted dark purple smudges beneath her eyes. Her bottom lip is caught between her teeth, and I want to reach out and tug it free, force her to go back to sleep and get the rest she so desperately needs.

"What are you doing here?" Lo asks again.

I let out a breath, knowing she's not going to let me off the hook, no matter how tired she is. "Camilla called me."

Lo fiddles with the hem of her shirt, dragging my gaze to the smooth, freckled skin of her legs. "I told her I would call you in the morning."

"Are you upset I came back?" I meet her gaze, suddenly desperate to know the answer. Time stands still as she watches me, and I hold my breath, waiting for her response.

When she finally shakes her head, my heart thumps back to life.

"Did you want me to come back?" I ask softly, sliding my hand across the sheets to touch hers. Her fingers trace over mine, as if memorizing the feel of them.

"Yes," she says, finally.

Her answer hangs in the air, and I can't help but ask, "Why didn't you ask me to come back?"

"I didn't want to make you choose."

I lean in close so she can see my expression when I speak the next words. "Lo, I will always choose you."

Her breath hitches, and the hand wrapped in mine clutches hard. Her wide eyes search mine for sincerity, and she must find it because in the next heartbeat, her lips crash against mine.

The kiss is hungry, frantic, and wild, like she thinks I might disappear if she doesn't hold on tight enough. I drag her into my lap gently, careful to not hurt her, and her legs settle around my hips. She feels so good, so right, like sunshine on a summer day, espresso first thing in the morning, dark chocolate on an ice cream bar, salt water on skin.

Lo breaks the kiss, pulling back to put her hands on either side of my face, and the cold metal of her wedding band presses into my cheek. Her nose brushes mine, and she's so close that her individual features are blurred. She's a haze of red hair, impossibly blue eyes, and freckles. So many freckles. I want to kiss each and every one.

"You told me you love me," she says, sounding a little breathless. "Did you mean it?"

I nod, dragging my nose across her cheek. Words aren't necessary when we're so close she can feel my every movement.

"You said you always did."

"Yes," I say aloud, not wanting to leave this up to interpretation. "From the first day."

"I've always loved you too, you know?"

My heart beats so loud I can hear it in my ears, feel it pounding beneath my chest. My hands settle on the smooth expanse of her thighs and slide upward, snagging on the hem of her shirt before stopping on her hips. She's so warm, so *real*, and it hits me all at once that all my dreams are coming true right beneath my fingertips.

Lo reaches over and switches the lamp off, leaving us bathed in darkness.

"What are you doing?" I breathe as her hands slide across my skin.

Her mouth hovers right above mine, and I can feel her words against my lips. "Just go with it."

Thirty-Seven

LO

A Few Weeks Later

THE BED IS EMPTY when I wake, the sheets cold and soft as silk against my skin. I stretch, thankful that, for the first time in weeks, I'm not waking up in pain. There's still twinges in my joints and tightness in my muscles, but nothing like the bone deep ache I've been dealing with. The only thing that has made it bearable has been Wes.

And now he's gone.

I sit up, letting the blankets fall around my waist, looking for any sign of my missing husband. A Polaroid on the nightstand catches my attention. It's a photo we took last weekend when I'd finally started to feel good enough to venture out of the house. We'd gone to a game night hosted by our favorite Tex-Mex restaurant, and spent the evening playing Monopoly with Rod and Camilla.

It's the inscription at the bottom that snags my eye, though. It says, *Hint #1.*

The corners of my lips tip up in a reluctant smile. I have a feeling I won't find Wes today unless I go looking for him, and I know just where to start.

SEARCHING FOR CLUES TAKES most of the morning, but I know when I pull into the coffee shop that Wes will be there, not another clue. This particular coffee shop is as familiar to me as my own bedroom. I spent countless hours studying here in college, many, many mornings laughing with Camilla, and even more staring over the rim of my mug at Wes, hoping he'd one day feel the same about me that I did about him.

But the most important thing to happen in this coffee shop was meeting Wes. It's where it all started—where *we* started.

A ridiculous surge of butterflies takes flight in my stomach, and despite the warmth of the late summer air, goosebumps prickle along my skin.

The bell above the door announces my arrival, and Wes looks up, meeting my eye. His smile is slow. It's the one I love, the one that never fails to melt my heart. His mouth twitches on one side first, a tug of those full lips, then spreads into a dazzling grin. The first time he smiled at me like that, right here in this coffee shop the day we met, I knew I was a goner.

I would have never, in all my wildest imaginings, guessed I would be back here right now, looking at him, with his ring on my finger.

His green eyes sparkle as he stands, walking toward me like he can't help it. His hands wrap around my waist, pulled by an invisible force, and I taste his kiss before I've even realized he's doing it.

Wes lingers there, his lips fastened to mine, and I think my heart might burst.

His thumb slips under the hem of my shirt, and swipes over the spot on my back that never fails to make my shiver. I feel his smile against my mouth before he backs up, pressing his forehead to mine.

"Hi," he says, and I don't miss the way he sounds a little breathless.

I grin up at him. "Hi."

He backs up, tugging me by the hand toward a booth near the back. I immediately recognize it as the place we sat that first day, and many times after. I remember feeling his shoulder brush mine and smelling that musky scent of his cologne.

As we sit now, that day feels simultaneously like a lifetime ago and like no time has passed at all. We could be two college kids stealing glances at each other across the table, or we could be wrinkled and gray, married for more time than we ever spent apart.

Reaching for the mug in front of me, I take a sip of the steaming liquid, savoring the familiar taste of vanilla and cinnamon and strong espresso on my tongue.

"What's the occasion?" I ask Wes, whose eyes are fixed on me, a warm, content smile on his face.

He ignores my question, lifting his hand to my face, one long finger dragging across my upper lip. "Foam," he says before licking it off.

A warmth spreads through my belly at the sight, and Wes grins like he knows exactly what I'm thinking.

"Think they'd notice if we slipped into the bathroom?"

Underneath the table, I kick his shin, and he chuckles.

I can't help my own grin. "Seriously though, I don't see any cameras. Why all the clues?"

Weston's brow crinkles. "I have to be filming to do something cute?"

After taking another sip of my coffee, I say, "Well, no. But today isn't anything special so I figured you were probably filming something if you were sending me all over Nashville."

Wes leans forward, bracing his elbows on the table. He's so close I can see the varied shades of green in his eyes and the pale freckles on his cheeks from spending the summer outside in the sun.

"You've been sick for the last few weeks," he says, his hand finding mine. The calluses of his palm scrape against my own. "So I haven't been able to romance you properly."

I swallow as he nudges my nose with his. "Is that so?"

"Yes, but I wouldn't want you to think there's nothing coming."

"Oh," I whisper, trying to focus on anything but my growing desire.

Wes's hot breath caresses my cheek, sending a delicious shiver down my spine. "Oh yes, I have *plans*."

"What kind of plans?" I pull back slightly so I can see his eyes. "Plans like the bathroom?"

He holds my gaze, his own smoldering. "Plans I wouldn't have enough time for in that bathroom."

I think I've been electrified.

"You're wrong, though, Lo," Wes says, his deep voice a husky whisper.

I blink, dazed at the change of subject. "About what?"

Wes leans back, snapping the cord of tension that formed between us. "Today *is* special." He stares at me, as if waiting on recognition to dawn, but for the life of me, I have no idea what he's talking about. "You really don't remember?"

Shrugging, I say, "No idea."

His lips quirk in a grin. "We met on this day eight years ago."

My mind goes through the timeline, and I realize he's right. "How did you even remember that?" I ask, shaking my head.

"How could I forget?"

I don't know how *I* forgot, but I'm glad Wes didn't. Leaning back against the booth, I ask, "Did you ever imagine we'd end up here one day?"

His eyes twinkle at me. "I was counting on it."

Normally, I'd think he was joking, but I can see the sincerity there, in every line of his face, in every angle of his body. He's so familiar to me, so dear, like a memory that you hold so precious that it's almost painful to look back on.

Reaching forward, he threads his fingers with mine. "I love you, Lo."

Tears prick at the back of my eyes, and I feel *completely and perfectly and incandescently happy*, as Jane Austen would say. "I love you, too."

Wes reaches into his pocket. "I have something for you," he says, pulling out a small, black velvet box. He slides it across the linoleum table. "An anniversary gift."

My fingers tremble slightly as I reach for it. It's so soft beneath my touch as I pry it open. Inside is a thin gold band inlaid with blue green gemstones. "It's beautiful," I breathe.

Wes, for once, looks a little unsure of himself. "The gems reminded me of the water. The beach, the lake, and the pool," he says quickly. His face softens a little, the pinch of concern leaving as I look up at him. "And your eyes. They mostly reminded me of your eyes."

I look back down at the ring, noting the varied shades of the deep, blue-green. "What kind of stone is it?"

"Aquamarine. But if you don't like it—if you'd rather have diamonds—we can return it."

I press the box to my chest as if he's going to snatch it from my grasp. "No, it's perfect. I love it."

He smiles then, his face relaxing. "I thought you needed an actual wedding band."

It hadn't crossed my mind, actually, to have anything other than my engagement ring, the one we bought when this was all just an arrangement. This feels right, though.

Gently, I pull the ring from its velvet-line foam bed. It's cool to the touch.

"Wait," Wes says, right before I slip it on my left finger. "There's an inscription."

Grinning, I flip it over in my hand, expecting it to say *Just Go With It*, but I find two other words instead. Etched in the precious metal are the words *Most Ardently*.

My gaze flicks back up to his.

"I read it, you know," Wes says. "That day after we left the coffee shop, I went to the library on campus and asked the librarian to help me find it." A small chuckle escapes him. "I didn't realize it was such a popular book—the librarian looked at me like I was an idiot."

"I highly doubt that," I say, thinking of how that librarian must have felt when this tan, muscular man showed up asking for help finding the most romantic book ever written.

He grins. "Anyway, I checked it out. I had to renew it like five times, but I finally finished it. I wanted to see why you would read it so much."

"And did you figure it out?"

"No," Wes says with a sardonic tug of his lips. "But I still felt like I'd gotten to know a little piece of you." He reaches for my hand, swiping his thumb across my knuckles. "You were so reserved for so long, and it took you forever to open up." Shrugging, he says, "But I felt like I knew you a little more after reading it."

My heart swells in my chest, almost painfully so. The sunlight pouring through the windows catches on the aquamarine gemstones, sending a sparkle across the hard lines of Wes's face.

"I know that line isn't actually in the book," he says. "It's in the movie."

I nod, holding back a smile. I can't help but remember watching this movie in bed with him, grease from my *In N' Out* burger covering my fingers.

"'You must allow me to tell you how ardently I admire and love you,' wouldn't fit on the ring, though."

Leaning forward, I place a light kiss on his lips. "You don't know how hot it is when you quote Mr. Darcy to me."

Wes quirks an eyebrow. "Bathroom hot?"

My cheeks hurt from smiling. I didn't know I could be this happy. Sitting back, I hold out my left hand, the wedding band resting in my palm. "Will you put it on me?"

The metal is cool as Wes slips the ring on my fourth finger. It slides easily over my knuckle and comes to rest against my engagement ring. Lifting my hand to his mouth, Wes presses a kiss there, right atop the bands.

"I don't think I ever told you," he says, still holding my hand clasped in his. I can feel his warm breath cascading across my wrist.

"Told me what?" I ask, dragging my eyes from my rings up to meet his own.

"I almost didn't come to the coffee shop that day with Rod. I don't remember why, but I know I almost bailed last minute."

"Do you think it would have changed anything—for us—if you had?" I ask, squeezing his fingers reflectively.

His shoulders raise in a shrug. "I don't know."

I chew my lip for a moment, considering my next question. "Would you change anything if you could?"

I've thought about it a lot—all the time we wasted, all the time we could have spent together if I'd been brave or he'd been honest.

"No," he says after a long moment. "No, I wouldn't."

I let my eyes drift across the familiar lines of his face. It's so similar yet so different than it was eight years ago. Back then, he didn't have such deep laugh lines around his eyes and his stubble wasn't as thick. His hair was a little shorter and his skin wasn't as tan. He wasn't as broad or graceful. But his eyes are the same, and the way they look at me hasn't changed at all.

"I wouldn't either," I say finally.

He flips my hand over, pressing a kiss to my palm. "I think it worked out like it was supposed to. We may have missed a few years, but we have a lifetime to make up for it."

Those happy tears are back, welling in the corners of my eyes. "A lifetime," I agree.

Wes leans forward, his lips grazing over my cheek in a lingering kiss. "Now let's get out of here before I drag you into that bathroom, Mrs. King."

Epilogue

LO

One Year Later

"Where are you taking me?" Wes asks, squeezing my thigh, his rough palms scraping against my skin.

I smile at him over my shoulder before turning back to the road. "It's a surprise."

"A *just go with it* moment, huh?"

I nod succinctly, not giving anything away. Ever since I got the idea for this surprise one year anniversary trip, Wes has not stopped hounding me about where we're going. He would bring me a Weston Special while I sat at my computer writing, trying to coax it out of me. Or he'd follow me around the kitchen while I was making dinner, pestering me with questions, trying to get me to slip up on the location. One time he even barged in on my shower. But well, that time hadn't turned out all bad.

I snap myself back into focus. If I let my mind start wandering like that, he'd surely catch me distracted enough to spill the secret. Honestly, I'm not sure how he hasn't figured it out yet.

I steer the car down a dirt road.

"This area looks familiar," he says, sitting forward to get a better look out the windshield.

"Mm," is all I say. He's going to figure it out in just a minute if he hasn't already.

Suddenly, his bright green eyes swivel to me and his face lights up in that smile that, even after all these years, never ceases to give me butterflies. I don't look at him, though my lips tip up in a grin of their own.

I make one final turn and we stop in front of a somewhat dilapidated cabin—one right on the lake. It's familiar, even though we've only been here once before. Every single moment of that trip is seared into my brain. The feeling of Weston's skin, so new and intoxicating, now as familiar as my own, slipping against mine beneath the water. The way the moonlight swallowed the green of his eyes until they were stars themselves blinking back at me in the dark.

Weston and I had a lot of starts and a lot of ends before we finally shattered into one another last summer and built each other back using pieces of ourselves to fill the gaps we were missing.

This lake house itself was one such start and end for us, but I didn't want to leave it that way.

I climb out of the car on shaking legs. I'm not nervous for once—I'm much too excited for that.

Wes comes around the front of the car and meets me there. In the instant he is close enough to reach me, he pulls me against him, pressing his forehead against mine. "This is perfect, Lo. I can't believe you rented this place again."

I smile at him and push back far enough to grab his hand and lead him to the door. My fingers tremble as I pull the key from my pocket and try to fit it in the lock. Weston's steady hands clasp around mine, like they did one night almost a year ago, the night everything changed between us. He slips the key into the lock and turns it.

I push the door open and step inside. Through the narrow hallway, I can glimpse the great room beyond, with its tall windows that look out on the woods and lake beyond. It's serene, completely at odds with my wildly beating heart.

Tugging on Weston's hand, I pull him toward the back.

"Where are we going?" he asks, chuckling lightly at my obvious impatience. When I yank open the sliding glass door and push him out, he arches a brow at me. Then his mouth curves into a mischievous grin. "Mrs. King," he exclaims, pressing a hand to his chest. "Are you taking me out to the water for *scandalous* purposes?"

If I weren't full to bursting at this moment, I'd probably shove him down the stairs. But I can barely contain my excitement as I rush down them, kicking my shoes off before I sink my feet into the cool, gray-brown sand.

Wes trails after me, shucking his own shoes. I stop at the edge of the water and turn to face him.

His expression is finally serious now as he takes me in. "Okay, you've got me thoroughly intrigued now. What is it?"

I chew my lip as I stare up into his beautiful, familiar face. I love this man. I love every single thing about him, even the things that drive me absolutely nuts. Time and again, he has pushed me to my breaking point—in all the best of ways—only to help me rebuild myself as something better. I try to picture my life without him, to picture the existence I had before him. I was lost and too weary to wander. I was living, but barely. In this past year, he's shown me what it truly means to be alive.

"I love you," I whisper, my lips forming a trembling smile.

His brow furrows and he reaches for me. "What's wrong?"

I shake my head, despite tears forming in my eyes. They're happy tears. Tears that are so, so happy at celebrating a year of *living* this amazing life with him.

I sniff, pulling myself together, and spin around in a circle, tugging him with me by the hand. "Look at this place," I say, unable to hold back my wide grin now.

He smiles down at me. "Yeah, I know, right? This really is an amazing anniversary getaway."

"It's ours," I say, my voice finally strong and steady.

Wes stops swinging our arms and stares at me. "What?"

I move a little further down the beach so the gently lapping water covers my feet and ankles. "I bought it," I tell him and Weston's jaw slackens.

"You bought it?"

"The owners were looking to get rid of it, and when I told them our story, they actually lowered the price," I say, stepping closer to him. I place my hands on his shoulders, and his find my waist, pulling me until there is no space between us. "I bought it with my royalty checks."

His eyebrows inch up his forehead and I giggle. "Okay, also with money from some of your new sponsorship deals." My new book was selling well, but not *that* well. But after Weston hired a new manager, the sponsorships started rolling in. He's honestly had more brands reaching out to him than he knows what to do with—which is crazy since most of these same companies wouldn't even consider him last year under Brandon's management.

"You seriously bought it?" Wes asks, his voice soft and reverent.

When I nod, he looks around, taking in the land and the vintage cabin.

"It needs some repairs," I say quickly. "But..." I chew my lip and he turns back to me, that crooked grin lighting up his face. "I thought it might be a fun project for us when we just need to get away."

The last year had been full of many, many things, and a lot of them had been work. It had all been good, but neither of us wanted to get to a place again where we were barely making it, surviving day-by-day. A cabin couldn't do that for us, only daily choosing life and love and happiness could, but it might help.

"What do you think?" I ask, running my hands up his chest to lock around his neck.

His eyes light up, crinkling at the corners. "I think this is the most *just go with it* thing you've ever done and I'm absolutely in awe of you right now."

"Yeah?" I can't contain the smile breaking out across my face.

Wes doesn't answer. Instead, he reaches down, gripping my thighs and lifting me off my feet. I squeal, wrapping my legs around his hips, as he plunges us deeper and deeper into the water. He stops when the water is reaching our chests. "Do you trust me, Lo?"

Nine years ago, Weston King walked into my life and turned it upside down. Now, looking into his perfect green eyes, I know there's no one in this whole world that I'd trust more with my heart. It was always his to begin with.

Acknowledgements

I HAVE BEEN WAITING my whole life to write the phrase "it takes a village" at the end of my very own book. I'm here to tell you that the phrase is absolutely true. It does take a village, and I never understood how much so until I wrote my own book. For that reason, I have many people I'd like to thank.

First, to my husband, Josh. If I tried to write you as a character, everyone would think you are too good to be true. Thank you for being my Wes, Camilla, and Rod all wrapped in one. Without your support of me every single day, this book could have never been written.

Next, I'd like to thank my writer friends and beta readers who read a very different version of this book and helped shape it into what it is today. Kate, Emily, and Ashley, this book is better because of you and I cannot thank you enough. MaryLee, thank you for being my best friend, for always listening to my ideas at 3 AM, and for helping me through all the plot holes. I know you love these characters and this book as much as I do. Kelsey, thank you for being the best Internet bestie a girl could ask for. I will forever be grateful it was you who slid into my DMs and not some creepy old man.

Thank you to the Troop for your endless encouragement through every stage of writing this and for answering my thousands of questions over the past few months. I could not do life without you, and you all mean more to mean than I can say.

Thank you to my editor, Beth at V.B. Edits, for making this story shine. It would have been much harder to read without your touch.

To my parents and family, thank you for always encouraging my love of reading and writing. I would never have chased this dream without you first telling me it was possible.

Lastly, I'd like to thank God for giving me this dream and for making it come true at the exact right time.

If there is anyone I forgot, I'm sorry. To be honest, this book is only possible because of all of the love, support, and encouragement I have received from everyone in my life these past few months. If I didn't mention you by name, just know that your contribution has not gone unnoticed.

As a final note, I'd like to say a little something about fibromyalgia, the disease Lo and I both share. I did not expect that it would be so difficult for me to write about my chronic illness. There were many times I wanted to erase Lo's illness and find a way to write a story about her where she didn't suffer. But for Lo, this was her story, and it is also mine. Living with a chronic illness is *hard*. Writing about the most vulnerable part of my life was really tough, but I felt like my story and Lo's story needed to be shared. For those of you out there suffering silently, I hope Lo's story speaks to you. I hope you have a friend like Camilla who will stick by you even when it's not fun. I hope you know you deserve someone like Wes who *wants* to be there with you. Chronic illness is hard and devastating. I think you're really brave for just *being you*.

xoxo,

Madison

About The Author

MADISON WRIGHT IS A rom-com writer living her own happily ever after in Nashville, TN! After falling in love with reading at a young age, she always dreamed of being an author.

Madison spends most of her time with her head in a book—whether that be in the car, at the grocery store, or in her reading chair. When she's not reading, she's probably watching The Office, eating excessive amounts of chocolate, or spending time with her husband and dog.

Follow Madison on Instagram @authormadisonwright

Author's Note

ON THE NEXT PAGE, you will find a paperback exclusive bonus epilogue set a few years in the future. This epilogue contains spoilers for the ENTIRE series—nothing major, just who each main character ends up with in future books. If you don't want to know, feel free to skip it. If you love a good spoiler, enjoy!

Bonus Epilogue

LO

A Few Years Later

THERE'S NO FEELING QUITE like typing *The End*. And it's even better to do it with Wes. His mouth is stretched in a smile, and his arm is draped over the back of the couch behind me.

"That's it?" he asks. "We're done?"

A little laugh escapes me. "No, we're done with the first draft." I nudge his chest with my shoulder, my lips lifting in a grin. "But we're one step closer."

It turns out that Brandon had been fabricating *a lot* of things when he was Wes' manager, including the publisher interested in Wes's career. So when an agent reached out a few months ago, wanting us to write about our love story and how it played a part in Wes' brand, we jumped on it. We've spent every spare moment of the past few months working together to write our story. It's been kind of a revelation, seeing things from both of our points of view, but it's only brought us closer together.

"Coming to the lake house to finish the last few chapters was a good idea," he says.

"I'm glad you think so," I tell him, snuggling deeper into his side. His arm comes around me, fingers threading through my hair.

The lake house has come together in the last few years, becoming more like a home away from home than a vacation spot. Each year we find ourselves spending more time here.

There's always bright light pouring in through the floor-to-ceiling windows and sunshine glinting on the lake. We decorated everything in whites and blues and beiges. There's a photo hanging on the wall that Camden took on the shore at sunrise last summer, and every room features one of Hazel's paintings.

"We should celebrate," Wes says, and I know from the tone of his voice that whatever he has planned will be an adventure.

I close the laptop and set it on the coffee table. "What did you have in mind?"

Strong hands grip my waist, lifting me until I'm settled across Weston's lap, my knees cradling his hips.

I giggle. "Oh, so this is what you had in mind."

Green eyes sparkle back at me, twinkling like stars in the night sky. A curl slips over Wes' forehead, and I swipe it back, carding my fingers through his hair.

Wes makes an appreciative noise in the back of his throat and presses his nose into the space between my collarbones.

"So your plan is to smell me?" I ask, trying and failing to use a serious tone.

Wes answers by dragging his tongue up the slope of my neck.

I fight back a shiver. "Oh, tasting too, I see."

He nips at my earlobe.

"Hm, biting. I'm not sure what that could be for."

I feel his smile against my skin, even as he attempts to sound stern. "Hush, I'm doing my best work."

"Is that so?"

A laugh catches in my throat as Wes lifts me off his lap. One moment I'm straddling his hips, and the next his body pins me to the couch. The humor dies away as he settles between my legs, his lips landing on mine.

This is what was missing between us for so many years. We were friends, but this was always how we were supposed to end up—a tangle of limbs, friction and heat, hearts beating as one.

Wes' hand is just dipping below the hem of my shirt, burning a line against my skin, when there's a knock on the door. His head falls into the crook of my neck, stifling his groan.

"You forgot you invited our friends for the weekend, didn't you?" I ask, pressing my lips together to keep from giggling.

"Mhm," he mumbles. "I thought they weren't coming until tomorrow."

"Rod and Camilla aren't coming until tomorrow," I answer and wait for him to get up, but he doesn't move. In fact, he seems to settle a little heavier against me. "Are we going to answer the door?"

"I'm good," he says into the curve of my shoulder.

I push at his chest, unable to hold in my laughter any longer. "Come on, it won't be so bad."

"It would be better if I'd had a chance to—"

My hand covers his lips, and I can feel him smiling beneath it.

"We can hear you, you know," Cam yells from the porch. Someone, probably his wife, Ellie, cackles.

"At least they're not skinny dipping again," Ellie's brother, Alex, says as we make our way to the front door. "Remember that one time, Haze?"

Wes swings the door open, staring at our friends laden down with bags on our front porch. "We put a sock on the dock."

Hazel throws her hands in the air. "We've told you *so many times* that you can't see a *sock* in the dark."

Alex's arm comes around her shoulder, pulling her close to press a kiss to her temple. "It's fine. We'll just make sure to get out there first tonight."

"I hate all of this so much," Cam says.

Ellie pinches his stomach, her mouth splitting in a smile. "Maybe we'll get out there first."

A grin tilts his lips as he looks down at her.

"Okay, that's it," Wes says, hands circling my waist. Before I know what's happening, my world flips upside as he throws me over his shoulder.

"No one is stealing our lake!" His words are lost in the wind as he runs around the house, an arm banded around my thighs. A laugh bubbles out of me when I see our friends sprinting behind us, all heading for the lake.

Footsteps pound on the dock, and I know our neighbors will probably have something to say about the noise later, but I can't bring myself to care. Not as Wes launches us off the dock, time standing still for a moment as if frozen. Here suspended in air, I commit every bit of this to memory. Laughter dancing on the breeze, Wes' strong body curling protectively around mine, summer sunshine warming my skin.

In this brief instant, I can't believe this is my life. These are my people. This is my home.

This is *living*.

Printed in July 2023
by Rotomail Italia S.p.A., Vignate (MI) - Italy